Illusions

Illusions

MADELINE J. REYNOLDS

Entangled Publishing, LLC
2614 South Timberline Road
Suite 105, PMB 159
Fort Collins, CO 80525
rights@entangledpublishing.com

Entangled Teen is an imprint of Entangled Publishing, LLC.

Visit our website at www.entangledpublishing.com.

Edited by Lydia Sharp and Stephen Morgan
Cover design by Juan Villalobos
Cover images by
Ana Babii/shutterstock
AlexGate/shutterstock
Extezy/Getty Images
Wikimedia Public Domain
Interior design by Toni Kerr

ISBN 978-1-64063-563-0
Ebook ISBN 978-1-64063-564-7

Manufactured in the United States of America
First Edition November 2018

10 9 8 7 6 5 4 3 2 1

entangled teen
an imprint of Entangled Publishing LLC

To Eddie, who showed me that magic is not simply fictional (just like the cab driver said).

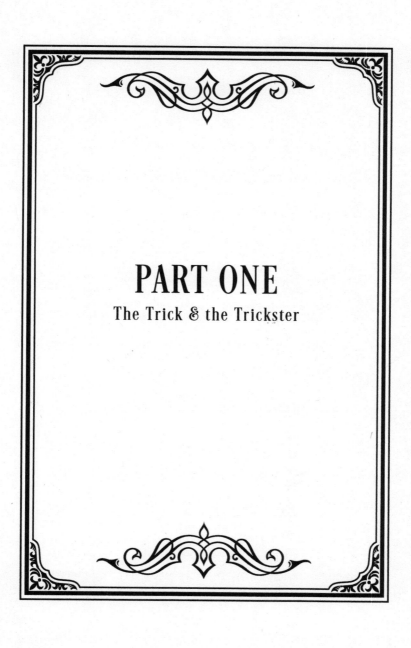

PART ONE

The Trick & the Trickster

The following is a collection of diary entries, public documents, and articles detailing the curious relationship between Thomas Pendleton and Saverio Moretti, apprentices to two of Europe's most renowned stage magicians. The excerpts featuring the diary entries of Mr. Moretti are not the original pages but rather transcripts featuring English translations. We've done our best to compile said documents in a way that conveys each boy's account of events in chronological order. This collection is for historical research and official use only.

—The London Metropolitan Archives
Courtesy of the National Archives

LONDON
METROPOLITAN
ARCHIVES

THOMAS

October 03, 1898

Twelve days. *Twelve.* Less than two weeks' time and Neville Wighton the Great will premiere his grand illusion for the city of London. It is his chance to cement his legacy. All he needs is for me to wait in the wings as I do my part.

October 04, 1898

Neville and I had our first proper rehearsal today.

It went about as miserably as I assumed it would.

The wild-eyed magician kept nagging and complaining, saying that I looked foolish—which I am certain I did—and suggesting I was unfit for the stage. Ha! I could have told him that. In fact, I am certain that I have, at various points throughout this "apprenticeship." I never had any desire to work for an illusionist.

Where I should be is at Oxford, studying literature and writing my poems. But my parents have insisted. Given my particular ~~gifts~~ talents, they feel it is the safest route.

As it is, it seems the only writing I will get to do is in here. Hence I have started keeping this journal. I have attempted to write some new poems between rehearsals, but the grueling schedule of a magician is not conducive to creativity—nor is consistently being insulted by one's mentor.

We are allowed access to the West London Theatre's auditorium only after normal service hours due to a performance of *Twelfth Night* that is currently running up until the weekend prior to our opening.

Having never performed on a proper stage, I kept bumping into Neville and standing in the wrong place—how was I to know which direction was meant by "upstage" or "downstage"? When he would call out "stage right!" I was never quite sure if he meant my right or his own. Needless to say, I had the same troubles with "stage left."

But all these other blunders were rather trivial. The real

atrocity was the final act: the headlining trick sure to astound our crowds.

Before making any attempt at it, he at least did me the courtesy of running through the mechanics of it all, step by step. He told me how he wanted it to look, where in the theatre he should appear once it was complete, even how I was to pose and smile during the moment of revelation.

I used this discussion as one last attempt at convincing him that a properly trained assistant should really be the one to share the stage with him. Not only would such an assistant be much more appealing to the eye than my scrawny frame, but it would also keep the greatly unwanted attention off myself.

He is convinced I need to be right by his side, seeing everything as he sees it, for the trick to go smoothly.

And then he did it. He leaped from the stage and out over the rows of chairs where the audience would soon be sitting.

I made an honest effort. But concentration was difficult at best, and my reaction was far too slow, causing Neville to fall onto the row of chairs below. His limbs were draped into awkward, unnatural positions, as though he were a marionette doll rather than a living, breathing man made up of bones and muscles and flesh.

As I stood watching him groan in agony, I was certain that he had broken at least some of those bones. But after pulling himself up, he claimed to still be in one piece.

When his eyes found me, he screamed insults and profanities, reminding me he'd seen me perform an identical feat just yesterday in his studio.

"Sir," I said. "Performing this trick on a small vase and performing it on a human being are two vastly different—"

He glared at me. "If you tarnish my good name by letting such a mistake happen on opening night, I will tarnish *your* reputation. You will never receive work again. Not as a magician's apprentice. Not as a street sweeper."

He was focused on the mistake, but what he truly did not like was my defying him.

I hope my reaction did not betray how unaffected I was by this threat of his.

I feel dreadful for what I am about to write, but being that this journal is meant for no eyes but my own...I shall confess, part of me wished that his bones truly had broken after his fall. It is terrible for me to wish injury upon the man, truly. But my dread in anticipation of this performance far outweighs any guilt plaguing my dark thoughts.

Mother and Father have retired to their bedroom for the night, so I shall get in some more practice. I was contemplating using a vase as my subject once again, but with the risk of having it fall to the floor and shatter, it would be best to use a small candle.

There are two scenarios:

One, I fail like I did in rehearsal today and make a fool of Neville.

Or two, even worse...I succeed.

I have to at least try to get this down. There is no reasoning with the man, and surely, if my secret does not kill me, he will.

SAVERIO

October 05, 1898

West London, would that you were as inviting to me as you are to everyone else. Yet here I am. Uprooted once again to a new city, with new streets to explore, new theatres to perform in, and a sea of new faces.

It comes with the territory. From growing up in the brothel, to doing menial labor as a stagehand, to being named apprentice to Paolo il Magnifico, I take one grueling step after another to finally improve my station.

Paolo thinks I am merely his assistant. He says I should be grateful for the opportunity. One day, he says, he will show me his tricks. His secrets. And then I, too, can be a magician. If I just wait.

But I am tired of waiting. All my life I've been waiting. I might only be nineteen, but I am meant for great things. I know it.

Until then, I follow Paolo, acting as his shadow, learning and doing all that I can. The constant travel means I am always alone, which is probably for the best. It's simple: no friends means not having to say goodbye once it is time to make our way to the next theatre in the next city.

I suppose I consider Isabella a friend of sorts. As Paolo's assistant, she is the only other familiar face I see on a consistent basis. But knowing Paolo, that likely won't last much longer. He has achieved the amount of fame that he has by being strategic, not generous. His sharp eyes are always looking for a younger, prettier face—much like my own. Ah, but all jokes aside, it really is a shame. Isabella and I were just starting to get along.

It is for the best. A true magician can open up to no one. But I won't always be alone, will I? Not truly. Just like Paolo, once I am a magician, the crowd will sustain me. Their amazement, their adoration. For the time being, I find my companionship with different bedfellows.

I offer a kiss, my bed, my body. And then, for my own trick, I disappear.

✤

As our carriage rolled along the cobblestone streets of London town, I scanned the crowds for prospects to contain my loneliness. Things did not look too promising, though. London's inhabitants seem about as chipper as the gray skies that hang over the city. And for some reason, they cover themselves from head to toe. No worry. I always do enjoy a challenge.

But as we continued onward, Paolo abruptly ordered our driver to stop. We came to West London for a reason, and it seemed he'd found it.

He exited the carriage, and Isabella gave me a knowing look—a wordless request to follow, so I did.

We had stopped in front of some square. A large column was plastered with local advertisements and notifications from businesses looking for laborers. And there was Paolo, staring at a poster. And from his glare, I could tell he wanted to rip the paper away and let it fall to the mud-caked street below.

Neville Wighton the Great. The whole reason we came here. We were originally supposed to perform in Munich, but while we were renting an apartment in Prague, I'd discovered a flyer for this "Neville Wighton the Great," making the same claims as that very poster. I had moved to throw the flyer away, but Paolo had ripped it from my hands and screamed, "Don't touch it!"

What is odd is I'd heard scarce little of Wighton before coming across the flyer. Any professionally working illusionist makes near-identical claims about their own performances.

A trick never before seen!

The greatest illusion on this earth!

Magic that will make you believe!

Paolo is never really one to notice or care, especially when it comes to performers who are so far beneath him. Yet this one commands every ounce of his being.

I was finally able to pry him away and usher him back into our carriage. Now we are settling comfortably into our rooms.

Why was my mentor in such a state? The advertisements make it seem that it will be a performance like most others. All I really know of the man is that he is older, so, as a veteran of the stage, he likely will not stoop to anything so simple as mere card tricks. Through the use of mirrors, cabinets with secret compartments, trapdoors leading underneath the stage, and a young woman with tantalizing good looks and a provocative, most likely sequined, costume (much like our Isabella), the man will entertain, confound, and possibly even amaze the simple folk who hand over their money in the hopes of seeing something that they cannot explain.

Still, this is not unlike many other illusionists performing all around the world. There is a man over in the States who refers to himself as The Alchemist who has his assistant collect simple copper pennies from volunteers in his audience and he then appears to turn the coins into gold before returning them to the delighted audience members.

There will always be competition, there will always be new illusions being tested and even perfected, there will always be some new (or in this case, old) face that captures an audience's eyes and hearts. I see no reason to spy on a performance that undoubtedly employs many of the same tricks or elements that Paolo currently utilizes himself.

I tried convincing my mentor of this to calm him.

"I have to see his trick," was all he said back to me.

He did not say he needed to see the performance as a whole but his *trick*. One singular trick. It is only now that I am remembering how the notice had advertised that Mr. Wighton will be performing a feat unlike any seen before.

I attempted to feed his ego various lines about how any tricks that the Englishman would perform could never hold a candle to Paolo's powers of prestidigitation. But once again, my mentor only had one response.

"I have to see his trick. For months now that stale old fopdoddle has been hinting at how *this* will be the performance to change his career and thus his fortune. A little late in life for that…"

My eyebrow shot up as I looked to my mumbling mentor. He was staring at the ground, talking more to himself than me, and only when our eyes connected did he seem to remember that I was even in the room.

He did not speak on the subject for the rest of the night, and I was left to wonder. Months? I had not realized Neville Wighton was someone Paolo had even cared to follow, let alone that he has apparently been corresponding with the man.

Paolo has been anything but an open book, a fact I accepted long ago. But it seems there are far more unread chapters in his story than I had originally suspected, and more characters who are integral to the plot.

THOMAS

October 09, 1898

Something happened today. Something wonderful, and terrible, and exciting, and confusing…o what does it matter? I am likely making more of it than actually exists.

And yet for something that will assuredly come to nothing… my heart ~~it was beating as fast as it does~~ the only other time it beats that fast is when my gift is making itself known, coursing through my veins like electrical currents.

This morning, Neville sent me off on errands in preparation for the opening performance, which is now only six days away. Specifically, I was to run to the tailor's shop to pick up his vest, tailcoat, and cloak that were made special for the performance.

Surely that was something I could not mess up…but of course, I found a way.

As promised, the pieces were magnificent. The tailcoat was sleek and cut in a modern style. The vest was black, lined with a midnight-blue satin, as was the cloak, which was also embroidered with a gold thread that twinkled as it caught the light, as though it were fashioned after the night sky.

Honestly, I was astonished. The idea that a man with an appearance as unruly and unkempt as Neville Wighton would have a mind for fashion was lost on me. What with his brown hair sprouting from his head in every which direction and graying in such a nonuniform manner, it looked as though his head were simply doused in ash. Not to mention his sharp, birdlike features, which are only hardened further by the scowl permanently fixed to his face.

There is certainly something to be said about a man who takes such special care when it comes to showmanship, and I suppose it was shallow of me to just assume that such details of a performance were of no significance to him.

With his costume in hand, I hurried out of the shop. I took a shortcut back to Neville's studio, and just as I was cutting through Manchester Square, I tripped over my own feet. Everything seemed to happen slower then, moment by moment. The gorgeous night-sky cloak was the first to float to the ground, and I followed, landing atop it.

I groaned into the lapel of the tailcoat, not ready to pull myself up and inspect the damage, when the sound of laughter pierced through the air. When I did finally look up, a pair of girls, probably not much older than myself, hung on either arm of a young man whom I'd never seen around this part of town before.

He was beautiful. Not just handsome — I've seen plenty of handsome men. But this young man, he was…striking. The way his dark curls hung loosely over even darker eyes had me at a loss for words. My stomach roiled in the strangest way. Not an unpleasant feeling — not at all. Just strange…confusing… unexpected. And yet, it was also welcome — as if something wonderful could happen at any moment just as long as he stayed near.

The girls he was with were giggling, but he seemed more contemplative than amused. He stepped forward and crouched down in front of me, then he picked up a part of the cloak and pinched it between his forefinger and thumb as he inspected it.

A cigarette hung from the side of his lips, and with him standing so close, a cloud of smoke created a veil between us. I did not know how to react, so I just lay there, frozen, letting the scent of the tobacco mixed with a hint of lavender oil filter through my senses.

He finally took his eyes off Neville's ruined ensemble, stood, and reached out an arm to help me up. At that, my heart was near stopping altogether. I pulled myself up quickly, hoping that if my movements were swift, the beautiful stranger wouldn't notice just how much I was trembling.

"What is your name?" he asked once I was up on my feet.

O his voice! A thick accent coated his words, and each syllable danced around my ears, sweet and melodic, as though he were singing rather than merely speaking. There I go again, as if I were sitting down to write another one of my poems rather than scribbling about the goings-on of my day in a journal.

"Thomas," I forced out in what was only incrementally louder than a whisper.

"Thomas," he repeated. It sounded so…right, when he said it.

He looked back down at Neville's soiled suit and cloak, and he smirked, the cigarette never faltering for a second. "That is quite the outfit." His eyes met mine once again. "I'm sure it looks *bello*… No, no. Fetching? This is the word you Englishmen use, yes? I'm sure it looks fetching on you—or it would have, anyway."

A surge of warmth shot through my face. Personally, I preferred the term "*bello*." Embarrassed, I was quick to admit that the clothing did not belong to me but to my master—which I then quickly switched to "mentor." That word still didn't feel right when describing Neville, because that would imply he's actually taught me something. But still, *master* makes it seem too much like I am his slave, rather than the young man who is about to either make or break his entire career.

He asked me who my mentor was and what sort of apprentice I am. I explained that I was working for "Neville

Wighton the Great." Though it sounded foolish coming out of my mouth, those dark eyes of his widened.

"Oh, I do love magic," he said. "Always so confounding. Do a trick for us, won't you?" His female companions were quick to agree, urging me to do an impromptu performance, right in the square.

I mumbled something about how I couldn't possibly and that I did not have the proper materials. I am not even entirely sure what I said and how much of it consisted of actual words, but it worked, for they relented. The boy shot me one last thoughtful smile, shrugged, then walked off, the girls trotting eagerly behind.

It is only now as I sit here that I am lamenting and cursing myself for being such a fool. He asked for my name and yet I never bothered to ask for his. Now he remains a nameless stranger, one I will likely never see again.

All I wish to do is to continue writing about him for the rest of the day, but I must be off. I promised Amelia I would accompany her to lunch—more specifically, Mother made me promise after our last two meetings were arranged by her. Both Mother and Father think it improper, since it gives the appearance that she is the one courting me and not the other way around.

I shall do my best to be decent company, but my mind is still in Manchester Square.

⚬⚭ ⚬⚭

Lunch with Amelia was fine. That is how all activities are with her. Just…fine.

Amelia Ashdown is a lovely girl, to be certain. I have never once denied that. But after my encounter with the handsome stranger, I know what it is to truly admire someone's features rather than simply appreciate them, as I do with Amelia. Amelia's beauty, while apparent, has never made me desire to be close to her. Today, with that boy, I felt the urge to be close enough that if I were to reach out, my fingers could trace his cheekbone down to his sharp jaw. As he walked away, an odd, immediate sense of loneliness rushed through me.

Oh what does it matter, anyway? It is not as if I could do anything about these strange feelings. Even if I had thought to ask him for his name, even if I knew exactly where in the city to find him at this very moment, *saints*. Even if I were able to muster up the courage—everyone says it is a sin. Each one of my thoughts about him more sinful than the next. I mean…just look at what happened to Wilde. I am already an "other"—something to be feared. The last thing I need is another secret. Another reason for the people of London to want to persecute me.

But is it so naive of me to want the type of passion I so often read about? Is it foolish to want a love that is so wholly consuming it causes me to ache? Fate is cruel that way, showing you exactly what you want even when it cannot be yours.

Passion or no, I shall continue to court Amelia, taking her out for tea and to lunches, for that is what is expected of me and what is proper.

SAVERIO

Something marvelous happened today.

I went against my own rule and put a name to one of the faces I met today. Thomas. It was in some square that I spotted him, just across town, near a café where I had successfully charmed two girls—sisters, if you can believe it. These Londoners are not as repressed as I figured. We were making our way to somewhere a little more private when a blur of ash-blond curls, pale skin, and elegant eyes fell toward the earth in an excitable fashion.

Even in his state, he was pleasant looking: slender, big gray eyes framed by those bouncing curls. He was clearly younger, though, even if only by a couple of years, and therefore not quite my type. I would have simply kept moving were it not for the articles of clothing he had dropped around him.

At first glance, they would have seemed like a simple black vest, tailcoat, and cloak, but the cloak and vest were each lined with a dark-blue fabric that had been embroidered with gold thread in such a way that the pattern looked like the night sky. No ordinary boy would be in possession of garments such as these.

And so I reached out a helping hand.

As it happens, the boy is also ~~an apprentice~~ a magician's apprentice. And he works for none other than Neville Wighton the Great.

It was a grand coincidence, surely. But could it be anything more than that? The more I have been thinking on it, the more I am certain: this is no mere coincidence; this is an opportunity.

You see, I have been waiting an eternity for Paolo to reveal his secrets to me. But I might now be able to claim something of my own, something Paolo wants so much that he will finally stop teasing me.

Paolo shifted our entire tour just so he could come witness this one illusion that Neville is claiming to be "unlike anything the world has ever seen." There is more to Paolo's curiosity than he is letting on — he knows something that we do not. But if it is true, and this illusion is unlike any performed before it, then how easy it would be to unlock its mystery with the aid of a certain magician's apprentice.

I could very easily have Thomas in the palm of my hand. From the look in his eager, shining eyes, and from the way he could barely form his words when I asked for something as simple as his name, it was clear I mesmerized him. It was sweet. And convenient for me. Just another coincidence working in my favor.

I've never actually used such methods to get what I want. Sharing my bed has only ever been a temporary cure for lingering loneliness. But as someone who considers himself a student in the intimate arts, would it not be appropriate to put what I have learned so far to good use? And I can think of no better use than positioning myself for greatness. Then many will adore me — and permanently, rather than by a single temporary bedfellow who is gone come morning light.

This plotting is likely all for nothing anyway. Perhaps Wighton's great trick is one that has already been done many different times with many different iterations. Paolo may simply be overreacting. All the same, I shall keep my eyes on this Thomas — keep him close, in case Paolo's hunch is all too real and this illusion is a prize just waiting to be won.

And even if Paolo is not wrong about this mysterious trick, what if *I* am wrong about the boy's feelings? It was only one chance encounter, after all. There was something in the way he stared, the way he fumbled for words (when he was even able to string some together). I have always considered myself a decent judge when it comes to the attraction, or lack thereof, of others. But what if the nervousness he was exhibiting was simply how he interacts with any new person he meets?

This is silly; of course it was attraction. It had to be. I am simply getting in my own head. I never usually analyze signals so closely, but then again, I suppose none of my other conquests ever really had any stakes. I've never had to worry much about whether or not the interest was reciprocated. Good Lord, is this what normal people go through with courtship? How can anyone stand such feelings of anxiety and insecurity on a consistent basis?

Ah, well. If he is indeed enamored with me, then the task will be an easy one. If he is not, well, then it will simply require more effort on my end. It will not be the first time I've built something from nothing.

I do feel a bit of remorse for what I may do. Then again, I did not set the rules; I am merely a player in the game.

All's fair in love and magic.

THOMAS

October 11, 1898

Mr. Wighton's temper is something I have grown accustomed to while apprenticing for him over the past month. Why, after showing him the damage done to his specialty garments, I thought he would damage his vocal cords permanently. Screaming I can handle. Insults I can handle. Even the constant degradation—I have taken it all in stride. It was not until today that his abuse switched from verbal to physical.

Though he may be reckless, Neville is not an unintelligent man. Getting splayed across a row of chairs once was enough to change his methods when it came to practicing our grand finale. Rather than leaping out over the audience, he has been simply leaping stage left—a concept I am still struggling with. After five failed attempts, I was expecting his usual chorus of name-calling as he searched for new and creative ways to describe my uselessness, but he was silent. Dead silent.

Without even looking at me, he moved offstage to where he had been keeping his props. He reached out for a cane that is incorporated in an act toward the beginning of the performance and gestured for me to come closer.

I remained where I stood, but still he did not yell. After an elongated exhale, Neville crossed the stage and, in one swift motion, he struck me. The cracking sound of the wood connecting with my shoulder blade resonated in my ears and set off something within me. Something I cannot explain, but even if I could, it would be far too complicated to write out here.

Most of the lights in the auditorium were dimmed, since our rehearsals take place after hours. But as soon as Neville pulled the cane away, winding back to deal another blow, a surge of white light illuminated the entire theatre. The blinding light swathed the auditorium for a second or two then began to flicker as a candle would, but it had a distinctive rhythm. The room dimmed and brightened in a pattern resembling a pulse. It was *my* pulse. Each small surge of light matched each beat of my heart perfectly.

My pulse was already more rapid than usual after the shock of Neville's outburst, but when I realized what was happening, my pulse quickened even more as fear took hold of me. It had been years since I had lost control like this. Usually, I am good at keeping my emotions at bay. But in that moment, a storm raged and roared inside me.

Faster and faster the light flickered, on and off, on and off. When I could take it no longer, the room went black. I could not see what was happening, but I did hear it. A sudden whirring filled my ears like wind, followed by the sound of two things crashing to the stage floor. The first was light but sharp, the second was heavy, more of a thud. Slowly, the gas lamps in the auditorium were brought back to life, and I saw what I had done with the thing that Neville so often likes to tell me is a "gift."

Neville was on his back and his cane was discarded, just a few feet away. Every instinct in my body told me to act, to flee, to do…*something*. In that moment, I was certain I had killed the man. My life fell apart around me as I tried to contemplate my options, but just as I was trying to calculate how much money I would need for a ticket on a ship leaving for New York, he arose.

I braced myself. If he had reacted violently because of my failure, I could only imagine what kind of reaction this little outburst was going to elicit.

But to my surprise and utter disbelief, he rose with a wide grin painted across his pale cheeks. Before then, I had not ever seen a smile on Neville Wighton's face. It looked…wrong, like a puzzle piece that was forced into a spot where it was not meant to fit.

He was thrilled—nay, *overjoyed*. He confessed he had been wondering at the validity of my parents' claims about the extent of my abilities. It was one thing to transport an object or man from one end to another. But this? This was something else. Something more.

Giddily, he paced around the theatre, clasping his hands together and, no doubt, making more and more plans for me.

For him, the incident was proof I could fulfill every dream he had of becoming the world's greatest magician.

For me, it was a nightmare brought to life.

Now, as I sit in the safety of my own rooms, I am flooded with horrid memories of incidents not entirely different from what occurred tonight. Though in those instances, I was a mere child, and so my fear was even greater.

None of this should even be happening to me. I should be at Oxford, with other people my own age. I should be apprenticing with someone whose career I admire or, at the very least, respect. I should be learning, exploring, finding my place in the world—hell, maybe even finding someone special to spend my time with. Instead I find myself indulging the whims of an opportunistic madman for my own survival.

SAVERIO

October 11, 1898

I read somewhere that boredom is the desire for desires. I cannot seem to remember who said it—I believe he was Russian. Anyhow, my desires have gone wanting here in London. Just as I knew they would.

Paolo il Genio, in dragging Isabella and myself here the moment he caught word of this damned performance, did not seem to realize that we would have a great deal of time left idle until the actual opening.

I have tried to find ways of amusing myself but have been unsuccessful. The young men here are so repressed and close-minded. The women are pleasant enough to the eye, but few have actually captured my interests. Which is not to say that they have not tried.

I indulge their flirtations all the same, and I will continue to do so. What other choice do I have? Sit around my hotel room while Paolo obsesses over something that is most likely nothing at all? I think not.

October fifteenth cannot arrive quickly enough. One of two things will occur that night: either Mr. Wighton's performance will be bland and ordinary and Paolo will realize he was worrying himself over nothing, *or* the man will premiere the most grand illusion seen by man and, with this, unveil my key to stardom. In moments of silence, I can almost hear the cheers and the whistles and the applause, but not for Wighton—for me. When I close my eyes, I can see the beaming faces of the entertained patrons. They are looking at me with adoration, with appreciation...

...with acceptance.

I have realized from experience, whether it be my mother, or potential romantic partners, or even my so-called mentor, the love of an individual is fleeting and never promised. Why waste my time on it? If I can achieve the *fama* and *notorieta* I so greatly desire, then I will have the love of an entire society—I could have the world! The history books would remember me, and people long after I have left this world will learn my name. If given the choice, I would gladly choose something as everlasting as fame over the affection of a single person. People are fickle. They change minds and they break hearts.

Does it make me a *mostro*, this conspiring behind Paolo's back? My plans to usurp his place center stage? I do owe the man *some* loyalty. From time to time I let myself think of where I would be had I not taken up work as one of his stagehands— probably still in that brothel in Perugia.

From that moment on, it was a quick education for me, learning how the world works. One of the most important things I learned was how easily things are acquired when you have a pretty face.

Is that all my mentor sees when he looks at me? A pretty face with no actual potential? And what if it's not just Paolo— what if all anyone ever sees is good looks and never bothers to look any further...see what's on the inside?

Since promoting me to be his apprentice, Paolo has told me on more than one occasion that my face was meant to be on the stage. I am not offended—on the contrary, I agree with him. The sneaking suspicion that my appearance is the only thing that earned me my position as his apprentice has simply fueled my resolve to become the greatest prestidigitator I can be. He's slowly taught me the basics, probably assuming I care very little or that even if I do, it will not matter, for all one needs to be truly successful is a basic grasp of sleight of hand and a gorgeous face, right?

Paolo doesn't see me in the wings, studying every move, every word, every smile during his performances. He does not realize how late I will sometimes stay awake reading volumes and journals detailing well-known secrets of the trade. Even a few of the lesser-known ones. And he does not need to know. Let him continue thinking I am some vapid, eager child blessed with striking features. One day, when I am headlining at the Palace Theatre in this very city, he will think on the days when the greatest stage magician of the century was nothing more than his smiling, empty-headed apprentice.

I am more than happy to continue on this path with patience and rigor. But if Neville Wighton and his sweet little apprentice offer me a shortcut to what is ultimately my destiny, who am I to pass up such favorable circumstances?

All will be revealed in a matter of nights.

THOMAS

Two days.

Two miserable days, which are sure to be the longest of my life.

I have been a complete and utter mess, and all the while, Neville has never been happier with me. Strange, since I *still* have not actually performed this grand feat he has planned out. One would think that would have him just as anxious (nay, *more*) as I. Or one would assume that at the very least, he would consider changing his mind.

I am not even suggesting that he has to cancel the performance—he could simply rework the set. Find another trick with which to close the show. A trick he has already mastered over his long career—one that he can pull off without as much magic and as much risk.

My accident in the theatre still has the man reeling. He is certain that our premiere will be just as spectacular as he first envisioned it. *I am making note now to take special care during the performance that he does not come anywhere near me with that cane.*

He is so confident in how smoothly everything will run that he canceled our final rehearsal. I hardly knew what to do with myself, but in these past weeks I have been making myself physically ill with worry, so I needed some sort of distraction.

Part of me wanted to return to Manchester Square. Perhaps

I would be so fortunate as to run into a certain handsome stranger again, but I quickly dismissed the notion as foolish. The chances of him being there a second time were slim at best, and even if I did see him, what would happen any differently? What new courage would I have now that I did not possess during our first encounter?

I ultimately landed on reading, which was sufficient distraction for a few hours' time, but now I lie awake in bed, restless once more. I have a life-altering decision before me. Do I throw the act entirely? Let Neville Wighton's good name and his career tumble down while I revel in his embarrassment and shame? I am quite past any guilt for these secret thoughts. The man has been tormenting me ever since he employed me. Not to mention, with his career in ruins, the magician would no longer need an apprentice. I would be free of him. And I certainly have the power to make it so…the real question is if I have the bravery.

Or, do I actually attempt the feat and risk exposing myself? It hardly seems worth it at this point, but my parents arranged this apprenticeship for a reason that I cannot ignore.

Perhaps I will not have to ruin the trick intentionally. Perhaps, even in an earnest effort, I will fail, thus ending this phase of my "career."

I should be attempting to get some sleep. But each time I try, each time I close my eyes, I see a tan face and dark-brown eyes framed by wisps of smoke. A face I will never see in person again.

SAVERIO

October 15, 1898

Tonight is the night. Paolo assumed that the abrupt nature of our excursion to London would alert few in the community to our arrival, but as it is, fame comes with its hindrances as it does its benefits. Neville Wighton personally sent Paolo and our company a special opening-night invitation with seats in the front row of the center balcony—some of the best in the house. Doubtless, he wants to ensure his rival has a good view of whatever is about to transpire.

Paolo's face has never turned quite so purple as it did when he opened the invitation. I did my best not to laugh.

I've been dressed and ready to leave for nearly an hour now. It's hard to say who is taking longer to primp and preen, Isabella or Paolo (quite possibly both).

I may or may not write about tonight's performance. We shall see if it is even worth my time.

 THOMAS

October 15, 1898

It worked; oh dear God…it worked.

No one can know. No one can know. No one can ever find out. No one can ever know.

SAVERIO

There are no words for what we witnessed tonight.

That was the most incredible trick I have ever seen in all my life. True, my life has not been very long, but even Paolo, who has walked this earth nearly twice as long, was completely at a loss for words.

I hardly know where to begin, but I shall do my best.

Upon entering the theatre, I noted that the stage was barren. No elaborate set pieces or decorations, no signs, no indication that anything significant or remarkable would be taking place.

Once all the patrons had found their seats, the house lights dimmed and a spotlight demanded we focus our attention to center stage. Neville Wighton the Great strolled rather casually out onto the stage and took his place under the limelight. He was even older than I thought he would be. His clothes were marvelous, but I had already gotten a sneak peek of the ensemble while in the square. Everything else about his appearance was slightly off. His hair was uncombed and sticking out in certain places, and his smile, if you can call it that, was awkward and strained. Watching him, I wondered at how a man with such poor presentation managed to gain as much fame as he has in London.

And then I saw a sight I had not been expecting—at least not upon the stage that evening. Young Thomas, who I already had the fortune of meeting, walked out and took his place—far enough from Mr. Wighton that the magician was still the center of attention and near the props that had been meticulously laid out on a table draped with purple velvet.

An apprentice taking over the duties of a beautiful assistant. (In fairness, I thought the boy was striking enough in his own right, but I was certain the audience had been expecting someone a little more feminine, in far more sequins and pearls.)

How many times now have I offered to lend a helping hand onstage with the especially complex illusions during Paolo's performances? But each time Paolo has told me that the apprentice's place is behind the curtain. I will certainly not let him forget this.

Even as Wighton initiated his first trick, my focus lingered on Thomas. The boy's nervous quivering proved more interesting than what Wighton was doing. For nearly the entire performance, I was completely and utterly bored. Simple levitation illusions and modern cabinet tricks had the crowd fawning and gasping. The difference between myself and these people is that I have seen all these tricks performed by at least five other illusionists and, in most cases, they were executed much better.

Wighton did not even have the sense to dress up his act with any sort of flair. Music. Colored lights. Hell, even a few articulated hand gestures would have done *something* to stir me. But he completed each trick with the calculated stoicism of a carpenter putting together a shelf.

I am surprised I did not fall asleep before he performed his final trick, but I am endlessly grateful that I was awake to witness it. Finally putting in some effort, Wighton started rambling, reciting a monologue about how the feat he would now perform cannot be explained through science or logic. Yet again, I was bored. I have heard some variation of the same speech a hundred times from conjurers all across the globe, assuring the audience that what they are about to witness defies everything they know to be possible and true about the world we live in.

I shifted in my chair, wondering how easy it would be to slip away to the bar before the theatre began to empty and the lounge would be flooded. As I was planning my escape, Wighton walked upstage, briskly brushing past his apprentice. Without another word, he turned and sprinted back downstage. Upon reaching the edge of the stage, he sprang forward, launching himself toward the audience and flying over their heads.

And then he was gone.

He vanished in midair. I was on the edge of my seat. Paolo was on his feet, scanning the theatre. I blinked multiple times, hardly able to trust my own eyes, but he had indeed disappeared. The patrons sitting where he should have landed had covered their heads and sunk into their seats, bracing for impact. Slowly they realized they were no longer in harm's way and began to inspect the area around their seats. A couple of men even stood and reached out above their heads but grasped at nothing more than empty air.

Heartbeats were all that passed before the words "Looking for someone?" were uttered in a surprisingly commanding tone. Everyone in the auditorium turned their attention upward to the place where the voice came from. From a private box above, which had been kept empty, Mr. Wighton was standing with arms fanned out in presentation.

In his advertisements, Wighton had promised his would be a trick unlike any seen by man, and surely, none of the patrons at the West London Theatre had ever witnessed such a spectacle. And so they reacted accordingly—with utter chaos.

There were those who did as was expected of a proper audience, standing and gifting the performer with hearty applause and cheers. But even more were going wild. People were gasping, looks of confusion plaguing their faces, and many clamored from their seats, thoughtlessly pushing and shoving past others to make their way toward the spot underneath where Wighton disappeared midair. Dignified members of high society were losing their minds as well as all sense of propriety as their fine gowns and well-tailored tuxedos blended together in a sea of elegant unrest. We would soon be witnessing a riot.

From our own vantage point, the people up on the balconies had little option to go investigate the scene below to try to solve the mystery, but that did not make for any less chaos. Just as those below rushed to the spot Wighton had been leaping toward, audience members seated in the balcony pushed past one another to get to the railing along the edge to gaze up at the box where the magician had miraculously reappeared.

Doing such a thing would serve little purpose in illuminating how the trick itself was actually performed, but at the time, I felt the urge to do the same. However, I was utterly frozen, my jaw still hanging open in disbelief. All I could do was stand there as supposedly well-bred theatregoers pushed, shoved, and pressed themselves against one another.

I was finally pulled from my stunned trance when a small cry managed to pierce the cacophony. My eyes darted through the waves of ruffled skirts and the rows of seats, and somehow I managed to spot a small figure, crumpled to the ground and quivering.

A boy, no older than five. Tears welled along the bottom of his big round eyes as he searched the commotion, undoubtedly for his parents who had not even had the decency to keep their own child close in the pandemonium. Though my head was telling me that Wighton's grand illusion was priority, my foolish, melancholy heart pulled me toward the frightened child. Besides, the illusion had already been executed. There was little to investigate at that point.

I maneuvered through the bodies and finally made it to the aisle where the boy was taking cover. I knelt down and offered my hand. He looked at it and me with understandable caution.

"*I tuoi genitori*. I…um, I mean, your parents." (I've been catching myself doing this lately, accidentally falling into my native tongue. It happens without my even thinking about it. I much prefer Italian to English; it sounds much more romantic. That said, I need to focus harder and not let these slips happen. It gives the locals here yet another reason to cast me strange looks. Another reason for them to assume I do not belong here.) "You've lost your parents, haven't you?" I had to shout my words for him to hear me. "I will get you out of here safely and we will find them."

He hesitated a moment longer, lip quivering, but then nodded and placed his small hand in mine.

I held on tightly as I led him through the shuffling crowd. I'd already lost track of Paolo and Isabella long ago.

As the situation in the auditorium escalated, I could only imagine Paolo's fury. He has performed some notable tricks of his own, but not once has he created such chaos.

Bursting through the entry doors felt like coming up from underwater. Other patrons slowly filtered out as we had, but it was not until some time later that the audience began to empty the theatre in droves. I looked down at the boy expectantly, waiting on him to spot a face in the crowd that was familiar to him.

Eventually, a woman with golden hair pulled into a braid and piled atop her head rushed toward where we stood on the nearby street corner. With gloved hands, she held back the skirts of her burgundy ball gown.

"Albert!" she shouted. "O my sweet Albert, come here!"

The boy ran into her arms, and as she lifted him up, she

cast me a dubious glare, as if I were some monster who had whisked him away from her rather than the one who saved him from being trampled after *she* had lost sight of him.

A "thank-you" would have been pleasant.

In an instance of unfortunate timing, Paolo exited the theatre at just that moment and had witnessed the small exchange.

"So good to see my hardworking apprentice was busy playing nanny after my rival just performed the most miraculous trick of his career," he sneered.

I am wise enough to know that his rage was simply the jealousy he was feeling at the time. As I think back on it now, I know he was not angry with me so much as he was angry about the situation. However, in the moment, all rational thought went out the window and the only thing I could think of was giving that gib-face a good tongue-lashing.

"I saw the trick with my own eyes. I was only distracted *after* the performance and was doing my best to help. You saw the conditions in there—it was complete hysteria!"

Paolo knows my history. He should know better than most my feelings when a child is left behind or forgotten by their parents.

The ride back to our hotel was silent.

Throughout my life, I have seen countless variations of the Vanishing Man, but this was…impossible. I can hardly believe I am writing this, but for once in my life I am truly mystified.

Usually every illusion has a very practical explanation— some clever methodology behind the curtains. But there is no explanation here, not one that I can wrap my mind around. There is no device, no mechanism that could pluck him out of the air and transport him to another part of the theatre. A trapdoor would not be viable—not above the audience's heads. That would be preposterous! Mirrors could be a possibility, but

I swear I saw him physically leaping off that stage.

If anyone were to procure this journal, they might think my scribbles to be the ramblings of a madman, and that's exactly how I feel, *mad*. All night I have been going over the illusion in my mind, again and again. This is what it must be like for common people when they go to see magic performances— simple folk, who have no prior knowledge of the tricks of the trade and tactics of misdirection.

We have to know how he did it. The difference is that I already have a plan for how to get my hands upon the knowledge. Thomas will be my key, my ticket to the kind of stardom Wighton will likely experience these next few months. I've restrained myself until tonight. Why expend myself before I know an endeavor is worth my time? But now that I have witnessed the illusion's greatness for myself, it is time to set the gears into motion.

THE ILLUSTRATED
LONDON NEWS.

MONDAY, OCTOBER 17, 1898.

AN OPENING WEEKEND SUCCESS FOR LONDON ILLUSIONIST

The Manchester Guardian.

Manchester: Printed and Published by J. GARNETT, No. 23, Market-street.

MONDAY, OCTOBER 17, 1898.   PRICE SEVEN-PENCE.

RENOWNED LOCAL STAGE PERFORMER
OPENS A SHOW UNLIKE ANY OTHER

The Daily Telegraph

LONDON, MONDAY, OCTOBER 17, 1898

LOCAL MAGICIAN CAPTIVATES WITH VANISHING FEAT

THE  TIMES

LONDON, SUNDAY, OCTOBER 16, 1898.

NEVILLE WIGHTON THE GREAT'S
LATEST PRODUCTION IS PURE GENIUS

THOMAS

October 18, 1898

Our first weekend of performances is complete, and we are an absolute success. Well, that feels odd for me to say. What I *should* be saying is that Neville Wighton is an absolute success.

The man has enjoyed various small successes over his long career. Even as someone who did not frequent magic performances, I had certainly heard of feats of Wighton's that had impressed the local masses: willing flowers to grow from a seemingly empty vase, placing members of his audiences under states of hypnosis, and so on. But I can safely assume that none of the attention he has ever received in the past is comparable to that which he is now receiving.

The constant accolades and affirmations of his talent allowed him to spend the weekend basking in his own glory, and I have to say, I am somewhat repulsed. I never thought I would be wishing for the temperamental shut-in I met when I first started working for Neville Wighton the Great.

Though my anxiety has somewhat lessened over the past few days.

I thought the plan to hide in plain sight was mad—suicide, even. But I cannot deny that it is now proving itself effective. All eyes are on Neville, and when he vanishes, it is his secret they are trying to unravel, not mine, for after all, in their eyes it is *his* trick. He's the master illusionist, the one with years of experience. Me? Why, I am simply the boy who fetches his props for him or locks the chains for the illusions that require he be bound or who chooses the volunteers from the audience before guiding them toward the stage. Why should anyone think twice about such a boy? Not a single audience member has turned a suspicious eye in my direction (for now).

Though I have finally had the chance to breathe a sigh of relief, I must remain vigilant. We still have until the end of the month before the run is officially over, and until that night, until I walk off the stage after our closing, I cannot let my guard down entirely.

It is a strange paradox. These people attending Neville's performance come to his shows, not only to be entertained but to be enchanted, mystified. The more I immerse myself in this world, the more I have come to realize that many of the patrons actually want to believe that Neville Wighton and his colleagues are truly able to perform supernatural feats.

But—and this is where the paradox lies—if any one of these delighted souls were to learn what I actually am, they would be horrified. The very same people who cheer and applaud his so-called illusions would cower in fear if they knew it was my hand plucking him out of the air and transporting him. And as history has shown us time and time again, fear can so easily turn to hatred.

Maybe they would be less fearful if there were others like me—and then I would feel less alone. It seems so impossible that in such a large world, with so many people, I would be the only one to possess such abilities. Yet all my life, ever since I had a concept of what I am and how different I am from the world around me, I have searched and scoured for any sign that magic exists elsewhere, with other people, but my searches have proved fruitless. If there are any others who wield such talents, they have done a magnificent job of keeping that fact hidden. Just another sign that I must do the same.

All I have to do is make it to All Hallows' Eve. Even more comforting is the idea (or hope, rather) that once our run of performances has ended, Neville's status will have heightened so significantly that he will no longer have any use for me. This booking was already more than he could have hoped for. A month-long engagement is an unprecedented amount of time for a stage magician to remain at one venue. Maybe he will be so grateful for all I have done for his career that he will compensate me with a cut of his earnings. I could use the money to start my schooling at Oxford in the spring and return my life to its intended course.

Wishful thinking, I know. After tasting the sort of success real magic has afforded him, my master will not let me out of his sight, let alone his employ. Booking agents from other venues and concert halls all across London are already vying for his attention and favor, sending postcards, messengers, and even shameless gifts in the hopes of securing our next booking. But wishes and dreams for my future are all I have now. I used to have poetry, but my creativity is still blocked, and I do not see that resolving itself anytime soon.

What would be really nice, what I really need, is a person to talk to about all this. Someone to empathize with, who understands—but even as I write that down, I realize how foolish it is. No one could even begin to understand my plight. I have done my research. Pored over old books and documents, newspaper articles, but have yet to find traces of phenomena as strange as my own. Still, I can't help my yearnings for someone living and breathing to spill my soul, my heart, and my secrets to. These blank pages will have to suffice.

SAVERIO

October 21, 1898

Tickets have already been purchased for Isabella and me to attend the rest of Neville Wighton's engagement at the West London Theatre. We are to pose as a young couple, and each night we shall study every inch of the theatre. Now that we know the routine, we can look where others will not, avoid the usual traps of misdirection, and stay alert.

Yes, he is leaving us behind to do the spying in his stead while he continues on with the remainder of his tour. My luck has been a spectacular thing lately. Honestly, I could not have planned it out better if I had insisted on the arrangement myself. I will get to study the performance over and over, without any supervision from Paolo, which could so easily lend itself to suspicion. All the while, he will be thinking that I am the loyal apprentice, working to steal the secret for *him*.

It is perfect.

He even managed to procure tickets to the sold-out final performance as well as an invitation to a gala being thrown on All Hallows' Eve to commemorate the performance. I shall also be attending the party in Paolo's stead to avoid the attention of Mr. Wighton. Imagine how pleased the Londoner would be to learn of the obsession that has taken hold of my mentor, an illusionist who, until now, was considered to be far superior.

I imagine this superiority to which Paolo has clung will not last much longer. The performance has made countless headlines already, and word of Neville Wighton's awe-inspiring trick is no doubt making its way to other cities, catching the attention of those in the magic community. It will not be long before other prestidigitators arrive to witness the feat and offer up their theories on how it is done—theories that, of course, will all be wrong.

I can already sense Paolo's desperation at the thought of being outshined. I do not blame him, though; I would be just as furious, if not more, if I were in his position.

It has been days now, and I still cannot remove from my mind the scene of Neville Wighton the Great disappearing in midair. It was so complex, so brilliant. If a young magician like myself were to learn the old man's secret and, shall we say, improve upon it…why, there would be no need to continue waiting in the wings as a mere apprentice. My future on the stage would be all but assured.

For now, though, I shall let Paolo assume what he will of my motives. After all, he is the one affording me the opportunity to unravel this mystery. Take the gala. The event promises to be an exclusive one, and thanks to Paolo's considerable fame, the door is wide open for me to complete my "research."

The party is being held at the home of Mr. and Mrs. Pendleton, some wealthy couple who, like most cultured people with sizable wallets, make a big show of supporting the arts. If what I hear is correct, they have a son: *Thomas Pendleton.*

Fate is a funny thing. When I happened upon a lanky boy fumbling over himself in the square not long ago, I hadn't the slightest idea what an integral part he would play in my future plans. Those big gray eyes looking up at me in equal parts embarrassment and interest…

And here I was thinking I would not be having any fun in London.

THOMAS

October 29, 1898

Only two nights left of our residency. I suppose I am feeling even more relaxed, for I let myself falter during the trick. Just as he always did, Neville jumped out over the rows of seats below and, as always, I successfully made him vanish before crashing down on the nervous patrons. My failure was in the act of transporting him where he desired to go.

Rather than placing him perched on the balcony of the highest box in the theatre (even now as we prepare to close out the run, no one in the audience seems to notice that we keep this box empty despite the "sold-out" status of the performances), he ended up dangling from one of the ornate chandeliers. My chest tightened, and it felt as if my rib cage were collapsing, no longer allowing my heart room to beat. My face felt hot and my breathing came out staggered. Even though all eyes were now on the flailing magician, I felt as though the eyes would soon turn on me in accusation. As if they would know, somehow, what I had done. A scene of Neville falling to his death played out over and over again in tiny instants as he continued to struggle. There was a chorus of nervous gasps from the audience and even a few shrieks, but being the veteran performer he is, he eventually regained his composure and a simple wave of his arm paired with a confident smile was enough to elicit uproarious, albeit relieved, applause.

Beneath his control, I could sense his anger, even from

my vantage point on the stage. I knew he would not dare say a word to me because no matter what illusion he likes to give off to his audiences, he and I know who is truly in control. This sudden surge of fame may be spreading like wildfire, but it is still new and still fragile and can so easily be stripped away. All it would take is one slip on my part for everything to shatter. He knows that doing anything to harm or upset me would come at the cost of his own good name.

Further evidence of this came tonight after the audience was ushered out of the theatre. I had already transported Neville back down to safety backstage. After the auditorium was clear of patrons, he stormed out to meet me, a look of murder in his eyes. I went so far as to offer him a shrug and half smirk in lieu of an actual apology. I could sense his restraint, I could feel him holding back, but he left the theatre without a word.

When he did, I nearly collapsed. My own boldness had caught me off guard, and I was trembling all over. I felt like I was going to be sick, but when I opened my mouth, expecting to heave, I instead began to laugh. The nerves were instantly met with a warmth that could only come from relief, beginning in my core and surging through the rest of my body. But there was something more than relief. Finally, after constant torment and degradation, I had finally stood my ground. It felt like I was an animal who had just shed a layer of skin—a timid, meek layer. I suddenly felt new.

Alone in the theatre, I let out an elated howl, enjoying the way it sounded as it echoed back to me.

Just two more nights. I will still be his apprentice, yes, and he will no doubt have agents and booking offices pleading with him to come perform all across the country (possibly even farther). But after All Hallows' Eve, I will at least be allowed a moment to step back, breathe, and think about my next steps.

SAVERIO

This is a complete and utter disaster! I have been to nearly every one of his damned performances, including matinees, and I *still* cannot fathom how he is able to pull it off. I have seen the show from many different spots in the theatre, and from every angle I have yet to see even a hint at how he is executing the disappearance.

There is no way for him to reappear in that box so quickly after leaping from the stage. A double waiting up in the empty box could potentially explain the seeming transportation, but it does not account for his sudden disappearance over the heads of audience members, nor does it account for the events of last night.

Last night I was seated at the dead center of the mezzanine level. All was going as normal while Isabella and I watched with keen eyes, anticipating his grand finale. My line of sight was already fixed upon the box where he normally appears before he even took the leap, in order to further explore my theory that he was using a double. If there was someone up there, then there was a chance he would make some sort of misstep. Maybe he would get a little eager and step forward half a second too soon. But no one appeared.

I heard groans and gasps all around me, and it was not until Isabella tugged on my arm and pointed above our heads that I saw Neville Wighton the Great flailing and swinging from one of the crystal chandeliers.

He played it off like a true professional, but to someone who had already seen the performance multiple times, the execution seemed sloppy and unplanned.

…And yet, it was still remarkable. More so, even. Immediately my theories were dashed. There would have been no way to have a look-alike stationed on or near the chandelier unseen.

He cannot simply be disappearing.

My own frustrations will surely only be surpassed by Paolo's.

I have tried to arrange for another "chance meeting" with the Pendleton boy, but every night while the more dedicated patrons wait to shower Mr. Wighton with their admiration and praise as he exits through the stage door, his apprentice is nowhere to be seen.

Tomorrow night's party *will* get me closer to divulging Wighton's secrets.

Thomas

October 31, 1898

Well, today is off to a *grand* start. I have torn a hole right through my favorite vest, and one of my old schoolmates is going to be published in a major poetry journal, meanwhile I have yet to write a single worthwhile piece in weeks, oh, and I have just been informed that Neville's engagement at the West London Theatre has been extended into November.

I do not understand. Tonight was supposed to be our final performance, at least for a short time. But letters have been coming in, and Neville has been receiving agents at his studio for private meetings. I am already hearing that the Adelphi Theatre is trying to secure a string of shows for Neville in December, and just the other night I overheard my parents discussing the possibility of a residency at the Grand Theatre in Lancaster come the New Year.

I have about as much desire to travel to Lancaster as I have to continue this damnable performance. Neville Wighton the Great's newfound success will quickly become my prison if I allow it to.

So I cannot allow it to.

I have made small gains when it comes to standing up for myself and my own interests, but it is time I draw a clear line. I love my parents dearly, and they felt they were doing what was best for me when they first posed the idea—they had found an answer to a problem that otherwise had no solution. But hopefully they will see that I have tried my best. Hopefully, they will trust me enough to keep my secret hidden from the world on my own terms. Have I not done so successfully for the past near seventeen years of my life?

The decision has been made. Tomorrow I will inform my parents that I no longer wish to serve as Neville's apprentice, and I will go to his studio to tell him of my resignation in person. Tonight I will let them have their fun at their party—let them revel in the success.

I am not so unreasonable that I will go forward without compromise, either. I am willing to see out the extended run through November, which will allow Neville the time to plan a new act to perform on his own (or with an assistant if he so chooses, but he will no doubt be far less qualified when it comes to magic).

I have done what I can for his career. Any other performer would be understanding of that—grateful, even. Not Neville Wighton. I have played through the scene dozens of times in my head, and each time it does not end in my favor. But this residency has heightened his name to new levels of respectability. After this year, he will be ensured regular bookings from theatres all across Britain (for certain, even other parts of Europe), and his pockets will not be empty. Much more than any stage performer is guaranteed in this world. In time, his anger will subside.

My new resolve has left me feeling lighter—dare I say it, even happy, or something resembling it.

I must go ready myself for the performance and for tonight's festivities. I was previously worried about the need to wear a mask of delight around our guests this evening, but now I have a strong feeling that the smile might actually be genuine.

⚬⚭ ⚮⚬

For the first time in what feels like an eternity, I am restless with inspiration. I have never felt such a strong desire to write, to capture the beauty keeping me awake this night.

The performance went smoothly and was met with a standing ovation from the crowd. Then, after we returned home, guests began to arrive. Some were wearing masks over their eyes or heavily decorated top hats in light of the holiday, but for the most part, everyone was in standard formal attire, doubtless their best pieces. Silk gowns that swept down to the floor, silk vests on the men to complement their female counterparts, strands of pearls and cut jewels, impeccably tailored tailcoats. It was a visual feast (rivaled only by the actual feast my parents had catered for our guests). Even those invited who are not substantially wealthy made sure they were looking the part.

Whenever my parents decide to entertain, they make certain that every detail is just right so that their social function is the talk of West London for weeks afterward.

I did my part in receiving our guests and welcoming them to our home. Many of Mother and Father's old acquaintances and friends made a point of telling me how much I resemble Father, even though it is not true at all. People generally assume that is what you are supposed to tell a young man, as if being compared to a woman were some sort of insult. But Katherine Pendleton is a lovely woman, and I am proud to have inherited her golden curls and her soft gray eyes.

The furniture was cleared from the parlor to make room for dancing while a harpist and violinist played throughout the evening. Meanwhile, space was also cleared in the drawing room for guests who had no interest in dancing but still wished to socialize. In the dining room, rows of tables were dressed with black tablecloths embroidered with a gold filigree pattern. Atop the tables were matching gold plates and platters offering an array of hors d'oeuvres.

Amelia spent the better part of the night at my side. She looked beautiful, but then again, she always looks beautiful. Under the weight of my mother's stern gaze (only slightly softened by the delighted smile she was flashing each new guest), I offered my arm to Amelia for more than a few dances. She is pleasant enough company.

It was during our third dance that I saw a face I had not been expecting to see—a face I had made myself forget.

It was the young man from the square. The one who had come to inspect me after I had fallen.

When my eyes locked on to his, I held his stare for half a moment longer than was proper. But even as I turned to face my eager dance partner, the heat from his dark eyes seared into me. Every spin in the dance, every turn, was a new opportunity to sneak a glance in his direction, and each time I did, the mystery guest had not taken his eyes off me.

I still hadn't the faintest idea who he was, and yet somehow he had managed to earn invitation to my parents' rather exclusive reception. I had to fight the urge to break away from Amelia right there on the dance floor and ask the man myself who he was and what he was doing there.

Once the music ceased, I bowed and slipped away. I made directly for the dining room where servants carried trays of sparkling wines. I swiped a glass and guzzled its contents, with little regard for the stares the act was eliciting, hoping that the wine would dull my sudden onset of nerves.

Mere seconds later, two fingers tapped gently upon my shoulder, and for the briefest of moments I was certain that my heart had stopped beating entirely. Slowly I turned and found the stranger standing behind me, far enough so as not to draw more stares from the surrounding guests yet close enough that I could smell that same subtle caress of lavender oil that had intoxicated me in the park, though now there was no smoke mixing with the scent.

In the hand he had not used to get my attention, he was swirling a glass of a far darker, richer wine.

His lips quirked into a smile and he raised his glass to mine. "Thomas! I do believe congratulations are in order. I was lucky enough to be in the audience during your show this evening. Spectacular performance!"

He remembered my name? I stammered something in response about how I am no performer, just a simple apprentice, and how Neville is the one deserving of praise (I am too embarrassed by my mumblings to even try to recall my exact words).

He said nothing to this, though. He simply looked me up and down, bit his bottom lip, then took a slow sip of his wine before casually strolling back into the drawing room.

All my breath escaped my body in a sharp, sudden exhale, and I was forced to grasp for another flute of sparkling wine. Disappointment hit me in waves. I had been hoping his compliments would have opened the door for a longer, more stimulating conversation. He probably thought me dreadfully impolite. I should have thanked him for his sentiments. And I figured I would have gotten a chance to ask for his name this time, but my opportunity came and went before I even knew what to do with it.

Even now as I mull over my own foolishness, I cannot help but feel a certain amount of inexplicable glee. I feel a strange yet delightful fluttering inside, as though moths are flying about within my chest. All I want to do is write about him.

I want to write about his thick, melodious accent that fills my ears when he speaks, just like a song that is written only for me. I want to write about his relaxed confidence, a confidence that I have never been able to attain myself, and envy with every fiber of my being.

New poems keep writing themselves at the back of my brain, and they do not stop. Ever since I began writing as a boy, I have never felt so artistically invigorated. My only regret is that I do not know more about my muse. I would very much like to thank him for this gift.

A sea of people, one face I see,
A world of sounds, one voice I hear.
A pair of eyes that lands on me,
A moment held forever dear.

A chance encounter, a twist of fate,
Two paths that now are crossed.
My mind left in a dreamlike state,
Now finding what was lost.

—An original poem by Thomas Pendleton

November 3, 1898

I must keep this brief, for I am off to meet Amelia for a luncheon uptown. I just had to note my suspicion that something is wrong. Something is very, very wrong.

⚜

Now I am home and can fully divulge my innermost suspicions. The day following the reception, I sat down to speak with my parents, just as I had promised myself I would. We took tea in the courtyard, and I calmly made a case in my own defense.

I explained to them that though I was appreciative of the opportunity to work one-on-one with someone so skilled, and though I knew that their intentions were in the right place when they made the arrangements, I simply could not continue as Mr. Wighton's apprentice. I tried to be as vague as possible when discussing the toxicity of our relationship—I did not tell them of Neville's verbal and physical abuse. That would serve only to make Mother feel terribly guilty, and that was not what I wanted.

And that is when the strangeness began. Even without a word of Neville's mistreatment, my mother's eyes began to fill with tears. She cried out about how I did not understand and that it was the only way they could keep me safe. With that, she fled from the courtyard, leaving me confused and speechless.

The two of us left alone, my father suddenly became quite stern with me. He told me I was still too young to grasp all that was at stake and that our arrangement with Neville was the only way for me to survive in this world. He got into a rambling speech about how they worried about me when I was a child. How they would throw lavish dinner parties for all their friends but would have to send everyone away because I would become upset, and whenever I was upset, objects would start moving about the room. They feared that others would think me a demon. They feared someone would try to take me away from them (although my father would not elaborate who they thought that *someone* would be).

I am beginning to understand what my parents must have gone through raising me. Always having to look over their shoulders—much like the way I live my life now. But I argued there were other ways of keeping my secret a secret. I told him that I was fully capable of blending into society by my own means and that I am no longer a child with no self-restraint (I never told them about my incident in the theatre with Neville just nights before our premiere, and now I most certainly never will).

But this is where my frustration took a sharp turn into suspicion. I remained steadfast in my arguments against my father and eventually told him that I was planning to see Neville later that afternoon and tell him of my intended resignation. My father rose from the table and told me that I would do no such thing. He then explained that if I did leave Mr. Wighton's employ, I would be cut off financially.

It was my father's turn to leave the courtyard, whilst I meanwhile sat in stunned silence. I can understand their fears for me, seeing that they are my parents and that they love me.

But to go so far as to disinherit me? No, no, no… Something is not adding up in this equation. This apprenticeship is a solution, yes, but it is not the only solution. My parents are not blind. And surely they can be stubborn, but so stubborn as to see me out on my own, without a penny to my name? Something more is at stake here than my safety. I am not accusing my parents of anything just yet, for at this point I do not even know what it is I would be accusing them of.

It all just seems so…dire. Needless to say, I did not give my resignation to Neville. Right now I sit in my dressing room (the success of our previous run has afforded me that much at least) preparing for this evening's performance. I hardly was given a choice. I was between two options: to be poor or to be miserable. I made the cowardly choice and elected to continue living in comfort at the expense of my own happiness.

My own cowardice is not the only cause of my current state of dread. I have reviewed my last entry in this very journal and could not help but cringe more than a few times as I read. I was acting foolish and naive, drunk on the allure of some handsome stranger. I let my sudden infatuation get the better of me, which I cannot allow to happen again. Just as I must control my supernatural abilities, so must I control my emotions. After the party, long after the guests had all left and the food and decorations were stored away, I was up scribbling lovesick poems and reveling in my own feverish delight. I even snuck a small vial of the lavender perfume that my mother likes to wear on special occasions and brought it up with me to my room. It was far more fragrant and sweet than the stranger's oil, but it was near enough to the scent that I closed my eyes and let myself pretend he was standing in the room beside me.

Every thought, every feeling buzzing through me that night are all things I should be thinking and feeling about a nice girl like Amelia.

SAVERIO

November 7, 1898

Just as Neville Wighton's residency has been extended at the West London Theatre, I have convinced Paolo to extend our stay. He and Isabella will be at the Midland Grand Hotel through the end of the month; meanwhile Paolo has already set about finding me my own apartment in the city. By the end of November, if my efforts have still proven fruitless (highly unlikely), then he and Isabella will return to Rome before making their way to Madrid for some variety show in which Paolo will be the headlining act. I will be left in London to continue my research, and at the middle of each consecutive month, Paolo will return to confer with me on what I have learned.

It took a great deal of convincing on my part, especially without so much as a hint as to how Mr. Wighton executes his vexing illusion. But ultimately, I knew Paolo would succumb. I mean really, what choice did he have? If I were not able to work my own magic, he would have to settle with never knowing Wighton's secret—always being baffled, always being confounded, and, worst of all, always being second best.

I was finally able to make him understand that patience will be key in this endeavor. His impatience is my own fault, of this I am painfully aware. I have conditioned him to expect immediate results with my past liaisons. He has become so accustomed to receiving answers the moment he snaps his fingers. But, to my own delight, I am learning that this will take much more subtlety and persistence on my part.

When I devised this plan, I was certain that winning Thomas's heart would be easy. This may be the first time I have treated seduction as a sport, but I figured I would have his affection as easily as if it were an object I could simply purchase from a store. But Thomas, much like the situation, is far from what I expected.

He was shy in Manchester Square; he was shy up on the stage beside the magician. And he was shy at his own party.

I like shy. Shy is a challenge.

His quiet demeanor may not be my only challenge to overcome, as it were. As I watched Thomas that night, though he was not exactly socially engaged with his guests, there was one…a young woman, who was on his arm practically the whole night, occupying his time with dances and chatter. There is no doubt in my mind that he is courting the lovely girl, but where my doubt does lie (and thus, my hope continues to flourish) is in whether or not he actually has any feelings of affection for her.

My focus was watching his eyes. At our chance meeting in the square, there was a certain shine and sense of wonder in the way he looked at me—it was there; I know it was. I am sure it was. When I watched him with his mystery girl, though, he looked thoroughly disinterested, bored, even. There is no way he could actually love this girl…is there?

Some might have taken his female companion and the distance at which he keeps himself from the world as a rejection or a dead end. Some might have given up already. But I have my own theory. I think he is afraid. Fearful of what he wants and what he could be, and so instead he is going through the motions and is doing what is expected of a boy his age. I am understanding, of course. I may be open with my flirtation now, but it was not long ago that I was confused or frightened when the sight of an attractive young man sent my heart racing.

The world conditions us to fear that which society and theology have not deemed "natural."

I have been attending each new performance and will continue to do so throughout the extended run. Paolo has made sure that now I am always seated in one of the rows under the spot where Wighton leaps before vanishing, giving me a better view of the trick. Unfortunately, being so close to the stage, I have to come up with a ridiculous disguise almost every night. Thomas knows my face now, and we cannot take any risks.

Paolo is doing his part, of course. He has made dinner plans with Neville Wighton later this week so that he may congratulate the man on his recent success. This will serve to prove to Wighton that his rival is not lurking in the shadows and will thus, hopefully, lure him into a false sense of security. At least when it comes to Paolo, many other magicians are also desperate to learn the secret of Wighton's breakout trick. A fact he is certainly aware of and most likely enjoying very much.

Paolo, meanwhile, is so focused on these other prestidigitators, he has yet to recognize an opponent in his own ranks—a mistake he will live to regret.

THOMAS

*A*melia has attended nearly every show, and when I do manage to get a day off, it is usually spent by her side. I have been escorting her to breakfast or lunch (depending on when I can stir myself out of bed), and our conversations, though hardly stimulating, are always pleasant. I must admit, it is good to be talking to *someone*. Other than functions revolving around magic and theatre performances, my social calendar has been wanting of late.

It is no one's fault but my own. Charles and Edgar have offered their company on more than one occasion. Though my friends mean well, they don't understand how seeing them nowadays upsets me. How their stories from academia fill me with envy and dread. Aside from performances and outings with Amelia, I am becoming somewhat of a recluse.

The weather has been unnaturally mild for this late in the year, and Amelia keeps begging me to go on a nice walk through the park. I would not object, but she keeps suggesting Manchester Square. So far I have been able to evade this request, but I am running out of sensible excuses. Of course, I cannot tell her the real reason I have no desire to go near the square…the memory of the chance meeting that both frustrates and excites me.

That brings me to the real reason I am writing today. There has been a development in my love life (if one can even call it that). A few days ago, after finishing a performance, I returned to my dressing room to find a gift waiting for me on the end table beside the door: a single red rose.

It is not uncommon for patrons to bring flowers, especially given Neville's rising popularity, but usually guests will hand them to him personally outside the theatre as he goes out to greet his adoring public. Even the flowers thrown onstage, though they are falling at *my* feet, are meant for Neville after he magically reappears up in the wings.

I had a good feeling it was not Amelia. Though, true, she is the one who has done most of the pursuing in our...situation, sending me a rose still seemed a bit forward, even for someone as bold as she.

My suspicion that it was not her doing was confirmed when I picked it up. A tiny white ribbon was tied around the stem. Attached was a small paper card, folded in half, making it no more than a tiny square. I opened the card expecting a note of congratulations on a job well done or an excellent performance, but the only thing written on the card was the letter *S* scrawled in the most excellent calligraphy I have ever seen.

I ran over any possible candidates, but there are few *S*'s in my life, let alone ones who I know well enough to send me such an intimate token.

Ever since that night, they have been arriving regularly: sometimes at the theatre and other times, they are waiting for me at my home. This has posed a bit of a problem.

My father is displeased because, as far as he knows, I am once again in the position where a young lady is courting me when it should be the other way around. My mother is also displeased, because she sees this "S" as some harlot for whom I have scorned poor, dear Amelia. What my mother fails to recognize is that my affections were never Amelia's to begin with.

I can see why she would want me to be with her. The

Ashdowns are a respectable family, with an even more respectable fortune. It is a good match, to be certain. And for reasons I still cannot fathom, she adores me. I wish that I could reciprocate her feelings, truly I do. Then at least one facet of my life could just be simple.

As for this mystery "S"…well, it could be code for anything: Samantha, Sarah…Samuel…~~Sterling~~. No, not Sterling, that doesn't feel right. It doesn't fit. I certainly know who I hope my admirer to be, but that only fills me with even more shame than I have already been struggling with.

SAVERIO

November 15, 1898

The seeds have been sown. My plan to lure in Thomas has been set into motion and yet, I have been feeling restless, like there is more I should be doing. My plan, though a genius one, will take time to unfold. It would be preferable to get my hands on Wighton's secret sooner rather than later.

And so today, with the free time I had available, I put together an outfit comprised of the more common items of clothing I own, and I made my way to the theatre. Before exiting the hotel, I stopped in the lobby and discreetly went to the grand fireplace. Just as I hoped, there was still ash and soot from the previous night. I grasped a handful and once I was outside, I smeared the ash upon my face like a lady would some fine powder.

Now I was fully in the role of a down-on-his-luck immigrant looking for work. When I got to the theatre, I went around to the back entrance, found a comfortable spot to lean, and I waited. I was ready to wait for many hours, if need be.

My plan was to linger around until one of the West London Theatre's stagehands, or other laborers, popped out and at that time I would inquire about a job. Even if the answer was no, it would give me an opportunity to ask about the sorts of mechanisms that had been loaded into the theatre recently for any current productions. Knowing what sort of apparatus Wighton is using will surely help solve his magical riddle.

As I had expected, it was hours before anyone emerged. I had gone over around midday to give myself plenty of time. It was dull, of course, just standing in the back alley, staring at the ground, but the desire to accomplish my goal was enough to keep me waiting.

Finally, a middle-aged man in a gray cap with stubble lining a pointed chin stumbled out into the alley. He jumped, clearly not expecting anyone to be outside the theatre door, and he shot me a strange look as he continued about his business, striking a match to light the cigarette hanging from his mouth.

"Bugger off, kid," he grunted. "We don't need no street rats loitering outside this nice establishment."

"I'm sorry, sir," I offered in my best meek voice, "I just arrived in town with my sister not long ago. We are almost out of money and are desperately hungry. I've been going from place to place in the city, hoping to find some work. I'll take anything you've got!"

The man let out a long exhale while giving me a pitying look. "Sorry, kid. We's gots a full staff here. And even if we did need some help, you're a bit skinny to be trying to lift heavy set pieces and building materials."

"I look thin," I was quick to answer, "but I've got strong arms and I'm young, so I've got plenty of energy. If you just give me a chance, I can show you all the things I can do."

He simply shook his head. "Strong or no, work is slow enough for those of us who *do* have jobs here. Things are kind of at a lull right now."

I pretended to look curious. "Isn't there some sort of production right now? I saw something up on the marquee — I admit, I don't know how to read."

Another look of pity from the man. "Aye, we got a show right now. One of the greatest we've ever had — it's a magician."

"A magician?" I gasped (I may have been overacting at

that point). "Well, surely you have plenty to do. With all the equipment it takes—large coffins, tanks for water, beds to put under the trap doors…"

The man shook his head. "Nah. None of that. It's just a magician and some boy who assists him." At this point he looked up toward the brick wall of the theatre, and his next statement was more to himself than it was to me. "It's unlike anything I've ever seen."

"That's not possible." I had not meant to say that out loud, so I quickly followed with, "Okay, well, what about help backstage or with the lights? Or even just cleaning up the place at the end of the night? I ain't picky."

He looked to contemplate my request and hope started to prickle in my veins. But that hope was extinguished along with the man's cigarette as he tossed it to the ground and stomped it out. He rolled up his sleeves. "Look, kid—clearly you're not hearing me, so how's about I make you understand."

But his saying that was all I needed to get the message. I ran back down the alley and out to the street, not even looking over my shoulder to check whether or not he was actually chasing me.

Now I am back at the hotel with no new information. Not even the beginnings of a clue. Apparently Wighton has the entire world baffled.

Thomas

Finally, a development! Not a clue but the promise of an actual answer. Tonight's rose came to my dressing room, only this time there was more written than just a simple but elegant *S*. Tonight's card read:

Simpson's Grand Divan on Strand.
I will be holding a table in the afternoon tomorrow.
Please do not keep me waiting.

My heart quickened with anxiety the first time I read the words. Especially that last line. "Please do not keep me waiting." Most forward, indeed. And yet that one word keeps echoing in my mind. Please, please, *please*.

I sit here now, wide awake, pretending to contemplate what I will do come tomorrow afternoon. But I am already perfectly aware of what I will be doing and where I will be going, for I fear if I do not figure out the true identity of "S," I will regret it for the rest of my life.

November 18, 1898

I was right.

Even as I tried to convince myself I was wrong or foolish, I had one very distinct guess as to whom S would reveal him- or herself to be, and I was correct.

Whether or not I wanted to be right is another matter entirely, and one that hardly seems to matter now.

Seeing as the card did not give a specific meeting time, I decided I would show up at one o'clock p.m. That way I would arrive in the afternoon but still early enough that I would not keep my admirer waiting, just as they had requested I not do.

I was dressed in some of my finest clothes. Simpson's usually caters to a clientele with a sizable income, although I had to admit, I was a bit perplexed. A chess and coffee house seemed an odd place for a (potentially) first meeting.

After giving my name to the host, I was led through the hall where rows of tables hosted men in top hats playing the game of strategy and contemplating their next moves. Though most of the tables were covered in the black-and-white game boards, others were laid out with silver plates of seasoned fish and potatoes, lamb, and greens. Aromas wafted through the room, mixing with the thick cigar smoke rising in small plumes.

I was led to the very back of the room, to a booth much smaller than the other tables. Already seated was the dark-haired stranger I'd encountered twice before. He was more casually dressed than he had been at the party and much more casually than anyone else at Simpson's, though no one seemed to notice or care, for he wore it well. His black vest sat over a cream-colored shirt unlike anything in fashion in London. The sleeves only reached about three-quarters of the length of his arms. The collar only reached the nape of his neck, and he'd left the top few buttons open so that a small *V* of his dark, tanned skin was exposed. His dark pants were slim fitted all the way down to his ankles. The only traditional part of his wardrobe was his shoes, and even those seemed to be more eye catching than any other pair of similar black oxfords throughout the room. There was something extra that I could not quite place, possibly in the way they shone like new while still giving off the appearance that they had been lived in and had earned some stories in their time.

Twirling the cigarette between his fingers, he flashed a toothy grin and nodded at the host. The man nodded in return and handed me a drink menu before returning to his post. I clutched onto that menu for dear life, staring wide eyed at the open seat across from the stranger I now knew as S.

I was clueless.

I did not know what to do.

I did not know what to say.

I could not breathe, let alone think.

I will try to recall the events of this afternoon and our conversation as best as I can, but I have lost some of the exact details. It was all just such a...blur.

He chuckled and nodded toward the open seat, which I was still staring at. "Are you going to sit down?"

I gulped. It took another moment for me to gather my courage, but I finally sat.

He took a drag of his cigarette and a sip from his coffee, never taking his eyes off me. He set the cup back down on the table and finally broke his gaze away from me, frowning down at the beverage.

"Certainly not as good as it is back home, but I suppose it will suffice."

"Where is home?" I finally asked, though I spoke so quietly, I was amazed he could hear me over the cacophonous activity.

He grinned, and his eyes widened. He was probably just as surprised as I was that I had been able to speak at all. He leaned back in his seat and responded, "*Italia*," embellishing his already thick accent.

I smiled but quickly raised a hand to cover my lips, as though I had done something improper.

"You came," he said simply.

"I hope I did not keep you waiting," I said, once again surprising myself. I had not been planning on making a joke. It just sort of came to me. I was feeling strangely comfortable around S.

To my relief, he laughed at the quip. I felt my muscles loosening at the sound of his laughter. He took another drag of his cigarette before offering it to me. I shook my head and turned my eyes down to the menu in my hands. I figured something to eat or drink might help with the nerves roaring inside me.

"So, Thomas, the magician's assistant," S mused, seemingly more to himself than to me.

"Apprentice," I corrected timidly.

"What?" he asked.

"Apprentice," I said, only slightly more sure of myself. "I'm Neville Wighton's apprentice, not his assistant. Well, I suppose… for this particular performance…I have been acting as his…I mean, I have been *assisting* him, but I…" (There was much more rambling like this on my part, but I suppose this gets the point across.)

Despite how thoroughly I was embarrassing myself, he did not mock me—something that would not have taken much effort. He simply sat there, smiling at me.

The waiter came by, and I ordered myself some tea with milk. I have never been much of a coffee drinker, myself, and from the look on S's face as he battled through another swig, it did not seem like I was missing out on anything too spectacular.

We sat in silence for a few moments—well, not silence, per se. What I know of chess, I never really thought it to be a rowdy game, and yet the room was filled with shouting, uproarious laughter, and even some cursing.

"Why here?" I asked, figuring I would start with a safe, simple topic.

S scanned the room. "I came across this spot not long after your party. I like to come here and just watch. I am something of an observer."

I nodded. I was hoping that would give us more to talk about, but it was a straightforward answer to a straightforward question. I waited for him to ask something of me, but he just continued to smile at me. Not expectantly but curiously.

Small talk was getting me nowhere, and I was resolved to leave with some sort of answer. I stammered, "So…um…w-well…the roses."

His grin widened again. "Ah, you liked them?" There was a hopeful gleam in his dark eyes, and something about it made me feel less nervous around him. It was sweet, like the look a puppy might give, seeking approval after performing a trick.

"No…I mean, yes! Yes, I liked them. They were…they are…lovely… It is just…well, why?"

"Why not?" he asked with a shrug. He turned his attention to a pair of men a couple of tables over who had fallen into a gridlock and were both grumbling impatiently.

I was less than pleased. It could not possibly be that simple, could it? And I certainly was not about to let him evade the question that effortlessly.

"But what were they for? What did they mean?" My voice

lowered as the waiter returned with my tea and a small plate of chocolate biscuits.

S watched him, slouching in his seat, and once he was gone he turned his smoky dark eyes back on me. "Who says they had to *mean* anything? I found your *prestazione*—it means performance"—he likely saw the question in my eye—"enchanting, and so I wanted to gift you with something even fractionally as lovely."

I could feel my cheeks getting hot, but I persisted. "It was not *my* performance. Neville is the magician. He is the one doing all the work."

"I hate that," S scoffed, flicking his cigarette at the edge of the plate holding his coffee cup.

"What?" I asked. Inside I felt panicked. I was certain I had offended him somehow, though that had certainly not been my intent.

"When performers sell themselves short like that, I abhor it."

"I am no performer," I argued, avoiding eye contact.

"You just said you were the man's apprentice. Which means you are studying the magician's craft, which can only mean one day you wish to be a stage magician yourself."

I did not have an argument for that. There was no way to explain the situation that my inherent abilities and my parents had forced me into. So instead, I just shrugged.

"Besides, are you not up on that stage alongside Neville Wighton the Great? You are a part of the show, you help sell the illusion, so take some of the credit—you deserve it."

He had no idea how right he was.

"Okay, but that does not explain why you left me so many roses—one might have sufficed—nor does it explain why you kept your identity hidden from me." I was getting bolder and bolder, and I was stammering less and less. I was full of surprises today.

He just laughed, finally putting out his cigarette on the saucer, the gray ash soiling the creamy porcelain. He raised an eyebrow at me. "I may not know much about stage magic, but I do understand the draw. Your audiences, they like to be surprised. I am still confounded by that amazing trick Mr. Wighton performed, but that does not mean I wish to know how he accomplished it. People love a good mystery."

"That does not answer my question," I said. Though it was a lie. I knew perfectly well what he was getting at. But I think he already knew that.

All the same, he leaned in close. I could smell that familiar, enticing scent of lavender oil on his skin, and as he spoke, the stark, dry scent of tobacco and coffee hung on his words. "Did you not like *my* mystery? Did it not excite you, trying to piece together the puzzle?"

Our faces remained close to each other for what could have only been a few seconds before I caught a mustachioed gentleman in the opposite corner of the room giving us a peculiar look. I immediately stiffened and took a sip of tea.

His sly smirk never wavered once. "Besides, I found you so… interesting. I hope that does not bother you. Ever since that night at your home, I have not been able to get you out of my mind. I wanted to get to know you, know more about you. It would have saddened me deeply if that were to be the last night we would ever see each other." He took another sip of coffee then looked me up and down. "Am I making you uncomfortable?"

I tried to answer him, but each word caught in my throat and stuck there like honey. I was rendered mute. So I just shook my head.

"Good," he said, another warm smile.

Warm in that it warmed me from the inside out, far better than my tea.

After that, we sat for a bit, taking in the activity surrounding us. I have to admit, I rather liked watching the various games unfold in their varying levels of competitiveness. He was right about observing; it was quite enjoyable. He had been right about many things, and I thought about what he had only just said about how saddened he would have been if we had parted ways that night and never seen each other again.

I agreed with him. I had been struggling with that same sadness and fear, even though I had been trying to push all thoughts of him from my mind entirely. I had felt so foolish that night for not having asked for his name. I was not going to make that mistake again.

As we departed from Simpson's, I worked up the last bit of courage that had not already been used and asked him what *S* was short for.

He cocked his head at me and gave a contemplative look, as though he were deciding if he should tell me or if he should let it remain a mystery. Finally he answered, "Saverio, though friends usually just call me Sav." After adjusting his cloak, he stepped in close, leaning his head down so that his lips were mere inches from my ear. "I would like it very much if you called me Sav."

With that he was gone, and I was left to wander the streets on my own. I had been so distracted by his words, I had not even noticed that he had managed to slip me a small card, much like the ones that had accompanied his roses. On it, in the same delicate calligraphy, was an address—one that I can only assume to be his own.

I have not had a day like this in a long time—a day where I have felt so happy, so free. I was so caught up in my own doings, I nearly forgot we have another performance tonight.

SAVERIO

November 18, 1898

I cannot believe how well this is all going. The poor boy is even more enamored with me than I could have hoped.

November 20, 1898

Tonight marks Neville Wighton the Great's final performance at the West London Theatre. I am not feeling panicked because the Adelphi has already confirmed and announced his residency in December, thus giving me plenty of time yet to learn the workings of the trick.

But if things keep going as well as they have been, I may not need much longer. Take tonight's closing performance. Yesterday a message arrived for me at my new apartment. I had no question as to who it was from. There are only two people on this earth who know where I am currently residing, and seeing that Paolo and Isabella departed from London less than a week prior, I was doubtful that my mentor was already checking in on me.

I had not really been expecting to hear from young Thomas so soon after our meeting. Usually, it takes a little more time for the results of my efforts to make themselves shown. Usually, the emotions have to ruminate a bit before the other party is ready to act on them.

It is almost sweet how new he is to flirtation. He does not understand the importance of playing coy—of not showing his hand too soon. If we really were playing cards, he would be robbed within mere minutes.

In a way, it is almost…endearing.

The telegram requested my presence at the closing performance, and the messenger also delivered to me a ticket. Sadly, it is not quite as good as the seat Paolo already had secured for me, but I cannot risk letting Thomas find me out, so I will gladly accept his invitation and sit in the seat he so graciously reserved for me.

He wishes to see me again. I cannot imagine a more perfect way for this all to be unfolding.

ෂ ෂ

Tonight did not go nearly as well as I had expected. It could have, but I slipped up. It is my own fault; I was too assured of myself—too certain. Earlier today I was scribbling about my own giddiness over how lovesick Thomas has become but I am the one who is acting like a fool.

Everything started out fine. I went to the theatre, just as I have been for the past few weeks, watched the performance, a performance I have seen so many times I could recite it my own self (save for one integral trick, of course). All in all, it was turning out to be a pretty standard evening. Once that final, maddening illusion was executed and the crowd's hysteria and wonder had subsided at least somewhat, the house lights were raised and we were being let out of the theatre.

An usher was standing at the end of the row in which I was seated, and when he locked eyes on me, he asked if I was "Mr. Saverio." The possibility that I had been found out was so incredibly slim, and yet it was enough to cause a strange, nervous heat to surge down the back of my neck as the hairs sprung up involuntarily.

Being the master performer that I am, I kept my composure. I nodded and informed him that that was indeed my name. He informed me that Mr. Pendleton had requested for me to wait in the theatre for him. I shrugged and moved back to my seat to wait for the rest of the patrons to exit the auditorium.

In my head, I was dancing and singing. This was too

delicious. I was left alone in the very space where the greatest illusion ever conceived was performed night after night. Once I was absolutely certain that I was the only person left sitting in the theatre, I made my way down to the main floor, barely able to contain the skip in my step.

I snaked through the rows of seats until I made it to the row I had been sitting in nearly every other night of the extended run. With nothing to inhibit me. I stood up atop one of the chairs, extending my arms and reaching out for the air above. The thought had previously crossed my mind that maybe carefully concealed mirrors were suspended overhead, reflecting the image of a leaping Neville. Was it a bit far fetched? Possibly. But nothing more bizarre than some of the scenarios I had already played through in my mind, and I was running out of theories.

Just as I had feared, there was nothing but empty air. I had to be quick; it was only a matter of time before Thomas would be coming out to meet me. After lowering myself back down off the seat, I was ready to cross over to the stage to inspect for any sort of apparatus that might explain the supposed midair disappearance. I was partially down the aisle, feet away from the stage, when I heard a soft, familiar voice.

Right before my eyes, only partially concealed by the crimson velvet stage curtain, was Thomas. I felt frozen, as if I had just been caught committing some criminal act (I was, in a sense, at least in the eye of other stage performers).

But Thomas simply craned his neck and, with a nod, urged me forward. He told me that he wanted to give me a private tour of the theatre.

Surely, I had to be dreaming. This sort of luck does not simply fall into one's lap. And yet there he was, extending a hand to pull me up onto the stage. It was as though he had a physical key to the illusion's secret and he was reaching out to hand it to me.

I had it all there…laid out at my feet.

And yet, I did not take proper advantage.

I curse my own idiocy. At first, I was on the right track. My eyes were alert, scanning for anything out of place, anything that might offer an explanation. But then we started talking.

Thomas, he is intelligent, thoughtful, curious. As we circled the stage, we began talking about the stage magician's craft — this required some nuanced acting on my part, pretending to not know most of what he was talking about. A few times I had to bite my tongue to keep from correcting him as he tried to explain how the most basic illusions and sleights were performed.

Our conversation then turned to other types of performances and arts. We talked a great deal about theatre, which transformed into a conversation about poetry, a topic that the boy seemed to know more than a bit about. He is quite well read, though that is not surprising for someone from such a wealthy, cultured family. I had not failed to notice the rows upon rows of bookcases that lined the Pendletons' estate, the night of their party.

Then, Thomas did something especially surprising for how timid he tends to come off. He started *performing* for me. Right there on the empty stage, he began reciting Shakespearian sonnets.

I was completely rapt. I should have been inspecting my competitor's territory, making mental notes, trying to piece it all together. But his words were so lovely; he had them memorized entirely and performed them with such charm and grace. At the time it was a joy, and I let myself get wrapped up in it.

Now that I am back at my apartment, left to stew over the night's happenings, I realize what a fool I was. I had a golden opportunity, and I let it go to waste. Who can be certain of the next time I will get such an opportunity, if I even get another one at all?

Thomas is just so heart-achingly sweet. And I allowed this sweetness to distract me from my objective.

This is why I never allow emotions to enter into the equation—a lesson that I inadvertently learned from my mother.

True, she was a prostitute and true, she shared her bed with many a man, but I was an observant child. I always noticed a certain longing in her eyes at any mention of the man who helped to conceive me (I refuse to acknowledge him as my father). Longing mixed with pain.

Since she would never actually tell me their story, I always had to make up my own. As a child, I invented some fiction detailing their short-lived romance. It changed every time I went over it in my mind, though at its core, most of the main details were always the same. I always picture him as a sailor for some reason, and French—in every fantasized scenario, he was always a Frenchman (I like to think it is where I inherited my fine tastes). His ship was in port at Civitavecchia and while passing through Perugia, he and his mates took a detour and made a stop at the local brothel for some fun. The man who fathered me was inspecting the girls, deciding who would warm his bed for the evening, when he spotted her—the most beautiful woman he had ever laid eyes on.

Now such a rare and delicate flower could not be kept in such a crass and lowly environment. So he whisked her away and rented a room in an inn just outside the city. It was a whirlwind weekend, making love, telling each other all their deepest secrets and wishes, and drinking their collective weight in locally grown wine.

The story always ends the same way: he promises her a new life, one with him. He tells her he loves her, even despite knowing her for such a short amount of time. Unsurprisingly, he breaks his promises along with her heart, and she spends the rest of her days in that same brothel where he found her. The son who is a constant living, breathing reminder of the man who shattered her heart to pieces is eventually sold off to a traveling stage magician, and the rest is no longer fiction but well-remembered history.

It is the memory of my mother's constant despair that serves as a reminder to me. A reminder not to allow something as temporary as love to cloud my judgment. It is the only rule I have ever set for myself, and up until now, it is one I have been able to abide by.

THOMAS

November 23, 1898

I am happy to report that I am finally allowed that moment to breathe I had been so desperately wanting. Now that our extended run is finally over, we have a lapse of time before our latest engagement at the Adelphi begins in December.

I already have more than a few ideas on how I would like to spend my newfound free time. Thoughts have been trailing into my head that should not be there. Wants and desires that are quickly ushered away by propriety and guilt.

It is lustful…

Sinful.

Hell, forget the questions of morality…it is criminal. I already have one secret that the court of public opinion would gladly see me tried for (if they had even the faintest idea)—I do not need to add buggery to my list of charges.

And yet, knowing it is wrong does not make me want to be around him any less than I do.

Oh, what does it matter, anyway? I have rightly embarrassed myself already. When Sav gave me the address to his flat, he most certainly could not have been expecting me to send a gram the very next day. But it was the last night of our performance (for a bit) and though he had already seen the show at least once before on All Hallows' Eve, I wanted to give him the chance to see more…to get to see the man behind the magician's apprentice.

Here is what I know of Sav at this point:

Much like myself, he is also an apprentice, but to a tailor with a workshop based in Rome.

His master, or as he referred to him, his "mentor" (I found this odd), sent him here to London with an allowance so that he may study rising fashions and new techniques for tailoring.

He was born into a humble family—not poor but not wealthy, either. I think he mentioned something about a sister… Isabelle, I think her name was.

He is older than me, by approximately three years. Like me, he was unable to attend university. He was told by his family to learn a craft and begin work immediately. But he has been trying different things, attempting to find the right fit. He said this is his third apprenticeship in a new area of expertise.

To his credit, he did not flee at my sudden, eager invitation. He obliged me, attended the show, conversed afterward for what ended up being hours. Time is nothing when he is around. It was the same feeling I had during our meeting at Simpson's and on the night of the party. It is a hard thing to put into words—the best one I can think of is "weightless." I do not feel the insurmountable pressure that my parents and Neville so willingly place upon my shoulders from day to day. I feel like, well, myself. A self I am only now being introduced to.

But as I said, it probably does not matter at all. I have not received word from him, and the roses stopped once the performances did.

I have to keep myself distracted. I have days to myself now, days of true freedom, and I am determined to enjoy them.

I am free of Neville for the time being and will not have to see him until rehearsals begin in our new performance space. This will not be for some time, since Neville has allotted only a few days prior to the premiere night for rehearsing. Our initial string of successes had made him confident, overconfident if you ask me. Although it is easy for him. The entire illusion does not rest on his shoulders—in fact, *none* of it does.

I have found reading to be a nice escape during my empty days. I made a trip to Mr. Wexler's shop to pick up an edition of *Fairy Tales from the Brothers Grimm*. I had been hankering for something more fantastical and was surprised to realize I did not already own a copy.

It has been nice, enveloping myself in tales where that which is mystical or unexplained is not immediately discounted as something malicious.

November 27, 1898

*A*nother tea date with Amelia today. Oh, the joy I feel...
    When she arrived with her family's carriage, I was busy making myself look presentable. Whilst I was still upstairs in my room, my mother took it upon herself to fetch one of my roses from Sav (to her, he remains the mysterious and elusive "S"). She picked the one that had dried out the least, one of the last I had received, and gave it to Amelia, saying it was from me before I had even descended the stairs. She was giddy over the token. When I realized what had happened, I stood wordless for a second, and then my father gave me a wink before we left. It was not simply a wink, though. It was a push—him pushing me in her direction.

It was a cruel thing for my mother to do. The rose was mine and had been a gift for me. I have been keeping them and, as they have been drying, I have been pressing them into the pages of one of my journals. This one will never join the others, and I feel a strange sense of loss. I suppose I am being overly sentimental.

It was a rather unkind thing to do to Amelia as well—giving her false hope and ideas about my feelings toward her. Although, I am doing a pretty fair job of that myself, what with these luncheons and tea dates.

When the heart is lonely, it will make a person do things they are not proud of.

To my new friend Thomas,

I want to take the time to properly thank you for inviting me to your final performance at the West London Theatre. It was an enchanting evening, and though I quite enjoyed Mr. Wighton's stunning act, getting the chance to speak with you alone afterward was what really took my breath away.

If it is not too forward, I would very much like to continue spending time with you while I am still here in London.

If you feel the same and would also like to see me again, meet me at our spot tomorrow at noon and I shall know your answer.

Sincerely yours,
S

November 30, 1898

It finally happened. Sav sent a letter for me that arrived only a day after my miserable date with Amelia. My parents are not so prying that they would read my mail, but I was still relieved to see that he had signed it with the moniker "S."

I was not entirely certain what he was alluding to when he said "our spot." I felt plagued by the overwhelming sense that I *should* know where he was referencing.

I had a few ideas in mind, so the following day, I left, giving myself what I felt would be enough time. Unsure if our activities for the day would involve a meal, I tried to sneak a biscuit from the kitchen without my parents noticing. I had planned on leaving without a word, but I stumbled in to find my father putting a kettle on the stove. It was an unfamiliar sight, and it was not until then that I realized the staff had not come in the day before, nor had they been in over the past weekend. I chose not to ask my father about it, since I was trying to slip away with as little conversation as possible.

He raised an eyebrow to me and casually asked where I was headed off to. Quickly, I created some fib about how Neville wanted to meet with me to discuss the new residency. It seemed to satisfy him, for he turned back to the stove, leaving me to make my escape.

I lie so rarely that, for the briefest of moments, I was actually rather impressed with myself. I expected to feel worse than I actually did. With my mother's and father's continued disregard for my requests or wants, there is little I feel I owe them, and this includes my honesty.

My first guess at our meeting point was the spot where we first laid eyes on each other: Manchester Square. The park was now covered in white snow, and there were few people out and about. I quickly inspected the figures lingering nearby, but not one turned out to be Sav.

No matter, I still had plenty of time.

I had some money with me, so I boarded a hansom cab and had the driver take me over to the West London Theatre. It was much more pleasant than walking in the cold. I half expected to see Sav there waiting for my arrival out in front, but he was nowhere to be seen. I had the driver wait while I went to try the doors but, as I suspected, they were locked. The staff would have gladly let me in, what with how much business Neville had brought them, but there was no one there. As it was, I severely doubted that Sav would be waiting for me inside a locked theatre. With brisk steps, I rounded the building and peered into the alleyway just to be certain that this was not the spot.

I pulled myself back into the cab and let the driver know that my next and (hopefully) final destination would be Simpson's. This had to be it; it was the only idea I had left… the only other place we had been together.

On a whim, I asked my driver if he happened to have the time. He rustled in his pocket for a moment, pulled out a watch on a small silver chain, and informed me that it was quarter past the hour. My heart skipped a beat. I opened the buttons to my coat so that I could retrieve my own pocket watch from my vest. There had to be some mistake. According to my watch, I still had a quarter of an hour until noontime. Either my own timepiece was running slow or his was running fast. My anxiety tightened my shoulder muscles and churned my stomach.

My mind played out the scenario: he had shown up, waited for me, and left thinking I had answered his question about whether or not I wished to see him again by way of standing him up.

Convinced that this was the case but hoping that I still had a chance to catch him and explain my tardiness, I urged the driver to stop right where we were on Exeter Street. I gave him a sixpence for his service, then ran the rest of the way to Simpson's.

As I walked in through the front door, I was dismayed when the oak grandfather clock in the lobby showed that it was indeed my timepiece that had been running slow, and now I was nearly twenty minutes late.

The host looked me up and down. "Ah, you must be Mr. Pendleton! I did not realize you were the boy from the magic show—I had the chance to see it with my wife, and we adored Mr. Wighton's performance. How ever did he pull off that miraculous trick?"

I gave a grin. "A magician never reveals his secrets, nor does his apprentice."

He laughed and made some remark about how fascinating being an illusionist's apprentice might be. Normally, I would have indulged the man, but I had no time for pleasantries. I was at least assured I had finally arrived at the correct location. If the man knew my name just from looking at me, I had only to assume Sav left a description of me with him.

My worries that I had already missed my companion were staved off when the host told me to follow him inside. Once again, the dining room was a cacophony of arguments mixed with pure delight. The afternoon sun was peeking past the winter clouds and streaming in through the windows, illuminating the cigar smoke that hung above each table as the chandeliers hanging overhead glinted and gleamed.

Instead of a secluded booth in the back of the room, like our last meeting here, the man led me to a table near the window, equipped with a full chessboard.

Sav was seated at the table, and to my surprise (and relief) he did not look the slightest bit perturbed. I can honestly say, in the few times I have seen him face to face, I have yet to see him look tense.

I, meanwhile, was tension incarnate. After the host bowed his head and left us to it, I immediately started babbling, retrieving my best excuse for why I was late. He took one look at my disheveled state, windswept hair and all, and laughed that warm laugh of his. He raised a silencing hand, and I stopped dead in my tracks. He then used that same hand to gesture toward the seat across from him and told me to sit.

It was not until I sat down that I realized there was already a cup of tea and a plate of what looked to be gingersnaps waiting for me.

"You ordered for me?"

"I hope you do not mind," Sav replied, "I know how you Brits like your tea, and I figured you would not want to wait. Although, I suppose you will need it warmed up now."

"You knew I would come."

"I hoped," he said before taking a sip of what by now was most likely his second or third cup of coffee.

I felt myself flush.

He pointed at the gingersnaps on my plate. "Those cookies are quite good. I finished mine rather quickly." He reached over and plucked one off the plate. "You don't mind, do you?" He tossed it into his mouth before waiting for an actual reply.

I shook my head and smiled. The truth was I did not mind, not in the slightest. In fact, there was something I found oddly charming in the way he was able to take what he wanted.

A waiter came by and took my tea to be refreshed. I looked back down at the table and nodded toward the game board. "I thought you liked observing."

"I do," he replied, "but I also like trying new things." He leaned in closer—not too close, just close enough. "Do you like trying new things, Thomas?"

I gulped. I genuinely did not know how to respond, so instead of doing so, I grabbed one of the gingersnaps and nibbled on it.

My genuine speechlessness seemed to amuse him, for he just chuckled and leaned back in his chair, apparently no longer expecting an answer from me. His eyes turned down to the chessboard before us.

He made the first move.

We played for a bit. He was good for someone who had previously claimed not to play much, but admittedly, I was better. Years of practice, I suppose. After a bit, Sav suggested we abandon our game. He claimed that our concentration was causing far too much silence, and he would much rather engage in conversation. This was perfectly fine with me, although I suspect that he was keenly aware of the fact that I was about to have checkmate.

Rather than a simple, hand-rolled cigarette, he had a small wooden pipe with him with a small band of ivory lining the stem. He filled it with tobacco and pulled out a small matchbook labeled with MIDLAND GRAND HOTEL. This time when he offered it to me, I decided I would try it. When I turned sixteen not too long ago, my father had invited me into his study and allowed me to smoke a bit from one of his pipes. I figured that experience would be enough to ensure I would not look foolish, but of course, the moment I tried to inhale, I was thrown into a violent fit of coughing.

Through watering eyes, I noticed Sav was biting down on his lip, containing his laughter. For what it was worth, I appreciated the restraint.

For the rest of the afternoon, we talked, we laughed, we drank (after a bit we switched from coffee and tea to warm cider). Every now and again he would turn the conversation back to my supposed "profession." He had questions about stage magic and sleight of hand, but even more than that, he had questions about Neville.

It is not that I minded…much. What I mean is, I understand. I can see perfectly clearly how someone looking from the outside in would find the man fascinating, especially for the feat they think he is pulling off single-handedly. I simply wish there was an aspect of my life, even just one, that did not involve Neville Wighton the Great.

As the afternoon turned to evening, a pair of gentlemen a table over from us invited us to join them. One of the men was heavily whiskered, his gray mustache nearly encompassing the whole of his mouth, and his companion was a larger gentleman with ruddy checks and eyes in a constant cheery squint, as though his face were always grinning even when his lips were not. They were a fair bit older than us, which gave them plenty of stories to delight us with.

With Sav's undeniable wit and insidious charm, they took an immediate liking to him, and I do not blame them. They laughed at all his quips and shared their whiskey with him (the offer was also extended to me, but I do not particularly care for the burning sensation it leaves in one's throat). As our socializing progressed, other men who were quite engrossed in their chess games started casting glares in our direction. The mustachioed man, who had introduced himself as Arthur something or other, protested that Simpson's was too stuffy anyway and suggested we move our activities to a nearby pub.

I was feeling uncertain at best. The hour was getting late, and I probably did not have much time left before my father became suspicious of whether or not I was actually with Neville. But all it took was a nudge in the arm from Sav and a wink of one of his dark, glimmering eyes and I was suddenly on board for whatever mischief we were about to get ourselves into—I likely would have agreed to anything at that point.

Snow had begun falling while we were still inside, but our journey was not an arduous one. The White Lion was the pub Arthur had been referring to, and it was in Covent Garden, a mere five-minute walk from Simpson's Grand Divan. We were greeted with a more joyous, if not already quite drunken crowd. Arthur, Roger (the ruddy fellow), and Sav all ordered more whiskey. What I really wanted was a simple glass of wine, but I felt ale a more befitting beverage of our new surroundings.

At one point, after they had enough drinks in them, Roger and Sav got up and started singing "Drink Little England Dry." Of course, being from Italy, Sav needed to be taught the lyrics (with some help from some drunken bar fellows), but I must say he caught on quite quickly. His enthusiasm was pure delight and his voice was melodious, even in his impaired state. His accent flavored the song in a way that made me wish for more and more verses. Pretty soon the whole pub was joining in.

I was more than content to sit in my seat and silently observe, but I was given little choice in the matter when you pulled me up to start dancing. At first, I admit, I was rather self-conscious, but the clapping and stomping from the crowd encouraged me on. You hooked your arm through mine and we began to skip around and around in time with each clap and stomp. It was somewhere between a schoolyard game children play as they sing nursery rhymes and a drunken Irish jig (more of the latter, I suppose).

The more we spun around the room, the faster we skipped, the more the world began to disappear. The pub was nothing more than a blur of lights and sound and all I could see was you.

SAVERIO

December 02, 1898

I am having myself plenty of fun, just as I was hoping I would, but time is slipping away from me. Thomas is falling under my spell, and yet there is still some reluctance on his part. Surely, we are getting to know each other better, bonding, even, yet during our conversations, I cannot help but feel like I am the one doing most of the speaking. And whenever I make an attempt to hold eye contact with him, he ends up looking away, as if something terrible will occur if he holds my gaze for a moment too long. If I want any shred of information on Wighton before Paolo's arrival back in London, then I shall have to double my efforts.

THOMAS

December 05, 1898

Something awful happened tonight. I am almost too fearful to detail it here in this journal, for writing it down will make it all the more real. That being said, I have decided that getting it out on the page will help me to work through what happened in an effort to keep it from occurring again.

Just a few days ago, Sav sent another letter for me, saying that he had a grand time and would very much like to see me again. He signed the letter with "S" once again, and as I read, my mother tried to get me to tell her who it was from. I told her that it was just an old mate from grammar school and that we would be meeting to catch up on our lives since we last saw each other.

Today I was able to leave without protest from my mother or father and once again, each member of the staff was absent from our household. I had a mind to inquire about it with Mother, but I was far too preoccupied with meeting Sav.

He did not have me meet him at Simpson's this time, or even the White Lion, but instead opted for an outdoor meeting point. We met at the north bank of London Bridge and walked along the Thames. The chill in the air was biting, especially near the river, but Sav seemed quite comfortable bundled in his winter clothes. His neck was wrapped three times over with a black wool scarf, and his head was topped with a matching black cap. He was wearing a vibrant red walking cloak that, from the looks of it, was probably designed for a woman but with his slender frame and confident gait, it suited him quite nicely. Even so, this did not stop others from staring.

I probably could have used my gift to warm myself, but I had performed such a thing so few times that I was uncertain how it would manifest physically. Ultimately, I made the decision the risk would not be worth the comfort.

Mercifully, after a bit of walking around, Sav suggested we take refuge in a nearby café. Once inside, he ordered himself a coffee, a tea for me, and a cranberry scone for each of us. I offered to pay for my own items but he waved off my words with a casual air. I told him I felt horrid and did not want him spending the money meant for his own living expenses on treats for me.

"It is no trouble," Sav said, sweet but firm, seemingly not wanting another argument from me. "My mentor will replenish my funds soon, and I am not struggling."

"Nor am I," I protested. "Not to be improper, but you have been in my home. Certainly that tells you enough about my own financial situation."

"Just because you can provide for yourself does not mean that I cannot do something nice for a friend, right?"

So I left it at that.

Sav took a bite from his scone and asked me a question about the upcoming headlining slot at the Adelphi.

I had no real interest in discussing the topic, but even if I did, it is not as though I have much to say. I have not seen Neville in weeks and will not see him for another few days. Our rehearsals are not so much for practice as they are for getting familiar with the new space. Nothing about the actual act is changing, though I am sensing that will not be the case for much longer. Neville has brought up the idea of "new material" on a few separate occasions. He says the grand illusion, while immensely popular, will grow stale after too long. He wants my help in creating new, impossible feats to wow our audiences. If he comes up with a new trick then by all means, I shall do what I can, but I will have no part in the planning of his next stage deception.

For now, our act remains the same. He has changed a few of the illusions leading up to the grand finale, but I have little involvement in those tricks, as it were. Still, Neville insists we must at least give off appearances that we are taking the time to set ourselves up in our new environment. If we did not, others in the theatrical community might grow suspicious.

Another magician would need to take the proper time to memorize the layout of their new performance space, to learn the advantages and limitations, and to set up a particularly complicated apparatus that cannot be easily assembled/disassembled. Of course, our grand act requires no such apparatus. We could perform the act tonight in a tavern by having Neville jump from a barstool, if he were feeling particularly whimsical or foolish. But we must act the part of the laboring performers, working to ensure every minor detail is in order. It is all part of keeping up the illusion—that what we are doing actually *is* an illusion and nothing more.

In this sense, the whole situation is something of an enigma.

I kept casually shifting the conversation to other matters, but it kept coming back to the world of magic, specifically my employer. He inquired about Neville's history, how he got into the profession, who his influences were, how he works...and more questions of that ilk.

~~I do not know where his growing interest in stage performance has come from~~... Actually, I know exactly where his curiosity has come from. Ever since we premiered that trick more than a month ago, it seems every theatregoer in London has a sudden desire to know the inner workings of Neville

Wighton's mind.

The problem? I am hardly the person to be asking. I know as little about the man as his milkman—nay, even less. When it comes to his method of work, well, that would require me actually seeing him work. And despite my being his "apprentice," the odd man has yet to actually teach me anything. I am the gears and cogs that allow the illusion to function.

I am actually quite baffled by Neville Wighton. From what I can gather, he is reclusive and awkward when it comes to social norms, and yet, he so desperately craves the fame and accolades that my magic has gifted him.

Sav must have gathered that I did not have much to say, for he eventually left it alone.

The bright winter afternoon quickly turned to evening, and I found my cup of tea transformed into a glass of Cabernet. It was my turn to start asking questions, and I had him tell me all about Italy. Every detail sounded so romantic as he spoke about his home country (especially the climate). I could have listened all night to him talking about the different cities and villages he has been to, but the staff started to clean up and we took this as our sign to leave.

Sav asked if I would walk with him to his flat, and I obliged. I was not feeling nearly as intoxicated as I had been during our last night of revelry and was certain I would be able to make my way back home without issue.

I knew we were getting close to his flat when his pace began to slow significantly. Something in his reluctance to allow the night to end made my cheeks grow hot and small beads of sweat form along my back, even despite the harsh winter chill.

Number four Bedfordbury. That was where he had been residing. The building looked quite nice—quite nice indeed for a tailor's apprentice. His master must be most skillful if he can put Sav up in such lodgings for an extended time.

We had ceased our conversation as I looked up at the windows, silently pondering which flat belonged to my companion. The silence between us caused a rapid drumming of my heart that pulsed all throughout my body until it was thudding in my ears.

Sav stepped closer to me, breaking the silence by asking if I wished to come up. He apologized, saying that he had no tea to offer me but that he had cigarettes from France and half a bottle of Malbec he could share.

I said nothing, just stood there staring at him as flakes of snow flurried and fluttered around our heads. I focused on specific flakes, tracing them with my eyes as they landed in Sav's dark tufts of hair.

Was this truly happening?

I already knew I would say yes, that I would go with him. That if he were to reach out a hand, I would clasp onto it and follow him wherever he decided to lead me. Even in my doubt and fear, I felt certainty.

But I could not vocalize that certainty. I would try, open my mouth, waiting for a response to follow, but my words were as frozen as the snow around us.

Even without an answer, or any other indication that I wanted the night to continue, Sav was inching closer…closer… closer. Until I could feel his breath as it warmed my skin. The drumming of my heart quickened to a deafening speed, drowning out all other senses.

And then I felt it.

The pressure was building inside me, churning and screaming as it expanded throughout my being. It was the same feeling that had consumed me when Neville had struck me that night at rehearsal. It was the feeling that had made itself known when I was just a small child and Vivienne, my first nanny (first of many), had scolded me for sneaking a biscuit before finishing my potatoes.

The magic was taking shape within me, ready to lash out.

My heart was telling me that I could contain it—that with the proper amount of force, I could stifle whatever was about to occur. But my head already knew there was no containing it, no stifling it. When I was commanding my own gift, with intent and purpose, I could shape it to achieve the desired effect. But this was far different. Whenever I lose control and my emotions cause my powers to boil over and slide beneath the surface, I never know what effect it will have. It usually involves something violent and someone almost always gets hurt.

It was too late to correct the situation. The moment I recognized that raging storm inside myself was the precise moment Sav leaned down to match my height. Slowly he brought his face close to mine, and he…

He kissed me.

It was innocent enough—a simple kiss on my cheek, like I would bestow on a relative or longtime friend. And even had it not been so innocent, there was no one around to witness this tender moment.

But the racing of my heart. The rushing of my blood. The shortness of breath. It manifested itself before I could even try to control it (or, at the very least, wield it in a manner that would have been noticeable only by me). The pressure building inside me burst, and just a few feet away, the glass casing for two of the gas streetlamps shattered, extinguishing the inner light immediately.

Sav and I whirled. He seemed confused, and I could only blink in horror at the shattered glass decorating the street.

"How peculiar," Sav mumbled. He then turned his attention back to me as though nothing had happened. I muttered something that I hope sounded like an agreement before making up some excuse about how my parents were expecting me and would likely be waiting up. Foolish for a young man my age, but I was far more worried about what I had just let happen than I was about appearing more like a true adult.

He nodded, and before he could say anything to make me feel horrid or that would make me change my mind, I trotted back the way we had come, not even looking down when my right boot crunched on one of the pieces of glass below.

I cannot fathom how Sav would have connected me to the glass shattering, but then again, I cannot be so ignorant as to rule out the possibility. He is an intelligent man, after all, but it is on this intelligence I must rely. Those with good sense and reason would think of a logical explanation for why the lamp burst—the chemical compounds in the gas keeping the lamps lit, a bit of ice falling from the rooftops above…something of that nature. Not something so childlike and silly as magic.

Meanwhile, I have only to lie awake and think of what could have been if I had not lost my handle over my abilities.

I was not expecting such a thing to happen for two reasons:

I had not been planning on Sav to show me any sort of physical attention.

I have never lost my control due to feelings of infatuation. Yes, in the past I have lost control due to intense emotions, but these were feelings of rage or dread. Never has something so positive caused such a chemical reaction in me.

I suppose it can only mean one thing: I have never felt for another person what I feel now for Sav.

SAVERIO

December 05, 1898

I was so close. So damn close.

I had Thomas right where I wanted him tonight and he slipped through my fingers like sand. If it were not for those cursed streetlamps breaking—he was startled, and like a frightened doe, he skittered and ran away. If the distraction had not pulled him back to the real world, he would have stayed in the one I'd created just for the two of us.

Perhaps it was not only the fright that pulled him to his senses. Perhaps I moved too quickly on this, frightened the boy all on my own. Perhaps I misread the signs of his infatuation with me.

The odd thing is I found myself more baffled over my own disappointment with the way the night unfolded. As I climbed the stairs to apartment 2E, a small bit of sadness tugged at me that I would not be spending my evening with Thomas.

I have just worked it out in my mind and am now realizing that since the first night of that miraculous performance, since I first decided that I would be setting out on this endeavor, my bed has been uncharacteristically empty. Throughout this whole pursuit, I have not even attempted to meet another soul, let alone invite them to spend the night with me.

This was not a decision that was made intentionally, so I am assuming it was more…subconscious. As I have stated before, I am like an actor putting on a role. Like any other actor would,

I must simply be staying true to this role of a man thoroughly enamored with Thomas Pendleton, seeking no other means of affection or fun.

And, as any other actor must, I shall have to be certain that I do not let the role consume each part of my life or soon, I will not know where one Saverio ends and the other begins.

THOMAS

My short-lived freedom was pleasant (mostly) while it lasted. Tonight I am to meet Neville at the Adelphi Theatre so that we may walk the space and get a sense of our new surroundings. No doubt he will also leap off the stage at some point (likely without warning) to make sure my senses are still sharp and that I can still execute the "illusion" with precision.

Sav sent a note for me. Supposedly he ran into our friends Arthur and Roger at Simpson's recently. Apparently they would very much like to see me again (almost as much as he would, according to his letter). The sentiment was quite nice, and it made me think happily on the night at the White Lion.

He did not mention the incident with the streetlamps, which is hopeful, I suppose.

Still, my cowardice took hold, and I never sent a response to his request for another meeting.

Surely, I will see him soon enough. He already expressed an interest in attending another one of Neville's performances. When he does, I will need to have already thought up some response for my rudeness. Perhaps he would have believed I had never received the note at all had it not been found directly on my doorstep. He must have delivered it personally, which makes it all the more strange that he did not simply wait and tell me everything detailed in the letter from his own mouth.

Though, I am glad he did not. Glad he is respecting the sudden distance I have wedged between us.

Perhaps "glad" is not the correct word. Still, being around him right now is too much of a risk. I cannot be certain of how I will feel the next time I see him, which means I cannot possibly know if or how my magic will manifest itself.

I cannot worry about that now. My current worries are all directed at my return to the stage with Neville.

Worry, worry, worry. All I ever do anymore is worry. For a bit there, I was certain I had found someone who relieved those worries and cured my heartaches and stresses. Someone I did not have to please or impress but who simply allowed me to be Thomas, nothing more, nothing less. Just another aspect of my life that magic has managed to ruin.

SAVERIO

December 16, 1898

I was so certain that Neville Wighton the Great would not slip, that he would not make a single false step. Tonight he did just that!

This is so incredibly brilliant.

I may not know where the blunder stemmed from or what it ultimately will come to mean, but it is something…and it fell into my lap just before Paolo's arrival. How fortuitous!

THOMAS

December 16, 1898

I would say that tonight was a disaster, but even that would fail to capture the true enormity of my mistake.

Our premiere performance at our new venue was a far grander event than the initial premiere at the West London Theatre.

Wealthy patrons filled every seat, even though most had already seen the show once or twice. To miss a premiere like this would be missing out on the event of the year (or rather, what was still left of it). Even though gaslights already filled the lobby, there were also candles adding a romantic glow to the space. Tables held glasses of champagne and small cakes for the patrons to enjoy before filing into the auditorium. In addition to the orchestra already set to play in the theatre, a cellist and harpist had been stationed in the lobby to welcome guests with their sweet melodies as they entered.

Despite all this pompousness prior to the performance, the actual show went mostly the same as it had more than a month ago (only, again, we now had live music accompanying each trick). Then it came time for what everyone was truly there to witness. Neville walked to his mark and stood waiting. As he readied himself to sprint forward, a single drumroll commenced, building in speed and tension. Neville ran forward to the edge of the stage and leaped, just as he had so many times before. And as before, he disappeared right over the heads of the astounded audience members seated below.

But that was all that happened.

I waited with bated breath, just like the rest of the audience, for the magician to emerge and reveal himself at the railing of the box we had kept clear of patrons. But he did not. He was nowhere to be seen.

I waited and waited, until I could wait no longer. Patrons had already started their whispers and murmurs, and I had to cover the horrendous blunder somehow.

I stepped forward from my spot on the stage and began applauding my mentor with a delighted smile, therefore praising the illusion merely as a disappearing act alone and not a reemergence.

Many faces in the elegantly dressed crowd still looked confused. Slowly, more applause began to break throughout the auditorium. It was timid and uncertain at first, surely because many of these people had already seen Neville Wighton's amazing illusion and knew exactly how it was meant to play out. But soon the applause grew in force and was accompanied by cheers and whistles. By the time patrons were being ushered out of the theatre, I overheard one or two exclaiming how wonderful that the magician had altered his act to add an element of surprise and keep his audiences on their toes.

My quick thinking had worked, but the relief was short lived. Neville was still gone. As they stood from their seats, I spotted my parents, who were each directing equally severe looks in my direction. Still, they knew better than to act as though something were amiss in such a large crowd, and so they left.

I paced back and forth, and once the theatre was clear, I tore through the space. Backstage was my first guess, but there was no sign of him. I climbed down the stairs that led to the alcove below, but nor was he there. I searched through every aisle, every row of seats, I checked his dressing room and any other dressing room that lined the halls, but no Neville. I scoured the lobby where I ran into the manager. He congratulated me on an excellent first performance and tried to guide me out the front door, but I told him that it was important I remain in the theatre for just a bit longer. He seemed a bit disgruntled at my refusal to leave but said that I could remain until the cleaning staff had finished tidying the theatre.

They finished their work and kicked me out before there was any sign of Neville. I waited in the cold for what felt like hours before his thin gray-haired figure made its way down the cobblestone street with a silver-topped cane in hand. His eyes were fire and ice all at once as he glared in my direction. Without a word, he grabbed me by the wrist and pulled me into the alleyway beside the theatre. Once we were safely out of sight, he seized my coat by the collar and pressed me up against the stone wall.

"Do you think that was funny, boy?"

I did not answer. Only glared back at him. The fool! Had he learned nothing about what provoking me could do? I did not necessarily desire to hurt him in that moment, but that didn't mean it wouldn't happen.

He pressed on. "Did you think you could make a fool of me? Make me the laughingstock of the magical community? Of all of London?"

I batted his hands away, and he let go with surprising ease.

This whole thing was an act, and I was a performer of sorts, so I knew I had to pretend to be someone else—someone brave. I thought of the most confident person I know. Sav. What would he say when backed into a corner by someone like Neville?

"No one thinks you are a fool, you old hornswoggler! Once again, you underestimate your apprentice's intelligence—I convinced them all it was an intentional change to the act. That it was a disappearing act and nothing more."

Neville had nothing to say to this. As I had guessed, he really *had* underestimated me. Since he had nothing to say, I continued. "Where did you reappear tonight?"

He gave me a cold stare. "My studio."

Strange. I had not been thinking of his studio. But then again, I had not been thinking of anything very specific at all. This is what happens when I allow myself to lose focus.

"You let anything like this happen ever again, and I swear, boy, I will—"

"You will what? Tell me, Neville. Are you threatening me? You realize I can just as easily threaten *you*, do you not?"

He reached to the ground, collecting the cane he had discarded when he had pushed me into the wall. He pointed it in my direction. "You would do best to watch your tongue!"

"I could walk away from all this...walk away from *you*. And then people might finally see you for the fraud you are. You would never get booked for another show as long as you live."

I expected him to be worried, taken aback even, but he just smiled. The smug bastard was grinning at me, and his grin was made all the more malicious by being backlit by the lights of the marquee.

"I guarantee, your parents would not like that very much," he sneered. "And you have no wish to disappoint them, now, do you?"

Did he already know I'd gone to them on the issue before? Did he know of how they had threatened to disinherit me? What sort of strange alliance has he formed with my parents?

He smoothed his cloak and instructed me to arrive an hour early tomorrow night so that we can go over the illusion and make sure nothing else goes astray. He then turned on his heels and walked away, leaving me breathless, my stomach clenched with rage.

SAVERIO

December 17, 1898

Paolo has arrived in London. Our meeting did not go quite as well as I had planned.

By the time he did eventually make it to my side of the city, it was just past three bells. I was attempting (rather unsuccessfully) to make tea. I figured if Thomas liked it so much, there had to be something to it. I bought some plain black tea at the local market but only later realized that my kitchen had not been equipped with a kettle, so I was trying to brew it in a tin pot. When Paolo came sauntering in unannounced, I swirled the translucent brown liquid around in the pot before offering him a cup. He looked down at the contents of the pot as though I had just offered him a cup of warmed saliva. I shrugged off his dismissive look and poured a cup for myself.

Paolo started the conversation by asking me why my door was unlocked. I never lock my door. I did not bring anything with me worth stealing and kept few of the things that I did bring when Paolo and Isabella left me in the city. There are my clothes, which are fine, to be certain, but clothing is quite easily replaced when you work for one of the most famous performers in all of Europe.

I explained this to my mentor (not the last bit about the clothing, of course), told him he was looking well, and then inquired as to how Isabella was doing. He made it clear he had no interest in such pleasantries, and so we got on to the matter at hand.

I tried to restrain my utter delight as I explained to him what had occurred the previous night at Wighton's Adelphi Theatre premiere. After I was finished detailing how the old man had disappeared but never reappeared, Paolo just continued to stare at me, stone faced and expectant. For a moment or two, we sat in silence.

"Is that all?" he finally asked.

"Is that all?" I mimicked incredulously. "What are you talking about? This is wonderful. The supposedly brilliant prestidigitator has faltered in front of one of his largest audiences yet. I assumed you would be pleased."

"And what did the audience make of this error?" my mentor asked, his voice as calm as his dark eyes.

"They… Well, they did not take it for a failure. They believed he'd altered it to make it only a disappearing act."

"And for all we know, it *was* the desired effect."

"But the boy! His apprentice. I was observing him, too. He looked nervous. When Wighton did not reappear as normal, his eyes were wide. Something was…off."

"You are convinced it was an error because the apprentice looked startled? That is your proof? Wide eyes? You come to me claiming to have seen Wighton falter, but you cannot even be certain he did. All you have done is recount to me what any other simpleton in that audience could have. If you had some actual proof, some way of being certain Mr. Wighton had meant to reemerge and take his bow, claim his applause, then yes…we might have something. If you actually knew there was a mistake, then it might give us a hint as to how the trick is executed. But you have nothing. You have a hunch—little more than what you had a month ago."

And he was right. I had not realized it until he laid it all out before me, but I still had absolutely nothing. I slunk back in my seat, feeling dejected and useless. I tried sipping at the tea, but my insides shuddered once the bitter potion washed over my tongue. I did not wish to give Paolo the satisfaction, so I fought the urge to spit it back out into the cup. The last thing I needed in that moment was another reason for him to think me foolish.

Paolo did not scream at me, and I knew he would not. His rage is a more silent one and therefore, even more unsettling. I could feel his disappointment seeping into my very bones as he looked me up and down.

The one thing, the one path that would lead me to Wighton's secret, was dear, sweet little Thomas. But even he seemed to be slipping from my grasp. I had called on him on a few occasions since the night he had refused to accompany me up to my room, trying to arrange a time for us to see each other. I had waited for him outside the theatre last night. I knew his parents were in attendance and was not planning on creating a scene. I simply wished to congratulate him and let him know I had been there.

But he refuses to see me, refuses to speak to me.

It has been distressing me.

I did not and will not mention any of this to Paolo. He need not know that all this time, all this hard work of mine, had been in ensuring that I (in the very least) had a friend in the magician's apprentice.

I was so certain of myself and my charms. So used to having any object of my desire fall willingly into my lap that when I set my sights on Thomas, I had not considered the possibility of his rejection. And when I found he was a poet…what luck! The boy was already a romantic with stars in his eyes and dreams in his mind. The work seemed to have done itself for me.

This is one of the things I have always despised about my mentor—one moment I am a king and the next, I am smaller than one of the mice currently taking residence in my walls.

THOMAS

December 18, 1898

Fiends! Liars! Oh cruel hearts…

Two nights prior, after my confrontation with Neville, I had a frightful time trying to let go of what he said about my leaving—about how my parents would not approve. This, in turn, had me thinking on their strange behavior of late. Two sleepless nights was all it took before I decided that I finally deserved some answers.

And oh, how I did find those answers.

Mother had plans to play bridge with some women in town and Father was off to breakfast with an "associate." He does not think I am fully aware that these friends and associates who keep taking him out for various meals are truly booking agents and promoters from all across London, but I have been keenly aware of their attempts to get to Neville Wighton through his apprentice's oblivious father (though he is far less oblivious than he lets on). ~~The fact that he~~

But I digress—I am losing sight of what is truly important here.

With an empty household this morn (heaven knows that not a single member of my family's staff has been seen in…well, to speak true, I hardly can recall), I seized my opportunity to have a look around Father's study.

By what I can attribute only to random chance, one of Father's ledgers happened to catch my eye. There was just something about it…the way it sat ever so slightly askew on the shelf, the noticeably smaller amount of dust that had collected on its spine, suggesting that the soft brown leather had been handled more recently.

I pulled the tome down and, lo and behold, small slips of paper were bookmarking a section in the middle of the ledger.

A moment. A pause. My hands shook and my own hesitation took hold of me like a sickness. In the moments before I chose to view the book's contents, I was still ignorant to my father's misdeeds and still held a modicum of respect for the man—respect that has all but vanished now.

As soon as I opened the ledger, the slips of paper slid from their place and floated to the floor, gentle and inconspicuous as feathers. A quick glance at the book's pages alerted me to absolutely nothing—just a handful of lines featuring shorthand that would probably mean something only to my father and his accountants or clients.

The slips were banknotes and, accompanying these banknotes, a handwritten receipt asserting proof of payment. The payee: Mr. Avery Pendleton…unsurprising. The surprise came when my eyes landed at the bottom of the receipt on a signature:

Neville Wighton

It was a blessing that my parents as well as the household staff were absent.

I felt the warm pulse of my curse as it coiled through my bloodstream and seeped through my skin. I heard it before I saw it: the low rumble. Upon looking up from the newfound evidence, I saw the small porcelain bust of my great-great-grandfather tremble. Pens rolled across Father's desk as if they'd become sentient and were now fleeing for their lives. What started as small tremors grew violent enough to shake a handful of books loose from the shelf I had just been investigating. I somehow avoided being pelted atop the head in the sudden downpour.

Once the earthquake subsided, I returned my attention to my discovery. Combined, the banknotes did not amount to a particularly awe-inspiring sum of money: £18. My family regularly spends this in a week's time, usually a bit more (I am not so naive or sheltered not to appreciate the fact that to someone in a less fortunate position than my own, the amount would be life changing)…but I just knew in the pit of my stomach that this was likely one of a number. There were undoubtedly many more banknotes with similar receipts made out to my father from Neville.

But one receipt was all I needed. One incriminating document will be more than enough to substantiate what I know now in my heart to be true… It all came together like a puzzle I had been so close to solving. The magician is paying my parents. Wighton cannot lose his magical "prodigy." I am the only key he has to any true sorcery and so to keep me in his clutches, he has tapped into my parents' greed…but what is worse is that they have taken the bait. No better than animals clawing hungrily at food dangled in front of their faces.

But why such desperation? To say my family has always lived comfortably would be putting things lightly. Neville has had a more successful career than most stage performers' paths. Even so, whatever he can offer on the modest income of such a profession, it would merely be supplemental to my family's fortune. Are a few added luxuries here and there truly worth more than their own son's happiness? They know of my misery, for this is a matter on which I have made myself painstakingly clear.

Now there is not much else for me to do but to wait…wait for my parents' return so that I may confront them. For so long, all I have wanted from them is simply answers, and now there will be no way for them to evade my questions. Not any longer.

~~I cannot recall the last time I was this angry~~>>> This is a blatant untruth. Every time I am in that damned magician's presence, I feel anger or something resembling it. I should choose my words more wisely: I cannot recall the last time I was this angry with my own parents. Why, when I left my father's study, I did not even bother to tidy up the mess that my outburst had created. Let him see. Let him be angry. His anger will pale in comparison to what I felt at learning that for the past few months, those who are meant to love me the most have been selling me out to a violent, controlling fool for an additional source of income.

It has taken all of what little self-control I do possess not to take the receipt and tear it into a million little pieces or allow the fire within me to burn it to a crisp.

❧ ❧

December 18, 1898 (continued)

Ɪ am bleary eyed, and my soul feels drained after tonight's events, and yet, sleep will not come to me. How could it? How could I possibly expect myself to sleep after all that I've learned, after all that was said?

After finishing my previous entry, I sat in the parlor and awaited my parents' return with dread.

I never wanted it to come to this, though. I never thought I would be viewing my mother and father in the same light that I view that awful man. I had not expected to think of my parents in such a way, but they are in cahoots with the man, which makes them no better than he. They are active participants in his abuse, though they like to pretend that feigning ignorance somehow makes them less at fault.

Mother was first to return. I had prepared so many words, a whole speech, really. I'd had enough time to run it over in my head like a rehearsal for a play. But when I looked into my mother's eyes, which had only ever looked at me with love and adoration (perhaps the occasional instance of fear when she thought my emotions were getting out of hand and would open the door I keep my magic so carefully locked behind), I could not bring myself to speak. All the words that I had selected so meticulously flew from my head as if they had sprouted wings.

So I held out the receipt with the banknotes folded underneath. Those gray eyes grew wider than I had ever seen them before, and her already porcelain skin blanched, making her look deathly ill.

Her eyes were wide, wet and glassy with tears and, despite my anger, I felt the sharp pang of guilt. She calmly explained that we would have a proper discussion once Father arrived home, though her voice trembled.

It was nearing dusk when my father did finally stroll through the door. He was in high spirits, but this was quickly altered when he entered the parlor to find a wife paler than a ghost and a son stricken silent and stern.

I again allowed the receipt to do the speaking for me.

My father swiped it from my hand along with the banknotes, though like my mother, he recognized what I'd found instantly. He looked from me to my mother then back to me, his eyes darting, scanning, searching…as though he would be able to find the right words written on one or both of our faces.

Finally, he relented, taking the seat opposite of mine, and his face told me what I had known long before he had arrived: that he was backed into a corner and, thus, defeated.

At first, my lack of speech was due to my own inhibitions

and fear, but now that my father was equally speechless, I would not be the one to speak first. Stubbornness was a side effect of the rage boiling beneath my silent, stoic surface. It was also one of the few traits I had inherited from Avery Pendleton.

Eventually my father found his voice and used it to ask what I had been doing in his study without his knowledge or permission.

The anger within me rose.

I had caught him in a dirty deal with Neville, and my father was actually trying to frame this as if *I* were the one in the wrong. The nerve! The unbelievable gall! How dare...

There is no need to write all the things that have already gone through my mind countless times tonight.

Rather than answer his question, I combated with my own. Why was he accepting Neville's money? Why allow me to continue on when he could clearly see how I've suffered? Why? Why? *Why?!*

I wanted to do so much more than ask these questions of him. I wanted to raise my voice—scream, even. I wanted to hurl accusations and call him the most horrible names my mind could conceive of. But even with this newfound sense of self-worth, I have not yet grown quite so bold. And even if I had, there is only one path that raising my temper would lead down, and as angry as I still am with them, I will not resort to such things.

And then something I had not been expecting occurred: my mother leaped up from her seat and she admitted it...*all* of it. My father could only watch in horror as Mother recounted the details of what had transpired behind my back.

Certainly, such an admission was what I had been aiming for, but I had not been counting on receiving it so willingly. Once she started, all the information washed over me in waves. I have decided to log all the major points of interest:

- Neville was the one who first found me and came to my parents about an apprenticeship (my mother's assumption is that one of her more gossip-prone confidantes who had attended a dinner party when I was a child saw something she had not been meant to. The current theory is that her loose lips let word travel through certain channels of the city until it guided the magician straight to our doorstep).

- It was years ago that Neville first approached my parents with the offer of payment for my "assistance." Long before I finished my schooling and long before I began my apprenticeship. When this first meeting occurred, my mother claims that both she and Father were insulted by such an offer and demanded that Wighton leave our home at once.

- Years passed, and if what my mother says is the Lord's honest truth, they had never intended to speak to the man again. Though the idea of a man so well known across London having knowledge of my secret troubled them greatly, so they had hired investigators to keep special watch on him and his whereabouts.

- Nearly three years ago, the bank started giving my father less and less work. At the time he thought very little of it and was still receiving a handsome salary, so he was actually quite pleased. (One would think this meant more time for a man to spend with his family, but looking back on this time, I certainly do not recall seeing my father any more than I had in the years prior. I suppose he found other ways to occupy those hours.)

- Gradually, the bank began to cut back on his pay as

much as they cut the hours they were having him work until finally, my father's boss admitted to him that due to the new system of bookkeeping and accounting that the bank was adopting, his position was all but rendered useless.

- It was at this point my father spoke up and admitted to me that none of his vast "wealth" had been placed into savings. To keep up with the lifestyle we had grown so accustomed to, my family had been spending just as quickly as my father had been earning.

- For months after being let go, my father scoured the city for hints of a new position, but his pride would not let him contact any of his many friends or connections. He simply did not want them to know.

- Once my parents' desperation became more than they could bear, my father did something he now claims not to be proud of…he got in contact with one of the private investigators whose services they had been using. Though it had been some time since my father had paid the man, he apparently was accommodating enough and agreed to give my father the address of Neville's apartment in South London.

It's obvious where the rest of the story leads from here.

For months now, I have been the only source of income for the Pendleton household. Was it not long ago that my father sat across from me in the courtyard, threatening to cut me off financially if I did not stay under Neville's employ? The sad, cruel irony here is that if I were to do so, it would be *me* cutting off him and my mother. The circumstances would be almost comical, if the whole thing were not so infuriating.

Once Mother and Father finished this series of confessions, my father looked me square in the eye and asked what I intended to do next. Quite honestly, I did not have an answer for him. I still don't. If I claim my freedom, I doom my own parents to financial ruin and destitution. I will be casting them out and leaving them to the mercy of London's unforgiving streets.

I may be angry, I may be hurt, but I do still love my family— as any loyal son would. What choice do I even have but to continue enduring my suffering to save those who brought me into this world? Is there even a choice in the matter?

December 19, 1898

I have had the night to think things through, and though my heart is still heavy with the weight of this betrayal, there is, perhaps, one glimmer of light: this recent turn of events has me feeling emboldened to go after what I want—what will truly make me happy.

For months, my parents have been planning an elaborate holiday party. Last night, after learning the truth of our financial misfortunes, I asked if this lavish event was still going to take place and with a noticeable degree of shame, my mother claimed that throwing the party as intended was the best way to keep with the status quo and to make it so none of our friends would suspect about our circumstances. Distasteful, but I already have plenty to be angry about right now—I hardly need to concern myself with yet another questionable decision on the part of Mother and Father.

A few weeks prior, we received stacks of invitations made up for the Christmas party. Maroon cards with the details scrawled by one of London's most prominent calligraphers. They were all the same, but my mother had pulled one out for me, suggesting that I add my own personal touch to the invitation, which I would send to Amelia and her family.

I confess now that very invitation still sits upon my desk. At first, I told myself that I was holding onto the invitation because I simply did not know what to write. Now, though, I am aware that the reason I could not bring myself to send it out is that secretly I was hoping…wishing that there might be someone else I could invite. That I could have someone else by my side.

And now that wish has come true.

Before last night's events, the idea of inviting Sav to the party in Amelia's place would have been an impossibility. But now? Now neither of them would have a leg to stand on if they were to try to prevent me. What right would they have to punish or scold me after their egregious actions?

Surely they will not be happy once they find out, and I do feel guilty for the insult to the Ashdowns, particularly Amelia. Having said that, the decision has been made, and I am not turning back. I will be delivering this invitation to Sav forthright. Either I act on my impulses now and get what I want, or I allow myself the time to think rationally and doubt myself until I do the respectable thing and inevitably invite Amelia.

Part of my desire to have Sav there is my state of weariness. With Neville's constant berating as well as his joint deceit with my own family, I feel as though I am surrounded by people who only do me harm, however intentionally or unintentionally. When I'm with Sav, there are no questions of intention or motive. There is just he and I, each of us enjoying the other's company, with our only thoughts being how we can make the other smile.

I am inviting Sav. It will be nice to have someone there I can trust.

Dear Sir or Madam,
Your presence is graciously requested at the home of Mr. Avery and Mrs. Katherine Pendleton on the night of Christmas Eve.
Come celebrate this time of holiday cheer with our family.
A four-course meal will be provided along with spiced wine and sweets.
Happy Christmas!

SAVERIO

December 21, 1898

I now hold in my hand the most beautiful scrap of parchment that could have possibly fallen into my lap. Well, to call it a mere "scrap" would be an understatement if there ever were one. The parchment has been carefully dyed a shade of deep maroon (a personal favorite color of mine) and was tucked inside an envelope sealed with wax the color of a golden sun — knowing the contents of the parcel now, it might as well have been sealed with liquid gold, for it certainly did contain a prize.

I have been personally invited to a dinner party the night of Christmas Eve, and not just *any* dinner party. This particular engagement will be taking place at the Pendleton manor house. Now how could I have come to be invited to such an event, but by the will of young Thomas himself?

Just as I was losing hope on the boy.

Just as Paolo was no doubt contemplating dragging me back to Italy in failure.

Anyone else in my position would have tried to concoct some new scheme — devise a different approach after going so long without any results or hints at progress. But in truth, the amount of time spent on this plan is one of the main reasons I have refused to change course. It would be too much of a disappointment to acknowledge that all this time spent and charms offered were a waste. It would be too heartbreaking to give up and concede that my plan to woo Thomas, which seemed so brilliant at first, was perhaps not so ingenious...

The timing of this invitation could not have been more perfect.

Of course, when I presented the invitation to my mentor, he scarcely showed any sign that he was at all impressed or even pleased (though I could spot a bit of relief behind those dark eyes). He still does not think that focusing on the boy will lead to anything fruitful, but one of Paolo's major flaws is that he focuses on singular battles rather than thinking of the grander war. This quality makes him a less than patient man (though he does not admit it).

Me? I have the gift of patience and the foresight to know where my efforts will ultimately lead. It is for this I am now rewarded. I have already started concocting a plan for the night. With so many guests and so much activity, Thomas will surely have points in the evening when he is more than a little distracted. I will be able to use one of these moments as my opportunity to sneak away from the festivities and find Thomas's room. Perhaps then I will be able to find some sort of log with notes from his rehearsals with Wighton. If I'm particularly lucky, maybe there will even be some device or mechanism that is used in the performance. I know that normally, such things would be kept in the theatre or the magician's private workshop, but for a secret as good as this one, people tend to get creative.

I do wonder how this invitation made it into my hands past the eyes of Mr. and Mrs. Pendleton. Though I do refer to him as "young" and "boy," Thomas is most certainly a young man and anyone his age is entitled to their own choices. This being stated, the home is still that of the snooty socialites, and I doubt they will be pleased welcoming some unknown foreigner to their table (and for a holiday, no less). Though I doubt the ignorant buffoons have the slightest clue of my intentions when it comes to their son.

I have little time to worry myself with what his parents do or do not think about me. What is important here is that *Thomas* wants me there. He wants me to break bread with his family and friends. ~~It is almost sweet in the sense that~~ No. I cannot allow myself to go there. If I start down the path of small sympathies and admiration, who knows where it will lead?

I have much to do. Only three days until Christmas Eve! I have to find the perfect outfit…and if possible, a nice little trinket for my host. But with the holiday fast approaching, the shops and boutiques that populate the streets will be infested with frantic Londoners.

O, the things I tolerate to portray the ultimate illusion: love.

December 24, 1898

Even with all the commotion plaguing London town during this merry season, I managed to find myself a most regal ensemble, if not a bit plain for my tastes. This night was not about drawing more attention to myself than necessary. There is only one person whose attention I required, and the invitation arriving on my doorstep was evidence enough that I had already acquired it. So with great restraint, I settled upon a plum-colored waistcoat made of a soft, reasonably expensive velvet with a long coat in a similar hue to match.

With suitable attire and the confidence of knowing Thomas wanted me to be there, I made my way through the cold, gray streets to the Pendleton manor. It was not until I neared the ornate stone fortress that I felt this strange fluttering inside. It was almost as though I was nervous, but even now it seems preposterous. I am not one to scare easily, nor do I ever get stage fright (not that I would know that for certain, I suppose, since Paolo will never let me out from behind the damned curtain).

I brushed off the odd sensation, as well as some snow that had collected on the shoulders of my coat, and brought myself to the mahogany doors. After a few raps upon the rich, dark wood, I waited for one of the servants to see me in, just as they had at the last social function I had attended at Thomas's home. I waited far longer than I had to the last time, and when the door did finally swing open, it was not some mere servant but the magician's apprentice himself.

I noted a quick intake of breath on his part as he looked

me up and down, and it caused my own breath to falter slightly. I silently chided myself, but on the outside, I simply flashed the boy a grin I had rehearsed probably as many times as I have rehearsed one of Paolo's signature illusions.

His smile had an apology behind his eyes, no doubt for his lack of contact and for not answering when I have called upon him in recent weeks. With my own smile, I attempted to convey that it was quite all right and that I was delighted to be seeing him again.

For a place that seems as stoic as a mausoleum, the home was surprisingly warm. Once again, I waited for a servant to rush to our sides, perhaps apologize to young Thomas for his lack of promptness, and take my coat. But just as he had been the one to let me in, Thomas was also the one to take my coat.

I raised my arms, allowing him to assist in slipping it off my back (though I was more than capable of removing the coat myself). When he brought his hands to my shoulders, I turned my face so it was near his. For the sake of being coy, I kept my eyes down toward the floor, not daring to connect with his, but I made sure my mouth was angled in such a way that he would be able to feel the heat of my breath as I exhaled. I did not have to look at the boy to observe his reaction...I could *feel* it in his very energy.

He lingered for a moment, and I let him take all the time he needed. Once he realized what he was doing, he pulled the coat off me with surprising force. It took a great deal of effort not to laugh—not for thinking him a fool, on the contrary. In spite of myself, I always find his nervous energy rather endearing.

Our footsteps echoed through the stark halls, and as we walked, I eyed each closed door, wondering which could lead to Thomas's bedchamber. I followed him to the main foyer where the other guests were gathered and mingling. The very aura was worlds different from the drab, shadowy hall we exited as we entered a room bathed in a golden glow of warm candlelight and cheer.

Just as I knew they would be, members of high British society were adorned in their finest fares: the women in ball gowns with silk gloves and assorted gems and pearls decorating their ears and hair. The men…well, there was not much to say about the men's attire. It is always the same with male fashion: similar black suits, cut into similar shapes, highlighting similar features of the male physique. In the sea of monochromatic clothing, my choice of dark purple pieces may have *still* been a touch too flamboyant—I have always held the opinion that women are far luckier when it comes to the world of fashion: so many more choices…but alas, I am forgetting myself here.

On the walls, strands of crimson fabric hung, meeting in the middle of each wall in a perfect bow. Green wreaths accented with pinecones and tiny fake birds were also hung in a neat order and caused the room to smell distinctly of pine.

This rustic, woodland scent danced alongside the aroma of freshly baked pastries. A pair of long tables on the far end of the room was covered with tablecloths more pure and white than the freshly fallen snow outside. Atop the tables were platters of the pastries: cookies, macarons, tarts, as well as fine chocolates (no doubt imported from either Belgium or Switzerland). Bowls of fresh fruit and what looked to be custard were placed in the center. Along the edges were flutes of bubbling champagne.

I looked to Thomas, expecting to meet his gaze, but his eyes were fixed on an older couple across the room. I assumed that they were Mr. and Mrs. Pendleton—it was only in the moment that I realized this was my second time being in their home and I had never been properly introduced. They were talking and laughing with a group of people, and the smiles on their faces looked anything but genuine.

My eyes wandered back to the boy, and I sensed a strain in his brow. I leaned in — not too close, of course; being in a room full of other people, I knew better than to push too hard — and softly asked, "Is everything all right?"

He jumped and turned to look at me with wide eyes, as if just remembering I was even in the room. The look lasted only for a moment before he smiled, sweet and warm, and nodded. He led me to one of the tables and reached for two glasses of the refreshment. It was as if the boy were a true magician himself and possessed the ability of a mind reader.

He then spoke his first words of the night. "I'm glad you are still in London. When you stopped calling upon me, I was not sure."

I smirked. "And yet you sent an invitation all the same."

He laughed. The kind of laugh one feels proud to have elicited from another. "I said I was unsure; I did not say I had lost all hope."

And then I felt it for the first time of the night: a strange warmth emanating from someplace within my chest.

"I must say, I was starting to. When you did not answer any of those calls…well, I was quite certain I would not be seeing more of you." As soon as I uttered the words, I worried that it might have been too much guilt to place on him for his silence, so I quickly added, "I'm glad that my assumption was wrong."

Another smile. Was it not days ago that I was so certain I had lost my grip on the boy's heart?

The woman he had just been scowling at then made her way toward us. She smiled politely at me, as any good hostess would, but there was a ~~question~~ in her eyes. Actually, it was more of an accusation. Like she wanted to say something along the lines of, "What in heavens is this oily haired Italian boy doing in my home?" Of course her breeding would never allow for such improprieties, so instead she merely looked to her son and said, "Thomas, dear, who is your friend? We have not had the pleasure."

Thomas took a sip from his champagne. "This is Saverio Moretti. Sav, this is my mother, Mrs. Katherine Pendleton."

She had a visible reaction to Thomas calling me Sav, as though his familiarity with me offended her in some way, but she offered a passably warm, "Welcome to our home."

At this point she pulled Thomas gently by the wrist so that he was right at her side. She leaned in to speak to him in "private." I took the hint and continued to sip on my champagne as I let my eyes wander around the room, appearing not to be listening to their every word (which I most certainly was). Some of it was hard to make out, but I caught the main points. In the most polite way she could, Mrs. Katherine Pendleton pointed out to her son that they would not have enough place settings or food for an added guest. Thomas informed her that a woman named Amelia would be unable to attend tonight's festivities, and surely it would be no trouble if I took her place.

This seemed to end the discussion, though I could tell that Thomas's mother had quite a bit more she would've liked to add. He excused himself from her grasp and passed in front of me, suggesting I follow him with a simple nod. I assumed we were off for more painfully uncomfortable introductions and mingling, but we wove our way through the partygoers, swimming through a sea of heavily ornamented skirts and dull conversations, to another stark gray hallway.

Even with a room bustling with people still so nearby, in the empty corridor it managed to feel as though we were the only two people in the house…in London…in the world. I walked right up to him, now with a shred of privacy. My intent had been to ever so suggestively inquire as to where he might be leading me. But my breath along with all my words caught in my throat, and all I could do was stare at the way his blond curls framed his innocent, hopeful stare.

Fool, fool, *fool*.

Since when have I *ever* been the softhearted buffoon to let a pretty face have me stumbling over my words?

I finally regained my composure and ran a hand through my hair, which had been expertly coiffed to look as though I had put no effort into it whatsoever.

"Don't you want to talk to more of your guests? Bask in their company?" I hoped the suggestion wasn't too blatant. I was getting eager to slip away and carry out my search. I would never be able to do so with him at my side the whole night.

Thomas shot a look of disdain back in the direction of the foyer. "You mean the sycophants who pretend to be friends with my parents because they have money? Or because they think…" At this point, Thomas bit his tongue, but he'd already said quite enough. It would not have taken much cleverness on my part to piece together that despite appearances, the Pendleton family may not be as successful in finances as such an extravagant party might suggest. And all at once, the severe lack of staff working the room made all the sense in the world.

His mind seemed to be elsewhere as he led me down the maze of hallways and stairs. Eventually he stopped in front of a closed door and opened it, waiting for me to step in first before following and closing it once more behind us.

It was a bedroom. His bedroom. He was taking me exactly where I had planned on going.

Dear God, I could not believe it. It was not actually going to be *this* easy, was it?

He strolled over to the bookshelf that stood opposite his bed with a humble desk of iron and wood beside it. I imagined the boy sitting at the desk to pen his poems, and the thought made me smile.

He pulled a small white book from the top shelf and turned

back to me with an eager smile, telling me that it was one of his favorites. He opened it and flipped a few pages before landing on the desired one, and then he began to read. It brought me back to that night when we were alone in the theatre, as he recited poems and sonnets from memory on the barren stage.

And the more I thought on that night, I remembered the feeling of failure that overtook me upon my return to my flat. The missed opportunity. All the things I could have done—could have learned. Well, another opportunity was now presenting itself at my feet, and it was not one that I was about to waste.

I let the boy read a few more poems to me in a voice soft and gentle. At a natural pause in his speech, I joined him at the bookshelf and grabbed for a tome that looked most like a journal. I innocently claimed that though his selections were lovely, I would much prefer to read some of his original work. That was the claim; my true intent was to accidentally happen upon the boy's private log—perhaps containing notes he had taken with his mentor on how to perform a certain illusion…

But as I pulled it from its place, Thomas also grabbed for the journal, knocking it from my grasp. It fell open upon the floor, right between our feet. I was not about to lose my chance to glimpse some choice information on Neville and his doings, so I bent down to gather the fallen book. As I reached for it, I noticed there was something in between the now-open pages. A flower, a dried flower, and not just any kind of flower…a rose. I looked up at Thomas and offered him a genuine smile, but he was avoiding eye contact with me. I turned my attention back to the book and flipped the page, even though I knew what I would find: another rose dried and pressed into the pages. He'd kept them.

All of them.

I closed the book, a wave of involuntary guilt washing over

me for my dastardly motives for pulling it out in the first place. As an apology in my own mind, I offered it back to Thomas, who still was not looking at me, but then my ears caught the sound of a low rumble. A fountain pen lying on the desk started to roll, and the books on the shelf shifted as their weight caused them to lean from one side to another. I looked to the ground, which seemed to be moving from under our feet.

And just as instantly as it all began, it was over. Inexplicable! I looked to Thomas, who let out a sigh of relief. The poor boy was spooked. But it was calming that he'd clearly felt it, too, and I was not simply going mad.

"Did you feel that?" I asked, just for added comfort and assurance.

He nodded, his gray eyes wide.

I stepped in closer, pressing the book into one of his hands, and with my other hand, I grabbed his free one and placed it over the top cover, holding it firmly in place. His milky-white cheeks turned the same color as the rose petals pressed between the pages.

He then informed me that we should return to the party, for dinner would soon be served.

So close, but once again I had not gained any information that would aid me in re-creating and perfecting that ever-elusive illusion.

Thomas exited his room first to investigate, ensuring that no stray party guest had drunkenly wandered through the halls and would see us leaving his bedchamber together. What a scandal that could cause. Once he was sure our way was clear, he led me back to the cacophonous foyer. The other guests were beginning to filter out into the connected dining room—although "room" hardly seems to be the proper term. The space was sleek and narrow, more akin to a hallway, but like a great hall. With chandeliers dangling from the ceiling, their crystal strands ornamented even further with cream and gold ribbons for the occasion.

Long tables, just like the ones serving up sweets and refreshments in the main party room, were pushed together, but with the tablecloths draped over their frames, it looked as though there were one expansive table stretching for miles down the narrow space. I could hardly imagine trying to hold a conversation with someone at the other end.

It was in that moment I looked to the other end and saw our esteemed hosts for the evening looking to their son expectantly. But Thomas made no move to join them. He stayed right by my side before taking an open seat near us, not even deigning to glance in their direction. I followed suit and sat beside him, surprised that such a high-class function did not have place cards assigning guests to specific seats to coordinate some sort of microcosm of the social hierarchy. But it only took looking back up to the few individuals who were hired as staff for the night scurrying around frantically to remind me that certain aspects likely suffered in the planning of this party.

One aspect that certainly did not suffer: the meal.

Once every guest had ceased with the mindless chattering, platters, trays, and bowls were ushered out from the kitchen along with the heavenly scent of roasted meats, vegetables cooked in lemon juice and various vinaigrettes, rolls and baguettes smelling as divine as if they had just been pulled from the oven in a French bakery.

After all the dishes were properly placed along the table, Mr. Pendleton stood and cleared his throat.

I will not take the time to scribble down here what he said. Just the same old nonsense hosts are always required to say: thanking everyone for attending, talking about what a year it has been (in the case of the Pendletons, I am sure it has been one for the books), and then throwing in some stale, forced jokes that no one truly finds funny but the whole room will cackle and roar as if they were utterances of comedic gold.

I paid little mind to the formulaic speech being addressed to the room. It was something under the table that had my attention… As his father droned on, Thomas's hand found its way into my own. He gave my hand a quick squeeze, and there was so much need in that small shaking gesture.

He needed me.

There is still so much to write on…so much that occurred. But the hour is ~~late~~ early? I grow wearier and wearier by the moment. If I do not retire soon, I shall be met with the unwelcome sight of dawn as its dim light filters through my apartment window. I shall continue recording tonight's events in the morn, after I have had some rest.

The winter morn is pale and the fresh-fallen snow pure white,
But there is nothing so pure as sweet love from thee.
The moon glows up above along with the stars in the night,
But there is nothing that burns so bright as the passion within me.

Whatever storm that rattles on across the sky,
Violent and relentless.
In your arms here as it passes us by,
A hurricane is no more than a caress.

—An original poem by Thomas Pendleton

December 25, 1898

Ah, the good a few hours of sleep can do. I feel positively refreshed. I did not miswrite in saying it was only a few hours, for the activities of last night had me anxious and eager to get back to writing and planning and...

I suppose that would make this Christmas morn! Whilst all the good Christians continue to celebrate and feast, I continue to dwell on last night's celebration.

Even now I can still feel Thomas's palm against mine. His skin was soft as velvet and surprisingly cold, save for a small, inexplicable pulse of warmth that surged here and there. It wasn't his blood...but I have no alternate reasoning for the tingle that ran through his skin and into my own. I simply gave his hand a squeeze in exchange.

A loud slamming noise put a sudden end to Mr. Pendleton's pre-meal speech and plucked Thomas and me from our own private version of the dinner party. Thomas wrenched his trembling hand away from mine and, just like everyone else in the room, we turned our heads in the direction of the noise.

Each guest held their breath in anticipation as the clacking of heels against marble alerted us to an incoming visitor. Mrs. Pendleton stood so that she was at the same level as her husband as they eyed the doorway. The footsteps grew in volume and echoed through each new room as the mystery guest neared the dining hall. Another pair of more frantic steps scurried to keep up with the first, and now there were two people making their way to join the feast.

Emerging through the open doorway was a young woman—younger than myself but likely no older than Thomas. She was a fair creature: raven-black hair tied into a bun behind her heart-shaped face. She had strong shoulders covered with a dark-gray cloak lined with rabbit fur at the collar. Her pale skin was complemented by flakes of snow that had gathered along her shoulders and in her dark hair.

I would have thought she was sweet as a little dove, but her eyes burned like embers as she scanned the assembly before her.

The second set of footsteps belonged to one of the few servants the Pendletons had working the affair. He was standing at the girl's side with his arms outstretched, likely trying to take her cloak for her, but she made no move to take it off. Her fiery gaze had landed on Thomas, and the way he shifted in his seat led me to surmise that this was the Amelia person he had been speaking about with his mother earlier.

"Amelia!"—right again—Mrs. Pendleton welcomed in her best hostess voice, but the greeting wavered with what was certainly a bit of confusion. She was already making her way down the table toward where Thomas and I sat, not far from where Amelia was now standing. "Happy Christmas to you! Thomas informed us that you would not be able to join us this evening."

"Is that correct?" She was talking to Mrs. Pendleton, but her gaze was still on Thomas. The fire in her eyes had now turned to ice, piercing and frigid. "Thomas told me that your party this year was going to be small…intimate…and was limited to members of the family only."

I expected Thomas's mother to give her son a similar icy look, but she avoided eye contact with him. She instead kept her smile aimed at Amelia (a smile that was likely difficult to keep painted on as she attempted to keep the girl from creating any more of a scene). "Amelia, darling, you know you are always welcome in our home. There was clearly some sort of miscommunication on Thomas's part…a misunderstanding! We have yet to start eating. We can have a place made up for you in no time. It is no trouble at all!"

→An interesting development considering how when she thought that *I* was the extra guest, it would have been all the trouble in the world.

The servant stepped in toward Amelia once again. "Miss Ashdown, if I may?" He reached for her cloak, but she wrenched away from his grasp. I saw some eyes widen across the table, but everyone was considerate enough to keep their gasps and whispers to themselves (at least temporarily). For me, it was utterly delightful. Better than a trip to the theatre. I resisted the urge to reach for the nearest dish so that I might have a little snack to pair with the night's entertainment.

Amelia shook her head. "I am happy to spend Christmas with my own family. Besides, I have been embarrassed enough." This was aimed at Thomas, but still he refused to look in her direction. "Thomas, I…" And that's when she caught sight of me for the first time that night. She scanned me up and down, and her words froze. She then looked to Thomas and back to me. This continued for a bit, and I knew exactly what she was doing. She was trying to piece it all together, find the proof of the scenarios her mind was so rapidly creating.

Had Thomas still been holding my hand, she would have found the evidence she had been looking for.

But she had nothing. We were just two young mates, enjoying each other's company at a Christmas party surrounded by plenty of other friends. I was just another guest in his home. She had no reason to believe me to be anything more.

At that point…this point…I'm still unsure *what* I am to the boy.

Dissatisfied, she turned on her heels and left with a huff

as her stomps echoed against the marble. It was only after the girl had gone that the murmurs started. Just a few at first, but soon the entire room was filled with the low hum of gossip in hushed tones.

Now he had done it! Thomas's folly had caused the Pendletons to be embarrassed in front of all their friends. Surely there would be some sort of discipline now, some anger. But Mrs. Pendleton smoothed her skirts and made her way back to her place at the head of the table, amid the sea of hushed chatter. Mr. Pendleton was also avoiding eye contact with Thomas. But I could tell from the way he now gripped his fork, he was holding back. He wanted to yell, to say something; hell, even throwing a glare in this direction would have satisfied the man. But he kept his eyes down toward the table.

What I couldn't understand was why. Why the restraint? Was he not the authority in these circumstances?

I looked to my companion for the evening, thinking, much like Amelia had thought when she looked at me, that I could find some unspoken answers. In a bold move, possibly even bolder than reaching for my hand under the table, Thomas took the lid off the nearest tray and began serving himself. Everyone around us paused their gossiping to stare at the boy, unsure of what to do or say. I decided to disrupt this tension by following suit and filling my plate—to be fair, I was far past famished at that point.

Eventually other guests joined in, and the whole table was digging in—although something tells me many of those people were not accustomed to serving themselves. The handful of servants who had brought out all the dishes were now eagerly working to try and assist, but the meal had already become a free-for-all. A frenzy. Chaos. It was delicious—oh, and the food was quite good, as well.

The whispers had all returned to normal conversations

about dull topics such as polo matches, or investments, or whatever it is people with such wealth choose to discuss with one another. Paolo has a handsome fortune, but luckily he has not allowed the money to make him boring like these old crones.

After the meal, there were Christmas cakes and coffee and, after the desserts, dancing. The guests were directed into a back parlor, which had been cleared of any furniture. At the far end of the room, four musicians were already awaiting our arrival: a harpist, a cellist, a violinist, and a flutist. As the guests migrated into the grand room, music fluttered sweetly like songbirds flying overhead to greet us.

Couples began to pair off from the crowd lining the walls and moved to the center of the room, dancing in perfect unison. Graceful and elegant, just as they were all bred to be. It was quite pleasing to the eye: pretty people in even prettier garments moving in such stylized harmony as the light reflected off the various jewels adorning the ladies' necks. Twirling and fawning about the room in the arms of those they loved (or pretended to).

Thomas and I just stood with the wallflowers who had elected not to participate. For a fleeting moment, I almost wished it were possible for Thomas and me to join each other in a dance. I am not so naive that I would have actually attempted such a thing in front of London's socially elite...all the same, the secret desire was there.

Once it was nearing midnight, most of the weary guests said their goodbyes; some offered up small thank-you gifts to the hosts and left. The few who stayed splintered off: the men followed Mr. Pendleton to some private library or study to sit around a fire, smoking cigars and sharing much darker shades of alcohol. The women stayed with Mrs. Pendleton and made their way back to the main foyer to peck at what was left of the pastries and gossip. Everyone had already seemingly forgotten

Amelia and had moved on to the next topic of intrigue.

Thomas led me to the front door, and then closed it behind us. The snow was still pouring out onto the earth. I had my coat, but Thomas had not stopped to retrieve a cloak for himself.

I reached for his wrist, tracing it with two of my fingers.

"Are you not cold?" I asked. But the boy did not need to answer the question. The touch of his skin had already answered it for me. Just like when he had grasped my hand before dinner, I felt an inexplicable warmth surging through his veins.

I smiled and thanked him for the most wonderful evening I'd had in a long time. The smile that brought to his face sent a pang of guilt stabbing through my side, and I had to turn away from him and flee down the snow-covered cobblestone.

And that brings me to this morning. In review: I still have no new information on Wighton or his masterful trick, but what I *do* have is an even firmer grasp on the apprentice's heart. Surely this will start opening some doors for me.

THOMAS

I was scarcely able to enjoy my holiday before Neville summoned me to his studio yesterday. It was not entirely unexpected, though, considering how soon our next engagement will be commencing. A new year ushers in a new string of miraculous performances for Neville and his assistant. Although I see no reason for him to call on me for preparations to be made. Planning the new details of his act so that it does not grow stale is a task that falls to him and him alone. As it is his audiences do not care about any of the preliminary tricks or odds and ends. There is one thing they come to see. Neville's talk of new tricks incorporating my "gifts" has increased, though his ideas are still rather vague. He mentioned something involving fire but I have openly refused. It is one thing when his is the only life we are risking; it is another matter entirely when a theatre full of innocent people is put in jeopardy. I explained this to him and luckily he seemed to find reason in my logic.

Wighton may be reckless and violent, but he is no murderer.

I do suppose I could use a little practice with the old trick to ensure that I do not grow rusty—or to ensure that I do not accidentally make Neville reappear on the roof of the building, at the bottom of the sea, or something else of the sort. That would just be tragic.

The Egyptian Hall will be the grand illusion's next venue,

and that suits me just fine. It is not very far from the Adelphi. Much preferable to venturing out of London to Lancaster to perform "our" godforsaken act at the Grand Theatre. Yesterday, during our meeting, I felt it the perfect time to inform Neville that I would certainly not accompany him anywhere outside of England's borders. If he wanted my magic, it would be on my terms. And if the theatregoers and magic lovers from other territories were so desperate to see Neville's logic-defying trick, well, then they would just have to travel to the United Kingdom in order to do so.

Since I had already started down the path of setting my terms, I decided I would not allow myself to lose this momentum. In a moment of what was either confidence or idiocy, I told Neville that he would be reducing the amount of money he was giving to my parents. They would still be given enough to live—much more frugally, though. The excess would be going to me (it did seem only fair, considering I was the one doing all the work—the entire reason he knew this much success so late in his career).

In addition to a wage for my services, I informed him that he would also be providing lodging for me and paying rent on a small flat I had already taken the liberty of finding for myself over near Hyde Park. I had decided even before that egregious party that I could not live under my parents' roof any longer— not that they will be able to live under it much longer, at the rate at which they have been burning through Neville's money.

After I relayed all my demands, there was a moment where Neville showed no reaction whatsoever. I expected him to be angry. And thinking on this anger, I started to feel the symptoms of my metaphysical curse manifesting within, but I reminded myself who had the upper hand here, and that was enough to keep the monster at bay. The only remaining sign of my fear was my hands as they trembled, but I did not worry about Neville seeing that.

But he never did get angry. His blank look morphed, and he wore a strange sort of half smile. In his eyes I saw something that could have easily been respect…admiration, even. Most young men in my shoes, the shoes of an apprentice, would have been thrilled to receive such approval from their master. But I am not most young men, and I care very little for what this man does or does not think of me. The continued promise of a roof over my parents' heads—and the new promise of a sanctuary of my own—is the only thing keeping me up on the stage night after night.

Ultimately, Neville met my terms. The magician is not really in a place to bargain or negotiate.

I left Neville's studio feeling lighter, freer. A place of my own! Though I am still in the prime of my youth, it feels so long overdue. My spirit has been restless, and the more I learn about my mother and father, the more I truly get to know them, the more I realize I do not belong in their world…or Amelia's… or Neville's, for that matter. There is only one person whose world I wish to belong to.

As I walked back to the house that would no longer be considered home, my mind raced with all the possibilities that my own flat would bring. Finally, I will have a place to go where I can truly be alone, where I can be away from potentially curious and questioning eyes. A place where I can read and write my poems in peace. And when I have had my fill of being alone, well, who is to say I could not invite a guest to visit me? It will be my flat, after all.

SAVERIO

December 28, 1898

No word from Thomas since the party.

Filled my day with a stroll around the slush-filled cobblestone streets. I was hoping for some decent people-watching as I went along, but there were no particularly noteworthy characters. Seems unfathomable in such a large, bustling city.

I have now retired to my quarters. Bored to tears.

December 29, 1898

Still no word from Thomas.

December 30, 1898

No word from the boy. Am I now at the point where a few days without contact from Thomas Pendleton has me as wound up as the gears on a child's toy?

'Tis quite sad on my part—pathetic, even.

Neville Wighton the Great will begin a two-week run at the Egyptian Hall over on Piccadilly. Most convenient indeed, as I have long desired to investigate this venue. Many notable illusions have been presented and premiered in the grand hall, and it has become something of a favorite of many working magicians today. Paolo is rather insulted that he has yet to have been invited to perform there—imagine his fury if I managed to secure a booking once I have established a career of my own.

Before I can have a solo act, I need the perfect trick. And there is none more perfect than Mr. Wighton's.

This engagement at the Egyptian Hall will be a rather grandiose welcome to the New Year: 1899. The turn of the century. And what a year it promises to be.

I just have to get past one more day of monotony and then I will be attending Neville's performances once again. Another new venue, a new chance to watch the illusion's executions, a new chance for Wighton to slip or show his hand.

For now, I just wish that Thomas would call on me, send for me…at least give me some kind of sign that he is still thinking of me, as I am sure that he is—I have never been more certain of anything. Or at least, that is how I felt Christmas morning. ~~But all this silence, it creates so many doubts in my mind…~~

I must keep reminding myself that the boy is a quiet, sensitive soul and that my effects on him are not immediately evident. But they are there. I can feel it whenever I am around him.

Patience, Saverio, patience.

December 31, 1898

It finally happened.

I had sent a message for Thomas at his home. Surely a young man of his social class had already made formal plans to welcome the New Year months ago. All the same, I requested the pleasure of his company and suggested we try to track down Arthur and Roger and enjoy another raucous night at the White Lion. It had been some time since our night there, and remembering Thomas's smile as we spun and danced to the choir of cheers and singing had me sure that he would not be able to resist.

All day I waited and all day I was left disappointed and painfully bored.

Around eight p.m. I finally decided I was being foolish. Sitting about like a sad puppy waiting on its master to return.

So I readied myself for a night of debauchery, with or without Thomas. I slathered my neck in oil, combed and fluffed my ever-curling locks, put on my favorite pant and vest pairing of emerald velvet with a cream-colored button-down. And I must admit, I looked even more dashing than was my usual standard. I certainly would not be spending the first moments of 1899 alone. Out into the cold final December night, I was headed to find a good gin, some mild entertainment, and an attractive bedfellow to keep me company.

But I did not even make it outside my door. I nearly had—I was reaching for the copper doorknob when I heard a soft rapping against the door.

Soft as it was, the surprise gave me a start as I jerked my

hand away. Even with the barrier of the wood, it felt as if whoever was standing on the other side could see everything I was doing. I felt thoroughly naked—and not in the way I enjoy.

I paused a moment. Maybe I had been mistaken. I mean, aside from Thomas, who did I really even know in London? The simple answer: no one. Sure, I have had my fleeting dalliances to pass the time, producing an occasional acquaintance (or two) here and there. But none so familiar that they would venture back here uninvited.

And then my steadily beating heart froze—of course it did not actually, otherwise I would not be writing this currently—as I pictured my mentor standing behind the door. Paolo had not informed me of a trip to London and would likely not arrange one until after Wighton has concluded his string of performances at the Egyptian Hall.

But was I so foolish that I had never considered the possibility of Paolo dropping in on me unannounced? Why, the element of surprise is not so uncommon a tool for a prestidigitator, and it would be the perfect opportunity for him to catch me wasting my time away along with his money, which is doubtless what he assumes I am doing here in London.

Another soft knock forced me to face whatever, or rather, whoever was waiting out in the hall. I twisted the doorknob and swung the door inward, bracing myself for the words of contempt my mentor surely had ready for me.

It was not Paolo.

It was Thomas.

The hallways in my building are improperly lit—by this I mean they are not lit at all (this has made for more than a few unpleasant returns from a night of drinking)—and the dark of the hall was touched with only the slightest measure of winter moonlight from a nearby window, making the boy's already pale skin seem like marble.

He looked delicate and chilled to the bone, and I felt a sudden urge to run my hands rapidly over his arms, warming him with the sweet, intimate friction. But instead I flashed him a genuinely surprised smirk.

"You sure do like to keep your distance."

Thomas smiled. He looked into the apartment, and it was in that moment I realized he had never actually been up here... only ever outside the building. I moved aside so he could step in, and as he did, it looked more like he was crossing an invisible barrier rather than a simple doorway.

He was trembling, but I have found that that is often the case with Thomas—his natural physical state. Still, he did not say a word. His eyes inspected the walls, the floor, even the ceiling, looking anywhere but at my eyes.

"Once again, I was starting to believe—"

But before I could finish my sentence, he was standing right beside me, mere inches away—skin upon skin, so close I could feel his breath on me each time he exhaled. I was taken aback by his sudden show of boldness. Even *I* would not have advanced so quickly. My plan had been to move slowly...steadily. But here he was, the shy poet, taking what it was that he wanted. For a few moments, my mouth just hung open, unsure of how to respond to his newfound boldness. In my astonished state, I stared at him, his already bright eyes illuminated by the traces of moonlight filtering in through the window.

"Thomas." I had intended to speak his name at full volume, but it came out as nothing more than a whisper.

He answered this by tracing his fingertips along my cheek. It was a struggle not to flinch away from his touch at first. His skin was as cold as ice, though, just as I had at Christmas, I could feel a current of warmth pulsing underneath. Luckily, I was able to keep myself still at the strange coolness of his touch.

Withdrawing would have only caused Thomas to do the same.

There was uncertainty in his movements. They were stagnant, trembling, and not entirely graceful. I could feel the tremors that his nerves were causing just below the surface. Somehow, his fear was all the more endearing. It showed to me just how hard this all was for him but that, to him, I was worth the effort.

I had been in this position many times before, and my standard play is to run a hand through my partner's hair gently before tightening my grip and pulling them in for a tender kiss. But Thomas had already taken the lead, and I wanted to follow him, wherever he wished to take me. Taking control now would have robbed him of courage I had not yet seen from him.

He hesitated a moment longer. Briefly, I feared that he had changed his mind and would not go through with it. The thought alone set off a painful, hollow feeling in my heart, but it was short lived. Before I could ask if everything was all right, he had one hand on my shoulder and used his grip to pull himself nearer to my own height as he pressed his lips against my own.

His kiss was more firm than tender (certainly not what I had been expecting). There was a want, a *need*, a hunger—a hunger I was more than happy to satiate.

We stood there for minutes, my door still hanging open. Another tenant could have walked past and spied us, but neither of us seemed to care. We were too busy getting properly acquainted for the first time since our meeting in Manchester Square. We moved in a steady rhythm of pushing and pulling as our lips made their way over every corner of the other's. I parted his lips with my own.

I was not sure how he would receive the move, but he did not pull away. Instead, he mimicked my actions eagerly, wrapping his arms around me and clasping them against my back.

Such boldness! This whole time I had been so positive that *I* would be the one to initiate any kind of physical intimacy. But here he was, having traveled through the city on this winter night for the sole purpose of kissing me.

When he did finally pull away, my mouth just hung open, mostly from the pure shock but also from wanting more.

In the aftermath, we stood and stared into each other's eyes. Then something beautiful happened, possibly even more beautiful than the kiss: we laughed.

We just stood there in the doorway, laughing like fools. In that moment we had connected, and it was a shared knowledge that neither of us was laughing because anything about the situation was particularly humorous. It was more of…a release.

The tension between us had been building for so long, and now it had finally come to a head. We were finally allowing ourselves to be comfortable around each other.

It was divine.

Thomas left some time shortly after ten bells, and I am alone in my apartment now, scribbling away by candlelight.

Midnight has not struck. It is still 1898 and, as it turns out, I will be welcoming the New Year on my own, in my own bed.

But this does not sadden me.

Tonight was a success, in every sense of the word.

Thomas

January 01, 1899

It is a new day of a new year, and as I write, my new flat is being prepared for a (somewhat) new life.

Mine is a happiness I never thought I would be able to obtain.

January 21, 1899

My, it has been a long while since I have recorded anything in this journal. Three weeks have now passed since my last entry.

We are preparing to close our run at the Egyptian Hall. It has been another engagement met with accolades from the local press, and it brought a great many more travelers from across Europe (and even a handful of Americans interested in magic). Everyone is still baffled as to how the old man is able to disappear and reappear entirely, and it will continue to baffle them for ages.

I have been finding myself less and less annoyed with Neville, but that has very little to do with him and much more to do with the happiness that has encapsulated my life over the past weeks.

Sav has attended nearly every one of the performances. His support is quite flattering (and would likely mean even more to me if it were support for something I was even slightly passionate about). Passion or no, he has been there.

When I am not in the role of assistant and when Sav is not in his role of captivated audience member, we have been spending as much time as we can together. It has become much easier now that I am in my own flat. There is no need to sneak away—I can come and go as I please.

Amelia has not questioned my lack of contact since Christmas, and to be honest, I quite doubt she has any desire to see me. Sav and I have been meeting up at small cafés during the day. Over lunch, he tells me stories from Rome and describes the Italian countryside in vivid detail. I am oft so envious when he speaks. I slave away over my writing and my poems, but the language of an artist comes so naturally to him. Every word is a song, every story captivating, every description like a painting. I could listen to him speak for hours and hours until the entire day manages to waste away. (Although a day spent with Sav could ne'er be considered a wasted one.)

The nights are even more glorious! On the nights I am not assisting Neville in fooling crowds of eager theatre patrons into thinking he is a masterful illusionist, Sav and I explore London's various neighborhoods and discover hidden gems that have been sitting right under my nose for years.

Why, the previous Monday—he and I ventured to the eastern part of the city over near Whitechapel. Mother and Father never came out this way and would always forbid me from doing the same. Their explanations were always that it is a working-class neighborhood so there was never any need for us to pass through such conditions, but I think their real trepidations had more to do with those gruesome murders that took place ten years ago. I was a boy at the time, and they tried not to discuss it in front of me, but I always sensed the discomfort in the room whenever a group of adults was talking about the Whitechapel murders. I could see the looks of horror on their faces whenever they were poring over the morning paper during teatime. I was well past reading age at that point, and it took only for me to peer over my father's shoulder to get a glimpse of all the chilling details for myself.

"That's not a part of the city I make a point of going to," I told him absently as we sat in my flat. I was attempting to write a new poem, but every line that came to me I scratched out almost immediately.

"And why not?" Sav was sprawled over the settee. He had a mixture of restless boredom and wild adventure in his eyes.

He wanted to get out and explore; meanwhile I was perfectly contented to stay indoors.

"Whitechapel has a bit of a…reputation." I decided to leave it at that. Growing up, I was always taught that matters involving things like gore were not to be discussed unless your wish was to repulse and repel your guest. In the back of my mind, I was sure Sav was the last person to mind such things. Still, the violent nature of the topic kept my tongue tied.

"A reputation? Hmm?" He rose to his feet and crossed over to me, then placed an arm around my shoulder and sent my heart racing. "You know…I had something of a reputation myself, back in Italy. Would that have kept you from getting to know me when we met?"

"That's entirely different," I scoffed.

"Why?" Sav was being stubborn. It would have been bothersome were he not so appealing. He has this face he makes when he is being wily and trying to get his way… It is irresistible.

"The Whitechapel neighborhood, a decade ago…you see… there were…well…murders. Did news of these crimes never make it over to Italy?"

Sav just shook his head.

"Ah." I shrugged. "Well, your reputation…whatever it may have been was not so gruesome as that, I am certain. Whitechapel is dangerous. We could be hurt."

There was a pause. "How are you certain that I am not dangerous?" He wore his usual sly smile, telling me that the question was a joke, but there was a shadow of concern in his eyes. Was he actually worried he was going to hurt me?

I felt bad about putting such thoughts in his mind, so I tossed my notebook aside and said, "It was ten years ago, so the area has likely changed a great deal since." I smiled at him. "Let us go explore."

The trek to Whitechapel was met with great effort. The cobblestone streets were covered with slush and soot. I made my best effort not to laugh at Sav when one of his Italian leather boots was caught in the snow and filth. He met my laughter with his own, and once his foot was freed, he chased after me, threatening to push me into the snow.

Upon arrival in Whitechapel, we were drawn to a large hall. Never having been to the neighborhood myself, I had no idea what it was used for, but there was a great deal of noise escaping from the doors and windows on each end.

Sav nodded, leading me closer. As the noises grew, I tried to keep my mind away from visions of violence and the drunkards and whores who might be filling the hall inside.

"Be brave," Sav whispered, his breath hot against my ear. And so I did just that. I stepped in through the large entryway, taking the lead. Upon entering the large hall, I did see blood, but it was not the blood of anyone in the hall.

It was an indoor meat market.

Vendors offered samples of all different types of fare, shouting out to any members of the bustling crowds who would listen. Without a moment's hesitation, Sav rushed to the first stand that caught his shining brown eyes. He took a small cube of cured pork and turned to me, cupping his free hand underneath so that none of the grease would drip. Although upon inspecting the floor, I realized it wouldn't have made much of a difference: the floor was already lined with dirt, tracked-in snow that was quickly melting, and even a little bit of blood from the more recently butchered offerings.

He nodded for me to come closer, and I obliged.

"Come now, open wide!" He grinned and opened his own mouth in example.

I gave a cautious look toward the man who had carved the pork for Sav, but his attention was already with a new set of customers. I opened my mouth and allowed Sav to feed me. The small snack was warm, tender, and spiced to perfection.

We wandered the contained market, trying different foods as we went, contemplating making a purchase for the vendors' sakes but without actually buying anything. Well, with two exceptions.

The first was when we happened upon an elderly Italian woman whose wrinkled face immediately lit upon hearing Sav speaking in his native tongue (as did my own, I am sure). I realized I had never actually heard Sav speak full sentences in Italian until that moment. As I stated before, listening to him speak is like music to my ears. But if his speaking in English is a song, then his speaking in Italian is an entire symphony.

The old woman (who Sav informed me was named Eloisa) came around to the front of her stall to wrap her arms around us and plant large, wet kisses on each of our cheeks. She then handed us slices of bread so that we could sample her "world-famous" olive oil flavored with raspberries. The taste was so subtly sweet and divine and her personality was so warm and charming that I could not resist buying an entire bottle.

The second purchase was one made by Sav. Just as we were about to leave for the night, we passed a stand selling fudge. No doubt, he saw the way my eyes widened with wanting at all the different flavors and varieties. He ordered two pieces. One was crafted from dark chocolate with pecans lodged inside, and the other was a blend of white fudge and milk chocolate. He gave me the one with white fudge, and we nibbled on our sweet treats as we stepped back out into the cold.

It was a perfect evening.

Most all of our evenings have ended with the both of us retiring to one or the other's flat. In the time since my last entry, Sav and I have slowly been getting more intimate physically. It all started on the eve of the New Year. No longer able to contain my feelings and with my new resolve to finally allow myself to be who I am, I sought him out and kissed him. I must admit, it was the most terrifying and thrilling thing I have done in my young life—even more terrifying than stepping out on that stage with Neville for the first time and making him disappear in front of a crowded house.

But for all my newfound bravery, I am still uncertain if I am ready to be *fully* intimate with Sav. There are more than a few things holding me back. I have exposed myself emotionally with him, yes, and one would think that would be the hardest part. But exposing myself physically? The notion has become much more daunting.

With how lovely and charming Sav is, it is not hard to imagine that he has had plenty of suitors...partners? Whatever I should call them... I should not be worrying myself with his past loves and former trysts, and yet I cannot help myself.

I mostly preoccupy myself with their appearances. Surely Sav could have anyone his heart desires. I have not shared a bed with anyone, male or female, but Sav? His confidence and flirtations lead me to believe that his sheets have seen a handful of bedmates already in his young life—all likely more striking than myself and more...experienced.

Never before have I concerned myself so much with my own stature and physique, but the thought of disrobing in front of Sav and allowing him to fully see me...would he like my frame? Or would he think me scrawny and awkward? Would he find my manhood...adequate? Or would he start to laugh the moment he realizes I haven't the faintest idea what I am doing?

But all these worries aside, even if I do give myself to him completely, body and soul, then I know in my heart that there will be no turning back; love in all its terrifying beauty will have consumed me. Although at this point, with how happy he does make me, would I even wish to turn back?

I am not sure why I continue to be so frightened of that which I want most. As of now, we have been simply lying side by side with the occasional shared kiss or gentle caress of the arm whilst we share our secrets (not all of them, of course), dreams, fears…these past few weeks have truly been the loveliest of my life.

The biggest fear that has taken root inside me with the arrival of the New Year: the idea of Sav returning to Rome to finish his apprenticeship. I have yet to express this fear to him, but it is one of the main reasons I refused to leave the country with Neville—for fear that I would return to London to find Sav had returned to Italy, to his old life. He hasn't mentioned anything about the tailor he works for but in his own small ways has tried to assure me that he has no intention of leaving. He discusses future plans, things he wishes to do and see in the coming weeks and months, and every time he does, my heart races with joy.

Dear Saverio,

I hope all is going well. My intentions were to travel to London to see you and gather what information you had for me at the end of this month, but I have recently been booked to headline a series of variety shows in Prague.

Given my schedule restrictions, any information that you do have for me should be delivered to the address of the theatre that I have enclosed along with this letter. To ensure security of the content, seek out my contact "Mr. Blue" at the post office on Baker Street. For added security, please also code the message using our predetermined guidelines.

I do regret to inform you that I will be cutting your monthly pay nearly in half. You will understand that seeing as I am no closer to learning Neville's secret than I was months ago, I feel that cutting down to the bare necessities might help you to focus. You will still have enough to pay for room and board and, of course, I will be providing a supplement for tickets to any of Wighton's upcoming performances.

Do not view this as punishment; instead view it as an opportunity. An opportunity to prove your usefulness and value. By the time this letter reaches you, you may already have obtained the key to my rival's success, and this measure will have been all for naught anyway.

I eagerly await your response.

Regards,
Your Gracious Employer

Dear Saverio,

It has been two weeks since the estimated arrival of my last letter in London. I must say I was quite perturbed when I did not receive a prompt reply. Surely after a three-week run at the Egyptian Hall you have <u>something</u> for me.

I am willing to give you the benefit of the doubt and consider the possibility that my last letter was lost in the post. Bearing this in mind, I have taken precautions to ensure that this letter arrives onto your doorstep and into your hands. If I do not receive a swift response, I will have to take matters into my own hands.

Once again, I have enclosed the address to the theatre in which I will be performing. Mr. Blue has instructions to man the post office daily until one p.m. until your letter is safely secured. I implore you not to keep him waiting long.

Regards,
Your Gracious Employer

SAVERIO

February 13, 1899

I now have an unexpected houseguest.

I should have known better than to ignore Paolo. The man has been writing to me from Prague, pressing me for information. I have been hopeful that I might be able to get away with avoiding a response and blame it on the incompetency of London's postal service. But I left him waiting for far too long, and who should show up at my door but...

Isabella.

Paolo has booked more performances, so sweet Isabella has come in his stead. I call her sweet, but what I really should be saying is naive. The poor girl. She thinks being trusted with acting as the illusionist's watchdog makes her so very important, but while she is here keeping an eye on me, Paolo has surely hired a new assistant—some pretty young thing with stars in her eyes. Once she has finished her spying, dear Isabella will likely be out of a job. If she were smart, she would've never left Paolo's side. Although, thinking on it, I am sure she had little choice in the matter.

'Tis a shame. Of all the assistants Paolo has had over the years, I had grown most fond of Isabella.

That said fondness is fading fast now that she is living in my home, eating my food (a precious commodity as now Paolo has been giving me less money), and demanding that I bring her with me almost everywhere I go. It has only been a few days now since she arrived in London unannounced, but it feels much, much longer.

I am just thankful that Thomas now has an apartment of his own so that I will have at least one place to hide from Paolo's watchful eyes.

I have been contemplating my situation, trying to make some decisions about how best to move forward. I have decided that I do not wish to involve Thomas in this whole mess, but I know that this revelation has ultimately come too late; I have already involved him. Something I deeply regret but cannot take back.

All the same, when I do get my hands on Wighton's secret, it will not be through Thomas. There must be another way I can piece the puzzle together without directly involving the apprentice. I have already left too many casualties in my wake when it has come to acquiring new tricks for my mentor—I will not add Thomas's name to that list. Even though this particular trick will be for my own use and not Paolo's...

'Tis so peculiar, how I have so suddenly found myself with a conscience.

Thomas has a strange effect on me indeed. What I feel for him...what I mean is, whenever he is around... I have such difficulty putting it into words. Surely the young poet already has the right ones in his back pocket. All I know is that when he is near, I get this inexplicable warmth that begins in my chest but radiates through my entire being. It is a sensation that is so foreign to me and yet vaguely familiar—like something precious you see in a shop through a frosted window in the winter. But you never step inside to try it on because you are sure it will never be yours in the first place.

February 22, 1899

I must think up a good excuse soon. Thomas is surely starting to wonder as to why I have not allowed him back to my apartment in recent days.

THOMAS

February 26, 1899

It happened. It really happened. I would write more but for once in my life, I am truly at a loss for words!

SAVERIO

Last night was momentous. It was a night of firsts for both Thomas and myself.

I already knew the boy was a virgin. That much was clear long ago. And for me? Well, in spite of my best efforts—as well as my usual code regarding such things—it would seem that I have...feelings for the boy.

I am a living, breathing contradiction.

How long have I fortified my heart against these exact types of feelings?

It was a night just like any of the others I had been spending with Thomas in recent weeks. We were at his apartment, of course, what with Isabella scrutinizing my comings and goings. She does not seem put off when I am out for an entire night, though, and why should she be? She was well aware of my habits in the time we had spent traveling with our dear Paolo. What *would* shock her would be to learn that I am spending these nights away with the same individual each time. Why, she would be just about as stunned as I am, myself.

Anyway, I digress. We were spending a quiet evening in. We had a small fire going in the fireplace, and Thomas had just poured us some black tea with honey. He was lying on the rug, busy scribbling away in one of his many leather notebooks. I was pretending to read Shelley but in all reality, I was sneaking glances at my companion, admiring the way the dim glow from the flames outlined his slender frame. He never caught me, not once, or if he did, he made no mention of it (which I am grateful for).

Out of nowhere, without a word, Thomas set the journal and his fountain pen aside and exited the den. I did not think much of it at the time, simply assuming that he was stepping away to use the facilities. But then more and more minutes began to pass by. First there was confusion, then concern, followed by curiosity. I rose from my resting place on the settee and strolled down the hall, only to find the door to the privy still wide open. Also open, I noted, was the door to Thomas's bedchamber—a room that always seemed off limits before last evening.

I had made a point not to rush any physical activities between us. In my experience, it is always more rewarding to have them come to you. And last night…well, you could say that Thomas was sprinting toward me.

Hesitantly, I gave the door a push. The room was alight with the soft amber glow from a single candle. Thomas was in the room and had clearly been waiting for me to come check on him.

He was shaking. Even from across the room, I could see his hands trembling as he fidgeted with the final button on his shirt. He looked up at me with a hint of a smile, though it was underlined with some natural uncertainty, as he pulled his shirt away slowly. One of his sleeves got caught as he tried to pull it off his arm, and after a few tugs, the shirt fell to the floor.

The glaring contradiction between his intended act of seduction and the nervousness that was merely a part of his whole nature was just so precious that it forced a laugh to escape my lips—something I immediately regretted. Even with the lone aide of the candlelight, I saw his milky skin blush. It had not been my intention to embarrass the poor boy. It was the unparalleled sweetness that had elicited my laughter, and by no means had it been meant in mockery.

I strode over to Thomas, and then cupped his soft cheeks in my hands. I gently placed a kiss on his forehead then looked at him, willing my eyes to say what would have been too awkward to simply speak aloud: that he had no reason to be embarrassed. I then stroked a hand through his hair and let my eyes scan hungrily over his bare chest.

Without saying anything, Thomas reached down to his trousers, but by this time his hands were shaking even more violently, and he could scarcely keep a hand on the buttons.

I reached down to grasp his hand and give it a little squeeze.

"Allow me," I whispered. I flashed him a smile that seemed to have a calming effect. He nodded his approval, and I bent down so that my eye line was level with his waist. In an instant, I could feel the same sort of nerves Thomas was just exhibiting in the very pit of my stomach—it was as if the butterflies had flown right out of him and into me.

Before pulling his trousers down, I looked up to examine his face. If he was frightened or rethinking this decision, I had to know. "Is this okay?" I asked. His naked chest was rising and falling rapidly, but he flashed me that sweet, shy smile and nodded once again. "Yes." So I slowly guided his pants down his slender legs.

I stood, so that we were eye level once more, and allowed myself the chance to take it all in. Take in his image, take in the moment, accept the fact that this was really happening. Even though I had been planning and scheming and ultimately hoping...the idea of actually being with Thomas had seemed like just that for so long: an idea. Nothing more. Not something that would ever come to be, and yet, there we were.

He bit his lip as he looked down at himself and he crossed his arms over his chest. I knew what he was doing. He was hiding.

"You're beautiful," I said. And I meant it. Just like that, his back and legs straightened as the awkward smile on his face grew fuller.

For a few moments, we simply stood in each other's presence, exhaling shaking breaths, neither of us knowing who would move first or when. Then suddenly, Thomas stepped forward and he kissed me, just as fiercely and full of desire as the night he had first done so.

The way his lips were urging me forward, I could tell he wanted to move quickly. I still remember how quickly I moved the first time I shared my bed with another male. I was so nervous, and the night had passed in a blur. That was why I wanted to move slowly, to take my time with Thomas and make sure he was comfortable throughout. I worried that if I moved too quickly it might be painful or he might not fully enjoy it all. That or, like me, he would scarcely remember all the details of his first time.

Usually, I let confidence take control and will guide the other person, move their hands where I want them to go, but I found myself letting Thomas take the lead. I wanted to see where he would place his hands, where his slender fingers would grab or tenderly trace, if his kisses would be soft or playful... Would he bite down? I was his to guide, as though it were my first experience rather than his.

I had never been so tentative before. It was hard to guess what he would or would not like, so each moan of pleasure, each sigh of release—they were all tiny victories in my mind.

I could feel the progression. Lust turned to passion turned to tenderness turned to... As I am writing here, I am finding I do not have the right word for what exactly I was feeling. Could it be, dare I say it, love?

No, no, of course not. That's silly and whimsical thinking. Given my history, I doubt I would even know if that is truly what this is becoming anyway. I know it's something. Whatever that something is currently, it's hard to say.

Now I find myself victim to the very emotions I had for so long evaded. I am now cursed with the affliction that has been the downfall for so many throughout history and will likely serve as my own.

For now, I am trying to allow myself to enjoy this foreign yet inviting sensation. After all, I did always enjoy trying new things. And this is most certainly new territory for me.

The earth moves beneath me, this I know,
And yet time itself seems frozen.
Down the road of love you and I do go,
A path that I have chosen.

I lay naked before you, this I know,
My heart more bare than my skin.
My defenses lowered, I let pretense go,
O, how could such beauty be sin?

—An original poem by Thomas Pendleton

THOMAS

February 27, 1899

The last time I wrote in here, I did not have the proper words to describe what I had experienced, but now I have had time to fully process my thoughts.

For the first time I have been with someone, truly been with him in heart and spirit. And nothing in the world has ever felt so right.

I had invited Sav to come spend time with me at my flat. I had posed the idea innocently enough, just a quiet night inside, sipping tea by a lit fire and enjoying each other's company, but I had already decided that I would make my boldest move yet in the chess game that Sav and I have been playing.

Over these past weeks, my bravery has been increasing. I have been standing up for myself with Neville, breaking away from my parents' hold, hell, I even kissed Sav! And I was ready for more. I figured the kiss would be enough to let Sav know how I felt, to show him how I wanted him. Secretly I had been hoping that I would then move forward with shows of more intense affection and devotion.

When he did not immediately try to sweep me off my feet, I was worried that maybe that was more than he actually wanted. Perhaps I was just a flirtation. Or perhaps he was holding back out of respect for me.

No matter the case, I needed to try something.

The other night, while we were reclining peacefully with

our tea, I made my way back to my bedchamber, a room he had not been let into before.

I slowly began to disrobe, but my anxiety caused me to fumble with the buttons on my shirt, and something I do daily suddenly became an insurmountable task. I was grateful he was not with me to see how clumsily I was preparing to seduce him.

The longer I was back in my bedchamber, the more foolish I began to feel. Should I call out to him? He did not know what I was doing or where I was. If he did venture to find me, what would he do? How would he react? Would he laugh? Turn away? Or would he take me in the way I had been secretly wishing he would?

This worry continued until finally, footsteps sounded along the wooden floor. There was no turning back now. The door to my bedchamber creaked as he pushed it open wider and stared at me with his big brown eyes.

He crossed over to me and finished removing my clothes before telling me that I was beautiful. It was then that I realized I'd never heard anyone use that word when describing me. Amelia and my parents' friends had called me handsome. But never beautiful. I could almost feel the flow of my blood as it rushed to my cheeks in a flush. I kissed him, firm and passionate as I had previously, and before I could get in my own way with thoughts of worry or if I would be good enough, I reached for the first closed button on his shirt and worked my way down.

This whole time I had thought that what I wanted was for Sav to sweep my off my feet. The other night I realized I wanted to be the one to sweep him off his.

I will not lie on this page and say that the entire act was magic and bliss. Discomfort and pain were mixed in with the pleasure, and there were many moments when I did not know what to do with my hands or my hips — this was all new territory for me, after all. But Sav was with me the entire time, asking if

I was in pain or frightened. His hand in mine erased any fear. I've never felt so safe.

I am so glad that it was Sav and not Amelia or another girl who I would pretend to love in my bed that night. Every movement, every word whispered, every feeling, it was all real and right. No matter what the world may think of it.

February 28, 1899

I saw Mother today.

She has asked me to tea on more than one occasion, and finally I obliged. It has been a handful of weeks since I was last at the house to see her and Father, and she did not need to say as much for me to know that this has been distressing her.

Though the last thing I owe Katherine is guilt (I truly do not owe her a thing), the woman is still my mother, and my anger has not hardened me against her entirely.

We met for tea — not at the house, though. She and Father will be vacating that house soon anyway, seeing as they can no longer afford it with the reduced sum they are receiving from Neville. This is *certainly* something I do not feel guilty for. If anything, it is likely that I am doing them a favor. It is my sincere opinion that living by more humble means will do them each some good. But we also did not meet at the house I called my home until recently because I had agreed to see only Mother and not Father.

She was complicit in the whole arrangement and, therefore, just as guilty as he. I know this. But for some reason, it is more bearable for me to be around her than it is my father, perhaps because she was the one to ultimately break down and confess their doings. I still have no desire to see my father, and I am uncertain if I ever will.

When she spotted me in the café, she looked close to tears. Tears of joy at how happy she was to see me, I could tell this much from the smile warring with the sadness in her eyes. All the same, it made my weak heart soften even more, and

I embraced her before we sat to catch each other up on the happenings in our lives. I would never have thought our affairs would be so…separate, so estranged.

Right away she made a comment on how well I looked and that I seemed happy, and she was right, because for the first time in a long time, I actually am. I admitted as much and could not fight back a smile. There was just something so delightful in knowing the effect Sav has on me is so immediately evident.

I contemplated telling her that I have found someone—not who, of course. Why, she would never understand. I toyed with the idea of just hinting at the fact that love had found its way into my heart but decided to just leave it be. She could make her own assumptions about what (or who) was making me so happy.

She did not bring up Neville, nor did she ask how work with the magician has been going, though I was surprised she did not. We are about to open an engagement at the famed Criterion Theatre. Neville has still been in contact with my parents, I am certain, but has made no mention of whether or not they will be in attendance. My mother did not bring it up today, but perhaps she knew better than to discuss the very reason for our newfound estrangement.

She was eating her biscuits in nibbles hardly suitable for a mouse. She was stalling. She did not want for the tea date to end. But after the last cups had been poured and the plates were all cleared away, she did inquire as to when she would be able to see me next. I told her that I was uncertain, as my schedule would be quite hectic in the coming days and weeks. And this is not false, what with the new string of performances (most of which are nearly sold out already) about to begin. The only thing I did not inform her of was the fact that the majority of my free time spent out of Neville's grasp I would be giving to Sav—I suppose she still only knows my love as "S" at this point.

Speaking of Sav, I must be off soon! We have made plans

to view a vaudeville show this evening. I was not too keen on the plan, since I have already spent my fair share of time in theatres these past months. The more time I can spend outside of them, the better. But Sav has already assured me that it will be a delight and has promised that if I fail to laugh once the performance is through, that he will take me to the nearest pub and treat me to whatever I would like to drink for the rest of the night.

I wonder if I have yet become a good enough actor that I could fool Sav into believing I have not enjoyed myself so that I still might receive those foolishly promised beverages.

SAVERIO

March 02, 1899

I have an issue that requires a solution, and quickly. Wighton's act is to open in just over a week at the Criterion. Isabella expects me to attend the opening night performance with the seats Paolo had already procured for us, as was originally planned. But Thomas has now invited me to attend the performance as his special guest—which includes the luxury of a private box in the upper balcony.

There is no conceivable way for me to decline Thomas's invitation, but I know Isabella, and working for Paolo has given her a taste for life's finer things. If she knows of this exclusive invite, she will surely demand that she accompany me, with a seat in the same box.

But any link to Paolo is far too risky. Thomas cannot know the truth behind our relationship. I have too much to lose now, and the idea of Thomas feeling the sting of my betrayal is more than I can bear. And even if no connection is made between Isabella, myself, and our shared employer, would Thomas still not be suspicious, hurt even, that I wish to bring a lovely young woman as my date to his own performance?

There is another risk I have to take into consideration. Just how long can I continue to act as an audience member at these performances when what I truly am is a spy? I have watched the act with an analytical eye for what feels like a thousand times, and I'm no closer to putting together the old man's confounding secret. Each new venue, I think I am going to be able to notice different aspects, view things in a different light. But no, he remains in shadows, his brilliance ever hidden from my sight.

Perhaps the key is not in scrutinizing the performance itself. There must be a way that I can enter the magician's studio without Thomas's assistance (or knowledge).

And now I have the added pressure of Paolo's assistant turned watchdog, viewing every step that I make. She and Paolo are so judgmental of me not having come up with an answer by now—why does she not study the magician herself whilst she is back in London? Let her see how easy it is!

Isabella will now be acting as the intermediary for any correspondence with Paolo. His patience grows dangerously thin, if he even still possesses any at all. He has made that abundantly clear through the continued reductions to my compensation. I have had to make some serious adjustments to my lifestyle. I have mapped out the routes that take me past my most favorite shops so that I can specifically avoid them and avoid the temptation to buy a new garment. I have been taking myself out for fewer lunches and dinners and buying ingredients at the local market for meals to make myself, from scratch. So far I have surmised that I am a dreadful cook. I know it is silly of me to expect for Paolo to continue paying me when I have given him nothing in return, and yet I still find myself annoyed with him over the situation I now find myself in.

Then again, he has already invested this much time in waiting for his prize. It would be even more silly for him to throw that time away and currently, I am the only thing tethering him to his foe. I am the only bridge.

Finding entry into Wighton's studio shall be the next step, but it is one that can wait. For now, I need to figure out how I can accept the invitation from my sweet while also appeasing my pest.

March 10, 1899

have been such a fool. Such a blind fool!
~~I don't understand how I~~
~~How could I have never known that~~

Tonight's performance has made everything so dramatically clear and yet at the same time has managed to perplex me even further than I had ever thought possible. I had already thought what Neville was doing on stage genius, due to sheer bewilderment and the secrecy that had previously been surrounding it. Now...

Well, now it is wondrous beyond words—beyond reason itself!

I had been fretting so about being seen with Isabella and provoking Thomas's suspicions that I had forgotten that I had already told Thomas about her, in a sense. Though in my depiction of her, I had told him that she was my sister. And to think, all this time I had been keeping her hidden when I had a perfectly good excuse for her presence already concocted. When I told her about the private balcony seating, she was more than happy to play along with the familial ruse. She already knew I was using the magician's apprentice to get close to him anyway, so I knew she would be complicit.

Rather than my "date," she was now my sweet sister, merely in town for a visit.

Lies. More lies. I had been trying to add as few of those to the list as possible, but my circumstances necessitate that they keep piling up, and now I am nearly drowned by them.

She was intoxicated from the excitement of it all—that or

the three glasses of champagne she had more inhaled rather than drunk. She had been talking about the illusion for days and could hardly wait to view it again, to get another chance at unraveling its mysteries. I had not chosen to partake in discussions of his trick. She tried to work through it verbally with me, thinking she could help, but all she had done was put my failure and my lying and scheming on a silver platter and served it to me so that I could feast on my own shame.

Once the rabble had all found their respective seats as well, the house lights dimmed and soft, elegant music began wafting from the orchestra pit all the way up to the theatre's rafters. A surprise, certainly. Usually Wighton does not seem to care for such flourishes to accompany his performances. But as soon as he stepped out onto the stage, I realized that this was not the only difference. His whole act had been altered entirely. Of course there had been changes made in the past to keep things fresh for those who had already seen him perform elsewhere. But the further he went, I realized that each trick was one I had never seen the man perform.

This being said, they were all variations of tricks I had seen performed by other men—and in the case of one trick, a woman who dubbed herself Madam Lydia the Strange. There was nothing particularly outstanding about this new lineup of illusions he had prepared for the Criterion. Standard acts of prestidigitation that, with just a bit of practice, I could likely accomplish on my own. None so enchanting as his grand vanishing trick, but I do assume that is entirely the point. It would be silly for a magician to try to overshadow the main event, his pinnacle achievement.

Once I realized that the new lineup had been comprised of run-of-the-mill sleights and uncomplicated prop work, the small surge of curiosity that had taken hold of me waned, and I found my eyes drawn to a much fairer thing.

Poor sweet Thomas. I could tell the smile on his face was forced, like that of a trained circus animal. His desire to please and his mild manner kept the grin painted on, and even in his clear discomfort, he was beautiful. To some, the harsh, bright electrical lighting would not be so forgiving. But Thomas was a beacon, his own light shining brighter than them all, from the inside out. I could not take my sickeningly lovestruck eyes off his waiflike figure.

I was captivated. I was entranced. I was falling even harder.

I had been so sure that allowing myself to be mesmerized in such a way would be the very cause of my undoing. The grand irony in all of this is that allowing myself to love the magician's apprentice is what has now brought me to discover Neville's secret (if I can even truly call it his).

The music ceased, save for a drumroll that started as nothing more than a light patter but grew in both volume and tension. Just as it was meant to do, the sound had Isabella on the edge of her seat in anticipation, and she clutched onto my arm, her nails nearly slicing through my suit coat. I should have taken her gesture as my cue to shift my gaze over to Mr. Wighton, but I continued to watch the object of my desire.

And that is when I saw it. Neville jumped, I knew that much from the abrupt halt in the drumroll. But as I previously stated, my eyes were locked on Thomas. Both hands were held firmly at his sides. His left hand was clenched into a fist but with his right, he was subtly raising and lowering different fingers as if he were counting but in no discernible order or rhythm.

His lips were moving. Down in any of the rows farther back, one might easily mistake it for quivering. But I have a trained eye, skilled in noticing what others do not, especially during a performance. Small words were forming in a soundless whisper.

But the sign that ultimately had me most curious was how at the precise moment Neville leaped from the stage, I saw

Thomas's hands open, both the left that had been balled in a fist and the right, whose fingers had been moving so rapidly and strangely. The fingers on each of his hands were suddenly splayed, as if in presentation, even though he was still holding them down at his sides. His eyes were open wide and his chest was still. He seemed to breathe again only once the magician reappeared.

All night I have been pondering his odd ritual on the stage. As I thought on it, I tried to recall any other strange phenomena or peculiar behavior exhibited by the boy. That's when it all started to come together for me, little by little: the lamp that shattered when I first showed him any sign of physical affection, the subtle feeling that the room was shaking when we were alone together in his house — like some small (and impossible) earthquake.

And then I started thinking more on the mystery that is Neville Wighton. I have been so consumed, thinking about the old magician, at no point had I thought of anyone who might be connected to him. Back when I had first met Thomas, back before the trick had even premiered, he informed me that he had only recently begun his apprenticeship under Wighton. It was only after acquiring this new apprentice that Neville Wighton the Great's fame soared to new heights in the theatrical community.

This whole time, it has been right in front of my eyes! I do not know how it never occurred to me before. There is no smoke nor are there mirrors, for Neville does not need such things.

I think Thomas may have magic. *Real* magic.

'Tis only just a theory at this point, and if anyone were to lay eyes on this journal and read this account, they would most assuredly think me mad. I myself can hardly wrap my mind around this new conclusion I have come to. Why, it throws into question everything I thought I knew about reality and the possibilities of what can and what cannot be.

And yet as baffled as I feel—as impossible as it all still seems—my heart is assuring me that my instincts are right, that the secret I have been searching for lies in Thomas. He *is* the secret. He is the key to all of this.

THOMAS

March 10, 1899

Anxiety has overtaken me tonight. Before tonight's performance, everything was fine—better than fine. It was as near to perfect as things could possibly be. Sure, it was another premiere of another string of shows, all of which I inevitably dread. Going up onstage to pretend to be what I am not—or rather pretend to pretend at being what I claim… Christ, it is all so confusing!

But the insurmountable glee from the start of this year has made all the ugliness with Neville and putting my magic to work for his gains…well, it has made it all seem so small. Why worry about such a man? Why fear what the people in the audience think of me? After all, I have found someone who makes me feel cared for.

Or at least, I thought I had. Now I am not so sure.

After tonight's performance, it had been my intent to take both Sav and his sister out for a nice meal. She is in town for the week visiting her brother, and I have yet to meet her. I did manage to spot her seated beside Sav during the performance. She was physically striking, but I did not need to see her to know this. One look at Sav is all one needs to know that anyone who shares his genes possesses such beauty.

What I was really hoping for was to get to know her a bit. I would not have let on to the true nature of our relationship. That is, unless she already happened to know about Sav's…

preferences…in which case, I still may not have said anything, for fears and insecurities of my own. Tonight I was simply going to be Sav's friend, just as he was mine when he met my parents. With any luck, I was hoping she might provide me with some hilarious stories and anecdotes from when she and Sav were young. Tidbits that might come in handy in the future.

But when I exited the stage door, Sav and Isabella were not waiting for me in the alleyway as he promised they would be. I skimmed around the building to the front, thinking maybe that they had come to hail a carriage and have it ready for us. But still there was no sign of them. I went back into the theatre to check if they had simply waited for me inside, but the lobby was cleared of people, as was the auditorium. It was so peculiar.

Now I am home, on my own, contemplating what I could have possibly done in the time since I was last with Sav.

Surely I am just overreacting… If he were cross with me, he would not have attended the performance at all. Why go to the trouble?

But then, why would he leave without a word?

March 12, 1899

Something is certainly wrong. Sav is now avoiding me. What I cannot fathom is why.

March 15, 1899

Ineed to keep my mind sharp! When I lose focus is when things start to go wrong, and when things start going wrong, I put myself at greater risk of being discovered.

Neville has noticed how distracted I have been lately, and he has voiced his own concerns with my preoccupied state of mind. He has his own neck to worry about if I happen to drop him from twenty meters in the air, or in some other city (not sure if I am even capable of that), or who knows what else? Maybe he could get stuck in the in-between space…wherever it is he goes for that brief moment he vanishes from our world… stuck…out in the ether. If such a thing is indeed possible, it would truly be a horror.

But how can I keep my mind on this performance when my heart is so distressed? Sav, my Sav, has all but disappeared from my life. And after things were going so well. Something is horribly wrong; I only wish I knew what. Part of me fears that his employer has finally summoned him back to Italy, like I have been dreading for so long.

But that would mean Sav left the country without a word of explanation or goodbye. I cannot imagine he would do something so cruel. Without any correspondence from him, I am left only to worry and wonder.

THE  TIMES

LONDON SUNDAY   MARCH 19, 1899

FAMED MAGICIAN TAKES FALL DURING
FRIDAY EVENING PERFORMANCE

World-renowned stage performer Neville Wighton the Great was performing at the Criterion Theatre in Piccadilly Circus on Friday 17/03, when during his final act, the man plummeted from the upper balcony and onto the theatre floor below.

Wighton landed in the center aisle and not on any of the seats below, so no patrons in attendance were injured. A man in the audience revealed himself to be a doctor. Dr. Chester Miller examined the fallen performer and immediately assessed that he likely had a fractured wrist, had twisted his left ankle, and shattered his left kneecap but would require further examination for anything to be certain.

Wighton was taken from the theatre and brought to St. Thomas' Hospital.

Theatregoers who have attended past performances believe that Mr. Wighton lost his footing on the balcony where he was meant to reveal himself. William Parker comments, "Usually the magician appears on some balcony or pops out of a corner in the theatre where he is least expected to be seen! When he does show himself, he makes a point to add some little flourish or gesture to draw that much more attention to the reappearance after vanishing and whatnot. Methinks he got a little carried away this time and gravity got the better of him!"

The Criterion Theatre has already canceled the remaining performances, all of which had already been sold out. Representatives from the theatre have promised full refunds to its patrons but have not addressed any intentions to book a new set of performances.

Mr. Wighton's injuries are not permanent and he is expected to make a full recovery.

THOMAS

March 21, 1899

Neville is so dramatic—no wonder he pursued a career on the stage. It is the perfect place for him.

I know the danger of going into a performance in such an excitable state. But last Friday it finally happened, that thing I have been fearing ever since Neville ~~recruited me~~ bought my services. I was off—my thinking was off, I mean—and I transported him in ever so slightly the wrong spot. He was so close to the balcony! Had he reached out fast enough, he may have even saved his own neck—not that it was his neck that broke, ~~unfortunately.~~

What is wrong with me? What kind of horrid creature have I become? Heaven forgive these dark thoughts that run through my mind and spill out from the ink of my pen.

As it was, even in his injured state, he somehow mustered enough willpower (or fury) to hobble his way to my flat and scream at me. Oddly enough, his bones were the least of his concerns. It was his pride and his reputation that he was most worried about.

Was I truly that surprised?

"Every night I put everything on the line and put my name— my entire career in your less-than-capable hands. And now look what you have done! It was only a matter of time! Bah! Such incredible, awe-inspiring gifts, they are wasted on the likes of you!"

At first, I took his stream of berating, for I felt it was what I deserved. Allowing him to yell and scream was my recompense for my life-threatening error. But there was only so much I could take, especially seeing he was well enough to make the journey to my flat. After a few more accusatory exclamations and insults hurled my way, I finally snapped.

"Consider yourself fortunate I did not drop you from the top of Big Ben, you old meater."

He opened his mouth, and the swift intake of breath told me that he was about to scream louder, call me more hideous names. I could practically feel his hand connecting with my face, that is how badly I knew he wished to strike me. But he paused, and I saw in his watery, wild eyes that he knew I was right. I could transport him anywhere my magic allowed, the extent of this neither one of us knew, and he certainly did not want to be the one to test it. And really, what was stopping me?

Well, plenty of things, in truth. Inside, he knew this as well. He knew I would never do such a thing to him intentionally. Maybe this is the reason for what he said next:

"You would do well to mind your tongue around me, boy. You may feel bold, may feel like you have power over me"—an ironic choice of words here, I must admit—"but like it or not, you need me just as much as I need you. You do not think I know how much you hate the stage? But without it, one too many people might see something they cannot explain—might start to ask questions. With my craft, you have the luxury of attributing any abnormalities to the guise of illusion work. I can be your protector, or I can leave you to fend for yourself in a world where fear and ignorance can cause people to do such vicious things. The choice is yours, so tread with caution."

The shaking and cold beads of sweat only began after he left.

I felt indignant. The nerve of him to suggest that I *need* him. There is only one person on this earth whom I need, and for some reason he has not been speaking to me. I went over to his flat the other day to see if my theory about his leaving London suddenly was correct. I had meant to go to his door but stopped when I saw his figure in the window from across the street.

He's still here. He's been here this whole time but has not even tried to get in touch with me. The heaviness in my heart far outweighed any relief that he had not been summoned back to Italy.

I was surprised when Sav did not even reach out to inquire about Neville's accident. Surely he has heard about it! It has been all over every newspaper in town.

Briefly I feared that he *had* heard about the incident and became frightened of me, feeling the need to distance himself. But that was merely an instinctual reaction, and of course once logic came back to me, I realized how silly and impossible that would be.

For Sav to have made such a connection, he would have to know that I was the puppeteer pulling the strings on the whole act. And there is no possible way he could know.

March 22, 1899

Sav has finally called on me. Oh sweet relief! I should have known better. I feel silly for getting riled in the first place. My heart is an anxious one, although this is far from a new development.

He has requested to see me at my flat for apparently, his sister has made plans to extend her visit. While I do appreciate his insistence on privacy, I would still very much like the chance to meet her. She is a part of Sav's life, so of course getting to know her…well, it would certainly mean a lot to me.

I must prepare for my meeting with Sav. Just thinking of seeing him puts a smile on my face that I simply cannot contain.

It is wonderful.

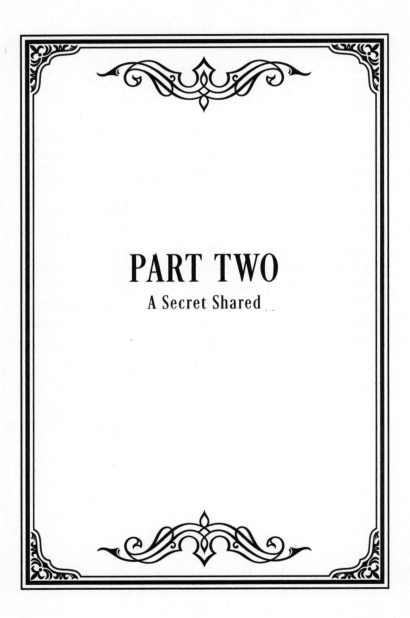

PART TWO

A Secret Shared

SAVERIO

March 23, 1899

I was right. I was so utterly and profoundly right.

Ever since that evening at the Criterion, my mind has been running, imagining, ruminating. When I pieced the puzzle together, I recognized the beauty in what was happening onstage, but now I have witnessed that which I have been dreaming of, and I now know what true beauty is.

Some time has passed since I last made the effort to write in here, and a decent amount of time had also passed since my last encounter with young Thomas. It was difficult...not seeing him, not talking to him... I wanted to—of course I did. But I did not feel ready to face him after the conclusion I had drawn after the performance. If I was right, and I was so certain that I was, then he was something more than I ever thought him to be. More than the sweet, nervous boy I have come to care for, more than a magician's apprentice, more than *human*.

The more I thought of what he was, what he could be, the more restless my sleep became, until it started evading me entirely. My crazed conspiracy was all I had been able to think on these past weeks, and I knew I had to see him. So last night I made plans to visit my dear Thomas.

After he let me into his apartment, I sheepishly apologized. But he did not appear to be cross with me. He looked...relieved. I know the feeling all too well. I remember the feelings of anxiety and dread when Thomas stopped communicating with me (however brief that period did turn out to be in the end). I remember thinking he had no desire to ever speak to me again and the sinking weight of such notions.

I felt remorse for putting him through these same anxieties and felt a gesture of comfort would be appropriate. It started with a stroke of his cheek, which led to a kiss on the forehead, which led to tender kisses elsewhere, and before I knew it, both our vests and shirts were off and strewn across the floor, our bodies locked in an embrace.

As I had stated, it had been some time since I had seen Thomas. There was certainly no rush to reveal to him what I knew. My theory would still be there, sitting in my head, waiting to be voiced, waiting to be confirmed. First I needed some fun and to give my love a proper greeting.

We were in his bedroom, and I was reclining on the bed, recovering from our bout of activity. Thomas was already on his feet in search of clothes with which to cover himself. Such modesty with these Brits. Even in the presence of an intimate companion, they feel they must hide themselves away as soon as the deed is done.

I watched him as he scurried about the room, wondering at what mysteries lived within him, even now. As I watched, I thought back on each time I felt a current of warmth pulse underneath his skin, even when it was cold as ice. It was all making so much sense now.

The words I wanted to say kept getting stuck in my throat, as though coated with molasses. How would he react? Would he be frightened—angry that I had discovered his truth? Or what if it weren't a truth at all? I had been so sure of myself, but what if I was indeed wrong? Was I about to make the biggest fool of myself that I ever had?

Finally, I pushed myself:

"Do magic for me."

He did not even look back over his shoulder at me, just kept pulling up his trousers while simultaneously exploring the room with his eyes, in search of his shirt. "I am afraid I don't have any playing cards. You don't happen to carry a stack on your person, do you?"

He glanced playfully at me, but I gave him only stoicism in response. The muscles in his chest tensed, and a frown twitched at the corners of his mouth. This was all I needed to see to know that he took my meaning. He knew that I was not presuming to be cute and that I was not requesting a simple trick.

We stared at each other for a moment more, maybe two, then he turned away from me to face his window on the opposite side of the room. He opened it, and he did not flinch away from the biting chill.

A sharp intake of breath sent me into a panic. I had worried that my revelation would upset him. But had I upset him so that he was willing to throw himself from the window? With a secret so monumental, it did not seem like such an unfounded fear. I ripped the sheet away and was on my feet, but before I even started toward the window, I noticed something. Thomas took in another breath, and then another, and then another.

He was not going to jump.

He was focusing. How did I know? All I had to do was look down at his hands to see that with his right, he was rapidly raising and lowering fingers again, just as he had been onstage. I looked back up, and his shoulder blades were rising and lowering in a syncopated rhythm. I longed desperately to reach out and trace the lines of his back, but I remained still. Something told me I was about to witness something important—something surreal—and I had no wish to interrupt or startle him.

He then raised his left hand in a beckoning gesture—not toward me, you see, but out into the world, to the night sky.

He was calling to someone (or something) and I watched, near breathless, waiting to see who (or what) responded.

And then it happened; I shall do my best to transcribe it here on this page, but I already know that my words will not do the moment justice. The stars, the very stars in the sky! That is what he was calling upon. And they answered! I could not believe my eyes. Twinkling specks of light floated through the sky and in through the window—now, at this point I know they were not the actual stars, just a replica of their image. For as the tiny orbs of light flew closer and closer toward us, they remained exactly that: tiny. As if they were still millions of kilometers away even though they were floating into Thomas's bedroom like smoldering fireflies.

Once Thomas had collected enough of these mini stars, he swiped his hand through the air and, using forces I could not see, he arranged the small bits of light into miniature constellations right above our very heads.

As I watched Thomas create these celestial paintings, I had to bring a palm up to cover my gaping mouth. I was focused on what was happening, unquestionably, but I still did not wish for Thomas to see me looking like a fool.

The beads of light flickered, danced, and glowed. By all rights I should have been frightened, but I felt completely and entirely at peace. I felt intoxicated without a drop of liquor; I felt pleasure without needing to be touched…I am certain this is what so many other people refer to as "bliss."

Completely speechless and swept away by what I had just seen, I moved for Thomas, then pulled him toward me and kissed him so hard, as if I would somehow be able to taste the magic upon his lips. We made love for the second time that night, but this time it was under a canopy of replicated starlight, softly illuminating the room.

So now my theory has been confirmed and the mystery of

Neville Wighton finally revealed. What I still cannot understand in all of this is why he continues to apprentice for a simple illusionist when he has magic, *real* magic! Were he to go out on his own, he could be the greatest in the world, just by virtue of being what he already is. He would never have to answer to anyone another day in his life.

I think it goes without saying that my quest to swindle the greatest illusion known to man has come to an end. I cannot steal that which I cannot replicate, and Thomas has a real gift, by some force of nature.

In showing me his magic up close, Thomas took an enormous leap of faith last night. He put his trust in me like no one ever has. Sure, there is Paolo, but the brand of trust that is required in having someone carry out your dirty work is far different from that which allows you to open up and reveal your deepest secret to someone. And I am making a vow, right here and now: I will never give Thomas another reason not to trust me. There is no need for him to ever know my original intentions, especially now.

I will never reveal Thomas's secret, for what would be the purpose? To what end? Other than to reveal Wighton's trickery—I must admit, I do have some respect for the man. He is a craftily minded bastard, masking an all-too-real phenomenon and passing it off as something that can be so easily controlled or easily explained. Why, it is *brilliant*.

Brilliant but terrible. If Thomas has been the secret to Neville's success this whole time, I can only imagine the amount of stress the magician has been placing upon Thomas—the amount of duress he has had to endure these past months. Not to mention the terror of always worrying that someone will find out his secret. Someone who is less likely to see his differences as something beautiful but rather, an ignorant, unimaginative individual, who sees the unknown as something to be not only feared but railed against. Someone far less interested in his wellbeing than I am.

My hunt for "Neville's" secret may have ended, but Paolo's will not. I am not sure how easily I will be able to dissuade him from his course.

THOMAS

March 23, 1899

I feel lighter, I feel weightless, I feel free!

For quite some time now I have felt that it is when I am around Sav that I can be myself. Now that is true in every facet of my being. He has seen the hidden bits and pieces, the one that others would normally view as darkness, and he saw beauty. He did not turn away but rather, he embraced me (both literally and metaphorically).

I have never felt so unburdened in my life, so happy!

March 23, 1899 (continued)

For so many years, I have spent my time living in constant fear of what I am. I only ever saw my magic as something to be hidden away, something to be ashamed of. I realize now that I have my parents to thank for that. My differences made me something they couldn't understand or control. And so they assumed others wouldn't understand or accept me, either. Always hiding me away, like some sort of terrible secret—that is, until they realized they could profit from what I am.

But being with Sav has shown me the loveliness of it all. I have accomplished things I did not even know were within my capabilities. I have created constellations in my bedroom; I have grown flowers from stone... Why, just yesterday, I was attempting to write some new poems (I have a lot of free time now that Neville is on bed rest, recovering from his injuries). Most of what I wrote was pure drivel—even the inspiration that has come from being in love does not always produce the most masterful of art.

Much of it was tossed aside into the waste bin beside my desk. I was starting to grow frustrated and a bit bored. I leaned back in my chair, letting my mind wander, and my attention landed on that pile of freshly crumpled paper sitting in the bin.

It got me to thinking...

A few nights ago, Sav asked me to do magic for him. But before he made the request of me, I rarely ever exercised my supernatural muscles. In fact, I spent a good majority of my time managing the "gift" so that it did not accidentally slip out at a less-than-ideal moment.

Upon Sav's request, I was able to create a miniature galaxy above our heads. Just what else could I do?

With this in mind, I directed the rest of my focus on those crumpled pages of paper. One by one, the balls of stationery floated out into the air and began to unfurl. Once they were back to their original shape (if not a bit more wrinkled than before), I focused as hard as I could on making the pages tear into smaller, more manageable shreds. And they did exactly as I commanded!

Now that I had several shreds of paper floating about me, I focused my energy on changing their form and, once again, the paper obeyed. I held my breath, waiting to see the final product. Dozens of white paper butterflies started to flutter about the room!

Though beautiful, even in its splendor, it was technically a failure, I must admit here. I had been trying to turn the shreds into tiny paper cranes.

All the same, I could not help my smile and even a bit of gleeful laughter as my paper butterflies flew around me in a sort of whimsical dance.

And to think all this time, the capability to create such things, to bring such precious moments to life had been lying dormant, merely waiting for me (or for someone else) to tap into it and bring it to life.

I know, and have known for some time, that my abilities are wasted on the self-serving magician. And I know that I must still keep my guard up and proceed with caution when it comes to the circumstances under which I use my powers. But it is a nice change of pace to actually appreciate what makes me different from the rest of the world, rather than ignore it. And I owe it all to Sav. The moment I first saw him, I knew he was an original, one of a kind. He is not the type who would ever let himself blend in with a crowd. And that is exactly what I have been doing: blending, hiding. And though I may still have to hide from those who would intend me harm, I can at least stop hiding from one person in particular...

Myself.

March 25, 1899

I have been thinking about Amelia more and more recently, and I decided it was finally time to get past my discomfort and call on her.

As my own happiness has been building, so has my guilt, for I think on what I had done to *her* happiness. Up until now, I had been so afraid to face her. The shame was just too much. But after leading her on for as long as I did, I knew I owed her an apology, at the very least.

I called on her to inquire if she would like to accompany me for afternoon tea. My assumption was that I would be rejected, if I were to even receive a response. To my surprise, she agreed.

We went to a café near the river that we had often gone to for luncheons and the occasional breakfast outing. In hindsight, perhaps picking a location that was once the setting for our "dates" was risky—a bit awkward, even, but I liked the idea of picking somewhere familiar.

She met me there. It seemed awkward and unnecessary to go to her home and walk with her, though it would have been the polite thing to do.

When she arrived, I was feeling a lot of different things: more guilt, of course; fear for what would come next; and even a little comfort in seeing a familiar face—even if that face belonged to someone who, at the moment, hated me.

We exchanged greetings, a few small niceties, and, once our tea was served, we got right on with it. I had apprehensions about having such a private conversation in public, but everyone in the café was so caught up in their own gossip and goings-on, my concerns were easily dispelled.

"Did you ever really care for me, Thomas?"

"Of course I did." This was not a lie.

"But you did not love me."

Saying I did *would* have been a lie, especially now, knowing what real love feels like. The euphoria it brings about. So I just shook my head, not brave enough to actually speak the word "no."

"How long would you have continued wasting my time? Both of our time?"

What exactly was I supposed to say to that? *For a great deal longer, most likely. In fact, if the love of my life had not shown up, I probably would have married you just to appease my parents.* So once again, I retreated into sheepishness, shrugging and murmuring something like, "Who can say?"

She frowned. This was not going well at all. I had to do something.

"I do not have any good reasons for you as to why I did what I did, and I think it is mainly because it was all so unnecessarily foolish. I should have been more forthcoming about my feelings—"

"You should have," she agreed, crossing her arms.

I nodded, resisting the urge to laugh. That was something I could always count on with Amelia: she was always right and she *always* knew it.

"Yes. And I feel terrible for any pain I might have caused you. I was being selfish—"

"You were."

"I was," I said, restating that which I had already admitted to. "I was not thinking about anyone else, which is why I had not considered how it might affect you. But any harm that was done was unintentional, please believe me. I know you have no reason to, and I know I likely do not deserve it, but I hope that one day, you will be able to forgive me."

She took a bite out of a shortbread cookie and examined it thoughtfully. "I must admit, it takes courage for a man to admit when he's done wrong. Especially when you could have easily just continued on about your life, ignoring me and never acknowledging your faults at all." She took another bite. "I will consider it—forgiveness, I mean."

I felt lighter, allowing a smile to show itself. "Perhaps we might even become friends, when all is said and done."

"Do not test the limits of your luck with me, Mr. Pendleton," she warned, raising a finger. "It is not something your family has a lot of these days."

Some might think it distasteful to comment on a family's financial issues. I actually sort of respected her for it. And this time, I let myself laugh.

SAVERIO

March 26, 1899

Isabella is growing more and more suspicious of me. I could feel it starting quite some time ago, but now she makes it perfectly evident in the way she demands to know where I am going and how long I will be. She has gone from being a nuisance to being an actual intrusion on my life. Oh how I wish I could tell her that all this time and effort was for naught and that no man will ever be able to re-create his feat. I would absolutely *revel* in her frustrations and dismay.

But as I have vowed on the pages of this very journal, I will not reveal Thomas's secret—not even to allow Paolo's spy to pass along the message that he has lost this battle.

Isabella has informed me that she spoke to our mutual employer shortly after Wighton's nasty fall, and it was agreed that she would be remaining in London until Neville's next engagement was announced. Though no such news has broken. It will only be a matter of time. Every theatre in town has been vying to get the magician on their bill like wild dogs fighting over a single scrap of meat. As soon as the magician can walk, he will be performing once more (probably even a little before then). Even now I am sure he is desperately awaiting the moment he can have all eyes on him again.

I told her that this is all fine and good, her remaining in the city, but she will have to figure out new lodgings for herself. I had expected her to be angry with me for suggesting such a thing, but she was perfectly calm. In fact, she seemed to agree that it would be necessary. The longer she has been here, the smaller the apartment has felt, likely for her as well. Besides, why would she want to stay in a meager little hovel with me when she can be put up in some lovely hotel suite as long as Paolo il Magnifico is paying the bill?

So now Paolo's coins will continue to fill her purse rather than mine. She will be outfitted with fine garments whilst mine become threadbare. She will stay in rooms with housekeeping while I can barely muster the energy to dust what few belongings I possess. She will have tickets to all of Neville's upcoming performances while I will scrape together what money I can to try to do nice things for my sweet Thomas. He insists on paying for every activity, every meal, and I know, given my current financial status, I should be fine with letting him, but it is also a matter of pride. It is embarrassing to not be able to reciprocate his kindness when he takes me out for a fine meal or to see a Shakespearean play. I fear that soon he may start to pity me. He is a prince and I am a mere pauper.

The old me would have been much more upset by the lack of nice things, but when it comes down to it, Thomas is what I care about. The only real reason I even want money now is so that I may spend it on him. It is nice, having someone who actually means something to fill the void that material objects and status once occupied. I would almost say that I wish I had allowed my heart to open up to love sooner in life, but the truth is...I don't. For if I had, who's to say if I would have found my way to him? Likely, I would not have. I would probably be leading an entirely different life at this very moment.

So let Isabella have the nice rooms and the clothes and whatever the hell else she wants. The farther away she is from me, the farther away she is from Thomas, and that is all I care about.

THOMAS

March 29, 1899

My heart is all aflutter with excitement! I did something today that I certainly should not have done. Not a few days ago I was discussing the importance of caution when it comes to my gift, and yet just hours ago I was as reckless as I have ever been.

I was over around Covent Garden and decided to take a stroll through the market. There was no intended purchase as I made my way past the stalls, but the fleeting thought struck me that I deserved something nice. And this thought comes around so rarely that when it does happen upon me, I have only but to seize the moment.

I was busy looking at scarves. One in particular had caught my eye—the fabric was a soft periwinkle and at the ends it was lined with a violet fringe. It was not something I would normally choose for myself. I'm usually drawn to the more subdued shades…they are what my father always deemed as "suitable" and my mother "elegant." But the moment I spotted it, it looked like something Sav would be wearing and, unsurprisingly, that immediately warmed me to it. I could stand to use some more color in my wardrobe.

As I was contemplating whether or not to make the purchase, the laughter of a handful of children pierced my deliberations. Two stalls down, a toymaker was selling his handcrafted playthings. Colorfully painted pinwheels, dolls with porcelain faces painted to imitate the way women paint their own, teddy bears that looked as soft as they likely felt, wooden horses... A wave of nostalgia broke upon me as I eyed the toys and the smiles upon the young ones' faces.

They were just so *delighted*. And then it dawned on me: why should they just be delighted when they could be positively enchanted? I scanned the market with a cautious, if not somewhat paranoid, eye. Then when the moment felt just right, I gently blew into the air, as though blowing a kiss.

A controlled, isolated gale swept over the children's heads and past the toys (I made sure that my little windstorm would not disturb any of the other stalls). As it went by, the pinwheels spun about, their vibrant colors blurring as they danced. The children all started to clap. I then centered my focus on the toys that were able to move thanks to gears that simply needed to be wound—only who needs such mechanisms when you have my gift? Little toy soldiers started to march, carved mice rolled about, and ballerinas twirled. The clapping quickly escalated to laughter, gasps, and even one cheer.

The toymaker had meanwhile been preoccupied, conversing with the parents. When all the adults craned their necks to see what had the young ones so excited, I forced the activity to a sudden halt. The look of confusion on their faces at the children's riotous (and, at that moment, unexplainable) laughter was enough that it sent me into a fit of giggles, my own self.

The whole thing had me wondering... For so long I have assumed that people would react with fear to my abilities—that they would think me a monster. But what if they didn't? What if people responded with joy and delight, like the children did earlier today? What if they showed me the same praise as Neville receives after one of his grand "illusions"? The thought is a hopeful one, but the problem is that there is no way for me to know. With no historical examples to base my decisions on, everything I choose to either reveal or hide about my magic could lead to…well…anything. As no one else with magic has made themselves known to the world, there is no way to know how such a revelation would be received.

Was it dangerous to act so impulsively in the midst of a crowded marketplace? Why, certainly! But heavens, was it fun!

SAVERIO

April 01, 1899

I am like a soldier, surrounded by the enemy, awaiting my own demise.

And such a shame, too, as the evening had otherwise been so lovely.

Thomas and I were out to dinner, and a nice meal at that—not the pub food I have become so accustomed to or the finger sandwiches I pick up here and there at the cafés. This was a five-course meal, the kind of food you almost feel bad about devouring for it is so elegantly displayed and costs an unseemly amount of money.

It was Thomas's money being spent. With past dalliances, I never much minded when the other person treated me to an elegant meal or bought me gifts—who am I trying to fool? I loved it! But with Thomas, I always feel as though I should be taking care of him. I have never told him as much, for even in my head I know how condescending that must sound.

As it is, Thomas has revealed to me in private that the magician has been paying him handsomely to keep up this charade. With such a gentle heart, I would have never pegged him for an extortionist.

This one just keeps surprising me—it is delicious!

Delicious, food, dinner—yes, that is what I was scrawling on about. We were out at some restaurant in the style of a French bistro. Everything was very stark and very white, the walls, the tablecloths, the curtains…the people (my date being no exception in this instance). We went because Thomas had been raving about it, claimed it was one of his favorite dining establishments in London. I did not have the heart to tell him that, having actually been to Paris, the menu was frightfully inauthentic, as was the ambiance. And besides, there was no need to spoil something as pure as his sharing something he enjoys with me, wanting me there.

Before I go any further, it is important that I note how increasingly difficult it has become playing at being nothing more than Thomas's friend whilst we are in public. What control it takes, keeping my hands to myself. To not kiss him when he gets that bashful little half smile, to not ruffle his hair when he accidentally misquotes a Greek philosopher, to not hold him close and assure him that I will not ever let go.

I, of course, have no issues with such displays of intimacy, but I know how uncomfortable it would make him if I were to be so forward. Still, in our own subtle ways, we have become more and more affectionate. I see it in him, but I also sense it in the odd stares we receive when we are out on an occasion such as tonight's. I notice them, and I have a feeling he does, too, but I feel he tries to mask his discomfort somewhat for my benefit. It is a pity, really, that someone as beautiful as he does not love himself, not truly, anyway.

It is fine, though, for I have decided that until he can accept himself, I will love him enough for the both of us.

Anyhow, tonight was one such night where a playful comment would lead to an equally playful grin then a touch of the hand, which subsequently led to a curious glance or an eyebrow raise from an adjacent table. Even so—even with these slips into affectionate behavior—my restraint was driving me mad. I remained on my best behavior, focusing on the gorgeous meal that Thomas was providing for me, kept my talk on matters of literature, philosophy, politics. It was when our dessert plates were removed from the table, the bill was settled, and we were out in the still-crisp night of early spring that I knew we were safe.

I took his soft, slender hand and guided him to a nearby alleyway. The heels of our boots clicked and clacked against the wet cobblestones as we made our way down the reclusive passage. I was not entirely certain that we were free from judgmental gazes, but I did not care. I had waited too long for his touch, his embrace, his kiss—I certainly was not about to wait until we returned to his apartment! With my palms on his cold cheeks, I pulled his face in close, at first only brushing my lips against his but then pressing firm, letting him have what warmth I could give.

When I pulled away I could not help but chuckle at the delighted smile spanning his face from ear to ear. He was positively beaming. For me, kissing a member of my own sex out in public where anyone could spy us is nothing so foreign, but I am not so forgetful that I cannot remember what it was like the first time it happened. Why, it was exhilarating. And I could see that that was exactly what he was: exhilarated.

It was such a delightful moment…until my heart felt as though it had come to a complete stop and my world began to spin. Something just beyond Thomas's shoulder caught my eye, a figure with a voluptuous form and a pair of watchful eyes aimed directly at us—something I had not thought to check for prior to leading him into the shadows of the alley.

Isabella.

She had followed me.

A roaring sound like rushing water filled my ears, and my kneecaps suddenly felt nonexistent—had Thomas not been there I probably would have allowed myself to collapse to the ground. My chest tightened, and no matter how I sucked in air, it never felt like it was quite enough.

She stalked away into the night, and I can only imagine what was running through her mind.

Yes, she knew I had planned on using Thomas, and certainly she had already had her ideas about what methods I would utilize. But she also knows how I have been evading the task at hand, the theft of Neville Wighton's grand illusion. Her suspicion has been growing stronger, and what she has seen tonight will only give her ideas about my true intentions—my purpose for remaining here in London.

I wanted nothing more than to go home with my darling, but my mind would not have been with him, not fully. Consumed with panic, I had to face this head-on. I sit now in my own apartment, but when I arrived earlier, Isabella was nowhere to be seen.

I can only wait.

⚬ℓ℮ ℮ℓ⚬

Three hours and she finally arrived. Devil knows what she was doing for three whole hours, though the pungent scent of whiskey gave me a few ideas.

I had started a small fire in the fireplace and was sitting in front of it, holding a book, though I was only pretending to read. I had tried desperately to focus on the words on the page, but my mind just kept returning to the look on her face when she spotted us. Equal parts knowing and triumph.

When she did finally stumble in, I did my best to maintain my composure. I looked her square in the eye, almost challenging her to say something about the incident, even though that was the last thing in the world that I wanted. Perhaps she would not call my bluff.

"Do you love him?" she asked in the most accusatory tone I had ever heard fall from her lips (slightly intoxicated or no).

What was I to say? Yes, I could have easily created some fable about the continued ruse I was participating in and even enticed her by claiming to be oh so close to discovering how Wighton had been pulling it off all this time. But truth be told, I was exhausted. No. More. Lies.

"Yes."

And in that moment, surprisingly enough, I felt lighter. I could breathe slightly easier. It was as though a giant sack of bricks had been sitting upon my chest. Revealing the truth of my love for Thomas to Isabella, while it did not relieve the weight entirely, at least felt like a few of the bricks had been removed.

She said nothing to this. She had a look on her face, a look of affirmation, because I was merely confirming what she already suspected.

I have spent the rest of the evening holed away in my bedroom. I heard some shuffling, steps, thuds, and then, at one point, the closing of the front door. She was packing her things and finally left my residence for the hotel Paolo is providing for her.

Paolo…that shall be the real concern.

I could lie and say that I am unafraid of him, for what is the worst he could do to me, correct? But no, this is entirely false. I have been draining his funds month after month, though his monetary gifts have significantly lessened as of late, and he has stood by patiently, for he knew that ultimately there would come a reward. With the information Isabella will doubtlessly supply him about my true intentions with the boy, he will know that I've had no intention of delivering on my promise. And he is a smart enough man that he will likely put together that this has been the case for some time now.

    I cannot say that the repercussions of tonight's events will be swift, but I have no doubt in my mind that there *will* be repercussions. Paolo il Magnifico is not one to take such insults lightly. He also does not have any patience for thievery (I must say, 'tis a bit hypocritical in light of the circumstances, but then again, I never did claim the man was perfect, now did I?). Even as well as I have come to know my guardian over the years, I cannot wrap my mind around what form of vengeance he will decide to take on me. It is why, as I mentioned at the beginning of my entry, I now feel as helpless as a soldier venturing unarmed into enemy territory.

April 12, 1899

I am only opening the pages of this journal to take note that I have yet to receive word from my mentor. What I should really be saying is "former mentor," but seeing as how I have not formally resigned and he has not formally terminated me, circumstances remain as they are.

Titles are irrelevant at this point, anyway.

THOMAS

April 13, 1899

We have a new residency booked, and now Neville has decided what his new illusion utilizing my magic will be. In the middle of his act, Neville will be standing center stage and will let out a birdcall. Once he has done this, I am to turn the paper programs into small birds, which will flutter majestically around the theatre above the audience's heads. Not unlike what I did with the butterflies. I finally relented and showed him what I could do with paper in order to get him to stop pestering me with other ideas that are more complicated and, assuredly, more dangerous. The transporting act will still be our grand finale and showstopper.

I did not immediately reject the idea as I likely would have if he had come to me with this only a few months ago. Now that I have been exercising my gift and using it for my own enjoyment, I feel somewhat confident in my ability to utilize my powers onstage. However, the risk of exposure still remains. I will have to be careful. This trick is quite risky, in that it leaves little room in the way of logical explanations for how the paper would be transforming. People will start to wonder…

Sav, meanwhile, has been acting slightly strange. When he is with me he manages to smile and keep conversation, but I can tell by the distant look in his eyes that his mind is off somewhere else, preoccupied. Out of my own desire to see him happy, I want to ask if everything is well, but then there is another part of me that believes if something were truly amiss, he would tell me (or at least, a part of me hopes he would).

I cannot claim to be entirely undistracted myself. I have not written anything of substance in what feels like eons. I should not get angry with myself for it, but it is difficult not to be frustrated with one's lack of creativity, especially when one is hardly lacking in inspiration.

I think what I truly need is a holiday, a break from more than just the stage. Just get out of London entirely. Go and watch the sunrise in a different part of the world, walk down Mediterranean beaches, hear songs sung in different languages, meet new faces... I want life and adventure in all its forms!

Perhaps Sav will take me to Italy. Even just the idea fills me with such romantic ideas. He and Isabella can show me around their favorite spots from when they were growing up. We can ride in gondolas down the canals of Venice, see the Colosseum in Rome, visit the Uffizi Gallery in Florence. How unfortunate that I should be struck with such a yearning now that my schedule will once again be placed under the constraints of routine.

My body may be stuck in London for the time being, but that does not mean that my mind cannot explore.

SAVERIO

April 17, 1899

The meeting I have been dreading is soon upon me.

Paolo has managed to arrange for a last-minute booking at the Gaiety Theatre, only a couple of weekends, to end his current tour. Though Wighton's fame has now surpassed Paolo's, my old mentor still has enough clout and plenty of connections that he can have his pick of theatrical venues—at least the ones who have not been able to rope in Wighton and are forced to find the next best thing.

Paolo still has yet to make direct contact. Instead he simply sent over a ticket for one of his performances. Honestly, I think I would have preferred some sort of letter to accompany it, even a brief note. Something. Now I have to sit and wonder what sort of verbal lashing will be awaiting me after the show.

I've contemplated skipping the performance altogether. But that would be foolish, considering Paolo knows exactly where to find me if I should try to evade him. And I cannot deny that there is a small part of me that is morbidly curious about how this reunion of ours will transpire.

In a matter of days, this will all have passed, and I can breathe easily once again.

April 25, 1899

Things with Paolo went about as well as I could have hoped, and that's certainly saying something.

His performance was entertaining. I had no doubt it would be. While my former mentor and I have had our differences, I have never once denied his showmanship or his skill for the craft. In the time since I have seen him last, he has added a rather compelling escape routine to his set where his assistant (golden haired and notably *not* Isabella) binds him in a straitjacket and locks him into a trunk. The rest of the audience watches in anticipation until the magician emerges unbound.

As I said, entertaining, but now that I know the existence of real, true magic, it's growingly difficult to look at such illusions and trickery with the amount of appreciation or respect I once did.

I sat in my seat until everyone else had departed after the performance. Once I was the only one remaining in the auditorium, the golden-haired girl came out to retrieve me. I followed her backstage, annoyed at how rapidly my heart was racing in my chest in spite of my determination to remain calm. I knew if I were to at least appear calm and unbothered to Paolo, it would irritate him to no end. I had to find my satisfaction where I could.

She left me outside Paolo's dressing room, knocked on the wooden door, and sauntered away before he answered.

"*Accedere,*" he finally said, beckoning me in our native tongue. His tone was neutral. I did not like that.

I took a steadying breath and made my way into the room.

It was modest but private, closed off from where the other performers dress and apply their cosmetics, which is more than many smaller venues would offer.

Paolo was seated with his legs crossed on a dark-blue velvet settee. He refused to make eye contact with me as I entered the room, no doubt trying to make me uncomfortable. I countered this by striding right in and leaning against the wall opposite him. There was no other seating in the room, and I was not fool enough to try sitting beside Paolo.

Beside him was the last place I wanted to be anyway.

"I suppose you think you're damn clever, don't you?"

His voice was cool with just a hint of darkness, like a cold breeze cutting through the night.

"In general, or…"

"You think you're funny, too, you always have." Paolo wasn't holding back now, his sneer fully evident. "But only so many can tolerate your type of arrogant wit and sarcasm. I tolerated it for a time because I thought you would prove useful to me. How wrong I was."

"I'm sorry I disappointed you," I said. It wasn't a genuine apology; he and I both knew that. So we just sat there, in unsettling silence, each waiting for the other to say something further.

"Isabella tells me you're in love." There was something so wrong about the way Paolo said the word "love." There was no warmth in it. Instead he hurled the word at me, like some hideous accusation.

"Ahh yes, where *is* Isabella? I was thinking I would see her tonight."

"Isabella has done her job and has been compensated generously for it," Paolo said. There was an unspoken understanding that she no longer had a place onstage with Paolo. I always knew he would abandon her as soon as he found someone younger, prettier. I do not take joy in being right about these things.

"Isabella, you see, has a sense of loyalty," Paolo continued. "Something you would know nothing about."

"I didn't plan for any of this to happen," I admitted. They were the first honest words I had said to Paolo in a long time. "I genuinely tried to discover the man's secret."

"And did you?"

How could I possibly begin to answer that? I remained silent, my eyes dropping to the floor, hoping he would take said silence as a "no."

Paolo shook his head. "*Inutili*," he muttered under his breath, though he fully intended for me to hear.

Useless.

I sighed and slowly raised my eyes, but as soon as I did, I jumped. I hadn't even seen or heard him move across the room, but he was suddenly right in front of me, his face inches away from my own.

"Do you have any idea how much money you owe me? And what if I decided to collect upon that debt? I could make your life a waking nightmare. Do you understand that?"

It was something I had considered but had been avoiding, like an ill man who thinks that ignoring his symptoms will delay the inevitable.

But then Paolo straightened, first smoothing out his vest, then combing his fingers through his hair, as if he were compensating for some social faux pas, even though he and I were the only two people in the room. He smiled at me.

"But I won't do any of that," he said, almost laughing as he did, as if I were an old friend and not some underling he utterly despised.

"I...I beg your pardon?" My head was screaming at me, telling me to keep my mouth shut and blindly accept this unbelievable luck. But I could not simply let this be. Paolo is not a generous man, and he certainly is not one to forgive or forget. It could not be this easy.

"I am not a cynic, Saverio. I believe that the universe, she is just. She rewards those who are deserving of her favor and she deals out consequences to vagrants like you, who think they can get away with damn near anything. I have no need to make your life miserable, no, because you are about to do that yourself by setting down this path."

"And what path would that be?" Though I knew exactly what he was implying.

He responded with a corresponding snort and shook his head again. "It is bad enough that you are choosing to give your heart to another man—but a glorified stagehand from a family that has gone bankrupt? You are practically begging for unhappiness. And what? Do you think Wighton will take care of you boys? I know a thing or two about my rival, and he is not so generous with his favors or his wallet as I foolishly was."

Paolo took another step so that his lips were right beside my ear. "Soon you will have nothing. You will come crawling back to me wishing for the life you once had, and that is when you will know the misery that you deserve. The misery that your actions have earned you."

There were so many things I wanted to say, so many things I wanted to do. He's completely wrong. I wanted to show him just how wrong he was, but I took my opportunity and I left. As soon as I was outside the theatre, I ran down the streets, not giving a care to the stares that followed after me.

As Paolo had said, he could have easily used the debt I owe him to ruin my life, but instead, he let me leave, trusting the universe to exact vengeance on his behalf. Now I am free of him, but his words linger. I am not a spiritual or superstitious man, like Paolo. I do not believe that fate is going to punish me for all my misdeeds. If that is how the world worked, I would already be frightfully unhappy. As it is I am the happiest I have ever been in my life. I have Thomas and we have a life together now, and nothing is going to change that.

So why can I not get Paolo's words out of my mind?

Winter has departed and spring is now in bloom,
yet my heart has been coated in a layer of frost.
Would I have still given myself so openly,
if I had first been told the cost?

The spark that I have held within was easily kept at bay,
But now it roars and scorches, much like dragon's flame.
My dignity, my heart, 'tis all in ruins,
But is it you or I to blame?

Ice and fire battle within me,
a war which will continue to wage.
The springtime sun cannot warm this heart,
Nor can kind words quell this rage.

—An original poem by Thomas Pendleton

THOMAS

My vision is fogged by misty tears, my throat aches from my involuntary cries, my whole body shakes — admittedly I can barely keep this pen steady enough to write a full, legible sentence. The storm within is raging and heaven knows I can only keep it contained for so long. Fear is the one thing keeping the leash tethered, for were I to release this fury into the world, I would likely collapse an entire building — perhaps several!

I hate him.

Such anger, such sadness, such raw and inconsolable pain. I had come to expect such things from someone like Neville or even from the betrayals of those who were supposed to love and protect me like my parents. But for some reason — some stupid, foolish reason — I allowed myself to believe that Sav was someone whom I could confide in and trust. What was it that had ever made me so certain? I feel like the fool I have been made to be; I should have known better, should have known that such blind faith in another human being could only lead to this very sort of heartbreak!

Neville and I had a meeting scheduled for today to tailor the details of some new tricks he had been crafting. Only a handful was to implement the use of actual magic. A majority would still be standard stage illusions that he had been practicing for years. He was not about to have me doing all the work for him—it likely would have made the old man feel useless or impotent.

But yesterday, just after afternoon tea, I was called down to the street where Neville had sent a cabby to deliver me to his studio. Such eagerness is not entirely unexpected from him, and though annoying, I had no plans for the rest of the day, so I saw no reason not to go ahead and get the whole thing over with.

When I arrived, Neville was standing at one of the windows in his studio with his arms crossed behind his back. Without even turning to look at me as I walked in, he nodded toward the table in the middle of the cluttered room. "You may want to sit for this."

I took in a deep breath and sat down, trying to brace myself for whatever dramatics he had planned for me—oh if I had known then just what manner of ugliness he was about to lay before my feet...

"I have been thinking about the trick you detailed, the one involving the—"

He laughed. In hindsight I now see just how cruel a thing that laughter was. "There will be time enough to discuss the act. That is not why you are here."

Then why was I there? What had been so important that he had sent a car to deliver me personally?

Only silence filled the space between us while he continued to stare out into London's gloom.

Finally, he turned to face me. "I have noticed you have been spending a great deal of time with an immigrant boy."

Sav? Confusion flooded my being, accompanied by the slightest bit of rage. What business of Neville's was it who I spent my time with outside of our performances?

"A friend of mine, yes. Though I don't see how that is any concern of yours." I felt almost protective in that moment—Sav was something good in my life, something pure. The idea of

Neville even thinking about Sav set my blood to boiling.

"I am a man who protects his assets," Neville explained. "You, my boy, are one of those assets." It was the first time Neville had ever referred to me as "my boy." It was a strange contradiction, hearing him use what is so commonly a term of endearment while simultaneously objectifying me, referring to me as nothing more than one of his possessions. "Your secret is my secret." Another sentence that sounded wrong from his lips, speaking as if my curse were instead some sort of bond that we shared.

"I still do not see what my friend has to do with anything," I said.

"Friend." He smirked, and in that moment I felt entirely nude, as though he knew everything, as if he had seen Sav and me in our most intimate moments. "What do you really know of this Italian boy?"

There was suspicion dripping in his tone. I knew where this was going. "He is apprenticing to become a tailor. A magician's secrets mean nothing to him."

"And you believe him at his word?"

I'd had enough of this. I stood to make my exit from the studio, but Neville continued on just the same. "Luckily, I am not quite so trusting and naive as you are. When a new player enters the scene, I feel it is best to have all the information I can—and so, I had him followed."

"You what?" I whirled on the old man, my hands clenched into fists. I could feel the faintest prickling as my abilities started to take hold. The cages hanging above began to rattle, sending the birds into a small frenzy of chirps and squawks. Neville had no doubt been anticipating such a thing occurring. He raised his hands in a gesture that, to me, was more condescending than it was soothing.

"It's a lovely little flat the boy has for himself…but tell

me, do you happen to know where Mr. Moretti was residing previously?"

He knew Sav's name. Not only that, he knew where Sav lived. It was such an invasion! My mind was too clouded by anger to attempt answering his question—one that was intended to be rhetorical, as it was.

"I had to do some digging about, but I was able to discover that before his current lodgings, your friend Saverio was living at the Midland Grand Hotel. A rather luxurious setting for a tailor's apprentice, do you not think?"

I blinked at him as I considered. Was it odd? Yes, of course. But Sav dresses in fine clothing, and his mentor has been sending him an allowance to live on. It was my assumption that Sav was always well taken care of. But I felt no need to defend to Neville the ways Sav spent his money, so I merely shrugged.

Neville nodded, as though he were considering my shrug like he would a verbal reply. "Yes, yes, you're right! It's just a hotel. We humans are allowed our indulgences here and there. Plenty of people enjoy the finer things in life. But you know what is strange. Saverio Moretti was staying at the Midland Grand Hotel at just around the same time when you and I premiered the greatest illusion known to man. And would you like to know who else was staying at that hotel at the exact same time?"

Once again, I shrugged.

Neville cocked his head. "Does the name Paolo il Magnifico mean anything to you?"

I hated to admit it, but it did. Even before my involvement in the world of stage magic and illusions, I had at least heard of Paolo il Magnifico. Where Neville, up until my involvement, had been famous only regionally, Paolo was a magician whose fame had spread worldwide. I had always wondered if Neville had harbored ill feelings toward men like Paolo who had more showmanship and more acclaim.

"Another performer," I said.

"Not just any performer," Neville continued. "A man I consider to be one of my great rivals."

This was where I was confused. "If that is true, then why am I only just now hearing of this rivalry? You never mentioned him before today."

"Ah." Neville lit up, as if I was finally catching on to something. "I never spoke of him in front of you because you were my key—you were the element that made me superior. Before you, Paolo and I would write to each other on and off; we would attend each other's performances, and for many years we had been at odds, trying to outdo each other. And more often than not, the Italian magician always seemed to best me. Not anymore, of course."

"And so you believe because of their shared nationality and the fact that they both happened to be guests at the same hotel that Sav and Paolo know each other?"

"I could see how, from where you are sitting, it seems like a leap," Neville admitted. "You have a gentle heart. You want to see the best in people—give them the benefit of the doubt. When you have walked this earth as long as I have, you'll realize that there is no such thing as inherent goodness. People are self-serving and are guided by their own ambition."

I wonder if Neville realized the irony, given that he was describing his own nature.

He continued. "All the same, I myself was not even entirely convinced that the boy might be trouble until the investigator I had following your friend reported to me that he had been lurking outside my studio at night—and on more than one night."

My pulse quickened and my brows furrowed, but I managed to keep calm. Lies. These were simply more of Neville's numerous lies, used to keep me under his thumb.

"I don't believe you," I replied.

He chuckled, smug as ever. "I suspected you wouldn't, not without sufficient evidence. Which is only fair." He moved over toward the table where I had been previously sitting. The tabletop was covered in papers and notebooks, and he reached for a small stack of folded-up papers atop the mountainous mess. "The boy did not break into my studio, though from the sounds of it, he had intended to. I figured that gave me sufficient reason to have his home searched."

"You broke into his flat?" The rage that had already been boiling within me was now tempered by the racing of my pulse. My mind felt foggy and my lip quivered as I waited with anxiety and dread for Neville to relay whatever it was he had discovered.

Instead of answering or elaborating, Neville just tossed me the folded papers. I unfurled them to find that they were letters. Each one was addressed to Saverio and each was signed "Your Gracious Employer." My eyes scanned the letters in a panic. Surely enough, there was talk of performances and discovering Neville's secret, but I would not allow him to poison me against Sav so easily.

"As I have stated," Neville began, "Paolo and I have written each other throughout the years. I can confirm that the handwriting belongs to Paolo il Magnifico."

No. I refused to believe it. No. He would not do this. ~~My~~ Sav could not do this to me.

"These are forgeries, by your hand or someone else's. I am just supposed to believe you when you say your rival wrote these letters?"

"I anticipated that as well," Neville said, "and so I procured one last piece of evidence." He held up an envelope. "Another letter. This one I intercepted as the boy tried to send it out to

Paolo. Have a look for yourself."

With a shaking hand, I ripped the envelope from Neville's hand, though it took me a few moments before I was ready to pull out the supposedly incriminating letter. I did not read the content, for I could already feel the strings of my heart tugging and tearing. No, my eyes merely traced the ink, looking for small details and flourishes that I recognized from Sav's penmanship. Sure enough, it was all there. I had plenty of notes and letters from Sav stashed away in my memory to serve as evidence, but even if my memory were not so clear, the element that proved it to me was one simple letter: *S*. The small cards that had accompanied all those roses I had received would ensure that I would recognize that letter anywhere. The little curls at the ends were so heartbreakingly familiar.

Still, somehow, I tried to protest. "It's not true. It can't be true."

Neville almost looked sorry for me at that point. "I have many connections in the world of stage magic. After my initial suspicions about this young man were all but confirmed, I started inquiring to my peers about any young men in Paolo's employ, and what did I find? My rival had just recently found himself an apprentice, a boy who had been working for years as one of his stagehands. A boy named Saverio Moretti."

I glared at the old man, the sting of his words almost unbearable.

Neville scoffed. "I understand your anger, but I am the last person you should be directing it at. In fact, you should be thanking me for finally revealing the truth to you. At the very least, you should be begging for my forgiveness."

"What?"

"You almost ruined everything we built! We would have been exposed, or worse, all because my apprentice allowed himself to become lovesick."

My blood was boiling once again, and yet my teeth began to chatter, as though I were freezing. My throat started to tighten, and though I was unsure of what to do, I could not be there with Neville any longer, and so I stormed out of the studio and into the streets.

The entirety of my night since has been fits of painful sobbing—and I do not simply mean painful in the emotional sense. The physical strain from keeping my powers locked in my internal cage was comparable to a sailor aboard a ship caught in a mighty hurricane. The elements thrash against his vessel (or, in this case, my own body) but no matter how furious the gods' wrath, the foolhearted, desperate sailor uses what little strength is left in his raw, aching fingers to cling to the ropes.

I managed not to crumble all of London town into nothing but dust, though I now have a broken picture frame, five shattered plates, and a scattering of nicks in the wall where some of the cutlery ended up lodged to show for it.

My mouth aches.

My eyes ache.

My heart aches.

My soul aches.

If there is any mercy in this world, this torment will be taken from me! What foolishness… Do I not know any better by now? Have I not learned my lesson through each new blow that life has dealt me? I am irreversibly cursed. At one point I had been so certain that my paranormal burden was my only curse. But it now seems that I am cursed in the way of love. Perhaps I was never meant to possess happiness. Perhaps what little joy I did feel (or thought I felt) was even more than I was ever supposed to find.

It is a terrible thing to know—especially at such an early age—that all hope is lost.

It would be so easy to be selfish at such a time of anguish

and yet, oddly enough, my mind has wandered on more than one occasion this evening to thoughts of Amelia. Thinking of her (something I have not done in an admittedly long time) has made me feel even more wretched. I can only hope that in misleading her, I did not make her feel as miserable as Sav has now made me.

SAVERIO

May 06, 1899

I feel at ease. My nerves, which were so recently dancing in a flurry of anticipation, are now settled, and I feel I can finally be at peace. I do not know why I never thought to disengage from Paolo's life sooner. Now that some time has passed since our encounter, I can fully appreciate the fact that he is finally out of my life for good. It is doing wonders for my mental state.

Though now I worry for the mental state of dear Thomas. Though I can sense the joy he feels when we are together, I still feel the weight of his burden and the sadness it causes him. The strain that Neville puts upon his life will surely end him if we allow it. I have to help free Thomas of the magician's shackles.

Unfortunately, I have finally reached a state of poverty that I can no longer ignore. My own money is nearly gone, and I cannot keep relying on Thomas to feed me. The thought makes me shudder, but it is time that I finally join London's working class. If we are to get Thomas out of Neville's grasp, then we will need a plan. As it is, most good plans require some sort of financial backing.

I have not actually decided which trade I shall take up… or what I am even skilled at outside of a theatre or a bedroom. Such concerns had never before troubled my mind. But if I am able to find a decent job and save up some money, then perhaps I have a chance at freeing Thomas from his entrapment.

May 10, 1899

Ihave begun my search for employment and thus far have not been met with much success. I suppose a life devoted to the stage, while also in the care of one whose wealth ensures that money is no issue, leaves many other skills wanting.

<u>Potential options:</u>

- ~~Blacksmith's apprentice~~ I refuse to resort to anything so filthy

- Waiter or Maitre d'

- ~~Cook or baker's boy~~ Also filthy—waiter would be much more safe if I *<u>must</u>* work in an eating establishment

- Tailor—perhaps I can turn my lie around to my own advantage and make it have at least a little truth. It's not like I've never had to patch up a cloak or re-sew a button in my lifetime

- Shopkeep

- Carriage driver—I must admit, I have not the faintest inkling what sort of training is required

Tomorrow is another day and my resolve grows stronger as my stomach grows leaner.

THOMAS

May 12, 1899

I have not left my flat in precisely a week and, if I am honest, I do not know if I ever will. Sav has yet to call on me since my terrible meeting with Neville, and I am glad for it (and yet, the part of me that still wants him in my life, the part that still wishes for his love to be true, is anxious about why he has not come to see me). I still do not know what I will say to him when I inevitably face him. The night his lies were revealed to me, I was certain that I would scream at him in a way that I have never had the nerve to scream at anyone before. I am not so certain that I would not still have a similar outburst—even in a week's time, none of the rage born in me has subsided.

Meanwhile, others in my life have been trying to stir me from my sudden reclusiveness. Mother wishes for us to meet sometime soon, and her invitation was not received with my usual apathy. Perhaps, in light of what I have learned about Sav, her own deceit seems far less severe.

And of course, Neville wishes to work on the new routine he is putting together. I cannot believe he actually has had the nerve to call upon me after the way he pulled the rug out from underneath my feet and shattered my illusion of happiness. No matter what he tries to claim, I know it was not in my own best interests. I may not know what the actual endgame was that he had in mind, but it was not to help me.

If anything, he has proven himself more foolish than ever

before. He wishes to utilize my abilities for his own gain, but his mind games and manipulations have me more distraught than ever before. If he were thinking strategically, he would have tried to keep me blinded to Sav's and Paolo's games, tried to keep me happy so that my mind was clear. Now my mind is clouded, my heart heavy, and performing is the last thing I wish to think about. But that would require Neville to actually consider the long-term effect of his actions—he is always far too preoccupied with immediate gratification.

Perhaps I should do some traveling, just as I had been desiring (of course, I had wanted Sav to be by my side for my adventures, but there is no helping that now). I do have some money in savings and could easily leave the city tonight, if I so wished.

But where would I go? What would I do? And who would I be in this new place?

⁂

I have thought on my earlier questions and have come up with my answers:

Anywhere.

Anything.

And anyone.

The more my mind fiddles with the idea of venturing out on my own, the more romantic the notion becomes. Nothing is certain, but if I do decide to go, I will take a series of trains across the English countryside. From there? Well, from there, I shall go wherever my wandering feet take me. It could be dangerous, yes, but it could also be exactly what my derailed life needs to get lined up on the right tracks.

Remaining here will only lead to a continued state of

lethargy and wallowing. London is just too full of hurt and lies. It will drown me if I allow it to. I must distance myself from the memories, the pain, and the people who once claimed to have loved me.

SAVERIO

May 14, 1899

Success! I have found work, and though it does not pay much, it should be enough to keep me here in London, close to my Thomas.

The job itself will be simple enough, which was, I admit, certainly one of the main draws. I liked the idea of adding a bit of truth to my fable of working as a tailor's apprentice, so I went to a lovely little store entitled McEwan & Clarke's. The boutique featured neatly cut suits, prim little dresses lined with lace along the collars and sleeves, petticoats, wide-brimmed hats, suede gloves, capes, stoles, and all in fashion. Nothing revolutionary or unique so to speak, but it was charming enough.

There was a bald, bespectacled man behind the counter, with his sleeves rolled up and a measuring tape hung around his shoulders in the way some ladies would wear a scarf. When I entered, he offered me a friendly smile.

"What can I help you with this afternoon, lad?" he queried in a subtle-but-present Irish accent. "A waistcoat, perhaps with a bowler to match?"

I nodded in greeting. "Thank you but no. I am not here to make any purchases. I wish to inquire about employment."

The man adjusted his glasses and pursed his lips thoughtfully. "And just what sort of work would ye be looking for there?"

"Anything you have." As soon as the words escaped, I

kicked myself in my mind. Could I have sounded any more desperate? I might as well have dressed myself in rags and come into the store begging for coin!

"Can ye sew?"

I shifted, not sure of how to approach this. If I lied and claimed to be some amazing craftsman with cloth and thread, then he might ask me to prove myself right there and then with what looked to be a suit coat he was attaching the sleeves to. But admitting to no skill at all would send me right back out the door.

"What about any previous work experience? Have ye ever worked in a shop before, lad? Have any apprenticeships under yer belt?"

Well, I have technically been someone's apprentice for quite some time now, but that someone happens to be a magician. And even if his profession were of no concern, it is more than a bit doubtful that my mentor would sing my praises to this gentleman.

So instead of mentioning anything about Paolo, I simply shook my head.

He heaved in an apologetic sigh and was about to open his mouth to tell me just how sorry he was that he could not hire me when a voice shouted something out from the back room.

"Harold! Harold, what's going on up here? You with customers?"

A tall woman with sharp features and tight ringlets the color of burning coals entered the room. When I had first entered the small boutique, I had assumed the man (Harold) was the shopkeeper, but from the way his shoulders tightened and his eyes darted about the room as she entered, I could tell who was really in command (it also made it quite evident that the woman was his wife).

She looked me up and down and then turned to Harold.

"What's all this now? Why've yah not started on measuring the lad?"

"He is not here for a suit, my turtledove, he is here for work. But as I was just about to tell him—"

She raised a hand, and he took his cue obediently. She cocked her head to the side, then to the other as she looked me up and down. "Do a spin."

I was confused at this point. I looked to Harold and he seemed equally so. All the same, I did as I was told. After giving her a full view of my "qualifications," she let out a "hmmph" then asked, "When can yah start?"

More confusion. Harold shuffled across the store to his wife. He leaned in and though I am sure he thought he was being discreet, I heard every word: "But turtledove, he's never worked as an apprentice, no experience in a shop, I doubt he's ever—"

"We don't need the boy to sew, yah dim lamp! You're a tailor married to a seamstress fer Christ's sake. We just have him work the storefront. Greet the customers, ring out orders. He doesn't need experience fer that. Maybe every now and then we have him stand out front or up by the window. A handsome face like that will bring in plenty of lasses, maybe even a few lads!" That last part was said with a wink in my direction.

I smiled to myself. Normally such things would have flattered me, maybe even excited me. But there is only one lad whose affections I care about now.

We agreed that I am to start in three days' time. I was so thrilled to have secured employment that I rushed straight home. But now I must find a way to properly celebrate my good fortune, and I have just the thing in mind!

It has been a while since I have been to visit Thomas. I felt almost ashamed, facing him in such a state of financial duress (even if he did not know about it), and I could not very well explain my situation given that he thinks I am here on the dime of some fine Roman tailor. But now I feel almost excited to share the news of procuring a position in town. It will assure him even more of my permanence in his city, and something tells me that the boy will be proud of me. I have never sought anyone's approval as I seek his.

Before today's good fortune, I had recently resorted to selling some of my belongings to put food in my belly. Just the other day I sold my favorite (and really, only) walking cane. I got far less than I should have for such an item—the handle was made from real silver—but I got a decent enough amount that I haven't gone hungry, and I even have some coin still jingling around in my purse.

Given the state of things recently, one would think it irresponsible to spend money on something so lavish as a bottle of wine. But I am now employed and the promise of income has me in celebratory (if not somewhat reckless) spirits! It is a well-deserved gift to myself—and to Thomas, of course, for he shall be sharing it with me. Perhaps I shall also purchase a rose for the boy, just like old times. It can be another to add to his collection.

It will be a celebration for both of us, in truth. Good fortune for me that I now finally have a job, but also for him, in that I will be working toward a goal: a plan to get us far away from London, far away from the lie plaguing the conditions under which Thomas and I met and grew close to each other, and far from Neville Wighton the Great.

∘৹ℓℯ ৡৎ৹∘

Something awful has happened. The most awful thing that could have possibly happened.

Thomas knows… He knows *everything*. And rightfully so,

he hates me for all that I've done. All that I've kept from him. I should have just told him myself—confessed my sins, lay at his feet, and pleaded for his forgiveness. I wanted to! There were so many instances when I came so close to revealing everything to him. But I was so certain that in doing so, I would lose him forever, as I likely have now.

I showed up at Thomas's apartment, wine bottle in hand with a rose whose stem was tied neatly to the bottle's neck. I was brimming with joy, eager to tell him all about the day I'd had. But when the door did finally swing open, I did not see the well-groomed, bright-eyed young man I had come to know so well. I saw unkempt, matted hair, red eyes that looked lost and confused, and a mouth turned into an unrecognizable scowl—one that felt off on a face that was normally so sweet and hopeful.

Without knowing then the reasons for his sadness, I rushed inside, setting the wine bottle down on the table, and turned back toward him, cupping his face in my hands. His smooth skin felt cold and clammy. I stroked a cheek with my thumb, but before I could get a word out to ask him what was wrong, he batted my arms away with surprising force.

"Do not touch me, Sav." His red eyes narrowed into a stern glare. "Although who's to say if that is even your real name… Saverio? Certainly not I! It has become apparent to me that I do not know the first thing about you!"

The world around me seemed to stop. The only thing that did not seem frozen was my heart, which was racing inside my chest. He knew. *How* did he know? My mind went into a frenzy, and the only thing that mattered was repairing the damage I had already done…if I could.

"Thomas, please, you must listen," I began, but I had made the fatal mistake of starting a sentence without knowing where it would lead me.

It seemed it would not matter, for Thomas yelled out, "Do

not tell me to listen! I have listened to you and believed you and trusted you from the moment we met, and what has that brought me? Woe and heartache!"

"It was never my intent to harm you. I only ever—"

"Stop! Just stop!" The pained crack in Thomas's voice broke my heart even more than his appearance. "The magician Paolo. You know him?"

I nodded. No more lies, not even to save our relationship.

"Do you work for him?"

"Not anymore. I have cut all ties to Paolo, I swear it."

"Oh forgive me, let me clarify: *did* you work for him?" There was some extra bite in that version of the question, and I deserved every bit of it.

His chest heaved up and down uncontrollably, and watching it was enough to send me into a fit of tears myself. I was at an impasse. All I wished to do was reach out and hold him until his pain withered away into nothingness. But he would hate me even more for it. My touch would not bring him any comfort…it would be more comforting for myself than him and, therefore, selfish.

But I did it anyway.

In my desperation, I reached out to pull him into an embrace, but naturally he resisted. "Stay away from me!" he kept screaming, as if I were some stranger or, worse, a monster, and not the very person who had been sharing his bed and his secrets. The man who had listened to his poems and his dreams. I was his and he was mine. And now it was all slipping from my hands as easily as grains of sand, no matter how desperately I tried to grasp at it.

Each move I made toward him, he either backed away or to the side to evade me. Each time I started talking or trying to reason with him or attempted to explain myself, he would interrupt me, telling me to stop talking or to simply leave.

I should have thought about him, and how what I was doing was affecting him. But I continued to push, and all my pushing culminated in a startling shatter that pulled us from our dance of hysterics. The wine bottle had broken entirely, leaving only a rose soaked in red wine and glass shards lying on the table.

"Get out," he said sternly. But it wasn't just a command, it was a plea. I could hear it faintly in his voice, but I could also see it in his watery eyes. He knew that was far from the worst his magic could do, and through all his anger and his pain, there was an inkling of concern. As much as he hated me, he did not wish to do me harm, and so I left with that knowledge being my one shred of hope to hold on to.

Now I am home, but the strange thing is, I don't remember the journey back here. My memory of the walk is hazy, as though I were walking back from the pub after a night of heavy drinking.

I wish that I were drunk. I wish I still had that bottle of wine so that I might use it to cure my pain. But turning to such methods would be fruitless. There is no medication for that which ails me.

I do not wish to sleep…I cannot! Not when across town, the one person I love—the one I gave up everything for—loathes me.

My little magic boy.

May 17, 1899

I cannot stand this. Today was my first day working at McEwan & Clarke's as the shop boy, but my mind was anywhere except the storefront. I had seriously contemplated just staying in my bed and ignoring my responsibilities for the day, but what good would slipping into poverty and debt do me? It would only add yet another problem to my already problematic circumstances.

So I went and I did as I was told. Thankfully enough, it was not very involved work. As the redheaded woman—Tilda, I now know—had told her husband a few days prior, I was to be little more than a decoration, something pretty for the customers to stare at. And this suited my needs just fine, especially today. Had any actual thoughtfulness or problem-solving been required of me today, it may have sent me running back for that bed I had wanted to stay in so desperately this morning (one I will no longer have if I do not continue to work).

I am now home, after an honest day's work. This is something that should have made me feel proud, but instead I feel nothing...not even misery at this point, only numbness.

What is worse, I have no one else to blame for my current state. As tormented as Thomas must feel, at least he has someone to hate and to blame, a name to curse each night before he falls asleep. Me? I am the cause of my own misfortune. Thomas did not break my heart; I broke it, right along with his.

I had to force my legs to keep to the roads leading to my apartment and not his. He would not have seen me; he would not have wanted me there. But I so desperately needed to see his kind face, even if no kindness would be spared to me now.

I am fully aware that I do not deserve his forgiveness. He trusted his heart and his secret to a con man, and were I in his shoes, I would likely be filled with a similar amount of hate (perhaps more).

Anyone else might quit the job at the shop, pack their trunks, and return to Paolo groveling and begging for forgiveness and a position at his side once more. Returning to a life of comforts and travel and luxuries might seem easy to most, but to me it would be the most difficult thing in the world. How far have I come in life, under the presumption that love was fantasy and certainly never meant for me? And now to have found a love so pure, so true—why, I would be a fool to give up without a fight.

And so, it would seem I have found new purpose here in London. I will work to undo the damage I have done—to unbreak Thomas's heart and win back my magic boy. No matter what it takes and no matter how long—even if it takes all our adult lives. I need for him to see that what we had was real. That my feelings for him were real. He has to know he was loved and that it was not all merely some deception.

The skies in my world now dark as a raven's eye,
a song once gleeful now a funeral hymn.
Fruits of our garden, they wither and die,
as all my thoughts turn to him.

Words lose their meaning, flowers their smell,
I chase that which I cannot find.
Like Lucifer, I am cast into my own type of hell,
With nothing but you on my mind.

—An original poem by Thomas Pendleton,
believed to be unfinished

My dearest Thomas,

I have been trying to find the proper words to say to you since last we met, though I know that even with a full speech prepared, upon seeing you each syllable would escape me. It is for this reason I have chosen to write out my thoughts and feelings into a letter.

But even now as I sit down to write, I still am not seeming to find the correct words. This is something that you would have no trouble with, what with your literary mind and lyrical heart. I know that with your skills with the pen I would easily articulate the turmoil I have been through in a way that is not only sincere but beautiful.

Please do not take those last remarks as my way of flattering you in attempts to get back into your good graces, for I would never stoop to such condescension. All I am attempting to do is be honest, something I have done a terrible job of since the moment we met.

Though it was under false pretenses, meeting you truly was one of the greatest moments of my life. I have never been much of a believer in fate or predesigned destiny, but after meeting you, knowing you, and loving you, I cannot help but feel that everything else that has happened in my life up until now was leading me here to you.

I openly admit that which I should have told you long ago: I was conspiring with Paolo il Magnifico to steal a secret I thought belonged to Mr. Neville Wighton, and courting you was an attempt to get close to him.

At least at first.

The more time I spent with you and the deeper you let me into your life, nay, your very soul, I was enchanted (please forgive my choice of words). It may have been your magic that first drew our paths together, but it was your kindness, and your thoughtful intelligence, and your smile ϰ (if I do not stop myself I will keep scribbling for pages and never get to the point) that charmed me and warmed my heart to yours.

You are good, Thomas Pendleton, more so than I think you know. Some people may see your willingness to open up and trust as naive in such a cold world, but it is one of the things that only brightens the light that shines from you. And in taking advantage of your trusting nature, I have dimmed that light, something I will continue to regret for the rest of my days.

I know you do not trust me now, and I have given you no reason to. But please, try to believe that when I say that the feelings I have developed for you are true and unlike anything I have ever felt before in my existence, it is with all the sincerity that I have to offer.

If you will see me, I would be eternally grateful just for the chance to be near you again. If this is too much for you at the time, I understand. Even just a letter in response would warm me. Something to know that you have read my words and are considering them to be truths.

Yours truly,
Saverio

My dearest Thomas,

I cannot say that I am surprised to have not yet received a reply to the first letter I sent you. The anger and hurt you must be experiencing now is likely immeasurable, and I, myself, am enduring a great deal of pain, just knowing that I am the cause.

As I freely admitted in my last letter and the last time we spoke, my motives in getting close to you were to unveil Mr. Wighton's big secret. Somehow, while everyone else's gaze was fixed on the magician, mine was only ever on you. And it was through this unexpected infatuation that I saw what no one else did and pieced together the puzzle of your mystery. This is how I know that you loved me, too, for instead of shying away or lying to protect yourself, you opened your heart and thus opened my eyes to a new world of magic — not the kind I had been brought up around but real, honest magic. I was mystified!

You owe me nothing, but if you could indulge me in just one thing, answer me this: when I did find out that there was no hidden key to performing such an illusion, when I knew for certain there was no possible way I nor my mentor could execute such a feat onstage, did I run away? Did I abandon you, knowing mine was a lost cause? No! I stayed by your side and continued to be your friend, your confidant, and, most importantly, the one who has loved you.

It was because that illusion was no longer what mattered to me: you were. If I am being honest, and (as stated in my previous letter) I am trying to be, the revelation that there was in fact nothing I would be able to steal turned out to be a monumental relief.

Another point worth making in my defense, if I cared nothing for you or your well-being, would it not stand to reason that I would have revealed your secret by now? The fact that you hide your gift from the world shows that there is real danger if it were to be revealed. And I am certain that there are plenty of folk in any number of industries (artistic, humanities, sciences) who would pay a handsome sum for information regarding the existence of actual magic.

Now please, do not take this last remark as a threat! I only point out this fact to further prove my devotion to you. I may have failed when it came to protecting your heart, but I will protect your secret with my life.

Though it is more than I deserve, I do wish to hear from you soon.

Yours truly,
Saverio

My dearest Thomas,

Still I have not heard from you and still, I am not surprised nor am I offended. A wound such as the one I have dealt you will take time to heal.

With that in mind, I can imagine this constant influx of letters from me has been less than pleasant. I'm sure you would love nothing more than to never see my name or hear my voice or see my face again—just do away with the memory of me entirely.

But I will not, nay, cannot relent. For ours is a love that cannot be so easily tossed aside or forgotten. Ours is a love that does not come around every day. For someone like myself, it has never come around till now.

You are the first and greatest love my cynical heart has ever come to know. I have shared my bed with plenty of partners—a fact about me that, though unspoken, I was sure you had gathered. But my life had never felt so full and complete than when you came into it.

In truth, this is one of the main things that allowed me to do something so manipulative and so cruel. The loneliness. The emptiness I had felt so long. I was so certain that fame would bring me the kind of love I had never before experienced. And because of that, I sought said fame by any means and at any cost. I genuinely believed that the adoration of masses would fill that void for me. When I first met you, you were a pawn that I was using to get what I wanted.

But then I fell in love.

Wholly unexpected for my part, since I had been so sure that love was more fiction than reality. A faerie story or a myth—an elusive object that was attainable only in dreams. Any intelligent man can admit when he is wrong, though, and I like to think I have at least enough smarts and enough humility to admit just how wrong I was.

Love is very real.

I feel it every day, pulsing through my veins like blood. And much like blood, I need it to survive. Without your love in my life, I will surely wither to nothing more than a husk of the man you have come to know and, hopefully, care for.

That is why I must continue my course. I will fight for you until the battle is won.

Yours truly,
Saverio

THOMAS

Saverio has been leaving letters for me at my doorstep. He has taken up his old habit of leaving said letters with a single rose each time. The only difference with this succession of notes is that now there is no need for anonymity. Rather than that lonely, familiar *S*, each envelope has his full name scrawled out.

I cannot seem to bring myself to dispose of the letters. I had thought to get a fire going, then set them aflame in the fireplace—the act of it alone would be cathartic—but I only got as far as tossing in a few newspapers. I crouched near the hearth with the unopened envelopes in hand, but there was something so heart wrenching about the prospect of never knowing the letters' contents (even though they remain in a pile on the mantel, unread).

One morning I had felt an urge to simply toss the envelopes out the window. Just let them into the world and be done with it. But once again, the idea of not ever knowing what he has to say for himself…well…there is a curiosity that always stays my hand when trying to rid myself of the letters. Also, though I owe him no courtesies, it would be terribly rude to toss such personal writings into the wind and allow strange eyes to view that which was meant for my eyes alone.

But he has been leaving them daily, and the stack is becoming harder to ignore. It is why now would be the perfect time to leave the city as planned. And so, I have decided to buy myself a train ticket. One of the few positives that have come of this whole mess is that my interactions with Saverio taught me to act on my desires. It may not have worked out favorably in respect to my love life, but I am willing to act on my impulsiveness once more and see where it takes me.

In a week I shall be on my way toward Edinburgh! I have already looked into securing myself a room in a hotel not far from the birthplace of Sir Walter Scott. From all the fantastical things Sav told me about Venice, I had been considering that or another city with winding canals, such as Amsterdam or Bruges.

There is no paved road that will lead Sav back to me now.

After much deliberation, I have decided that I shall start within Great Britain, and if my feet take me farther from there, then so be it.

I am hoping that this trip will not only mend my aching heart but perhaps will inspire me creatively. As of late, my only muse has been the dark lady, Misery, and though this has managed to produce some half-decent pieces, in my opinion, I am ready for lightness and joy to enter my writing once again (even if it has yet to enter back into my life).

My intended departure date falls just two weeks before Neville's next booking, and I have made the decision not to tell him of my travel plans. I do not need him fussing over whether or not I will be back with enough time to prepare, mainly because I cannot be certain if I will. Perhaps once I depart from London, I will never return! I wonder if my parents would miss me if I were to disappear. They already see me so rarely as it is, by my own choosing, of course. Still, I doubt they would even notice my departure. None of my plans moving forward are set in stone, and that is just the way I want it to be. I am tired of plans, and routines, and schedules, and appointments…I need spontaneity.

May 30, 1899

I now have a new subject for my feelings of hatred. Well, I suppose "new" is the wrong term, for he has always been a target for my animosity, but Neville has shown me a side of himself more treacherous than I had counted on—and this is a man who has subjected me to both physical and verbal torment.

He called me to his studio the other day. I was hesitant, to say the least, after what happened the last time I went to meet him in his studio.

He had a stern way about him when I arrived but was surprisingly hospitable. He offered me a seat, poured me a cup of tea (I had always assumed the stove there was merely for decorative purposes rather than actual use), and informed me that he had a matter that needed discussing—a redundant bit of information, since he had summoned me, but I sat silently, allowing him to regale me with whatever nonsense was bothering him this week.

But then he started speaking. He told me that he knew of my plans to travel to Scotland, and though his demeanor conveyed that of a calm man, I saw an anger burning within. He informed me that I would be canceling my trip and that I am not to plan any other such excursions. I was just about to scoff and tell him that he had no right to make such demands, but he likely saw that coming and informed me that if I did attempt to leave London, he would reveal my secret to the world.

I called him on what was surely a bluff. In exposing my magic, he would be exposing himself as a con man with no actual hand in the illusion that has brought him so much fame!

To destroy my life, he would have to destroy his career and reputation.

But he stated that he would willingly commit such self-sabotage if I dared to abandon him. It was such an interesting word to hear from his lips: "abandon." A word that implies such desperate need. I've always known that Neville needs me, but it did not make it any less strange to hear him stating so, even in his own roundabout way.

It would seem I have two options: test Neville's claim and see if he will actually reveal both of our greatest secrets in one detrimental blow *or* remain here in London, forced to assist him to ensure his silence.

I am intelligent enough to know that the latter is the only true option. Neville's knowledge of my magic has become a prison—a weapon that he can wield at will.

Meanwhile, Sav's letters continue to appear at my doorstep. I am running out of places to stash them all. If a stranger were to enter my flat, they might assume that lavender oil–scented envelopes were lining the very walls.

I still have yet to read a single one.

As for the roses? Well, they do add a bit of brightness that my flat has been lacking as of late. It is difficult being angry at something so beautiful.

June 02, 1899

¶ am glad that I kept the letters.

June 05, 1899

I have pored over every single letter Saverio has written me, some multiple times, and my resolve is weakening.

I thought I could do it, I thought I could stay angry with him until he was out of my life for good, but with each letter, every word penned, I felt myself giving in. That combined with the memories of what once existed between us had me yearning to reclaim that happiness that until so recently had been mine.

I will not recount in this journal all that he has said, considering he has left a letter every day. I will note that he made an excellent point in one of the letters, stating that if he did not care for me, he could have easily shared my secret with the highest bidder. It is hard to ignore the fact that Sav, unlike Neville, has not attempted to use my magic against me.

He has also made claim that I am the first person he has ever truly been in love with and oh, how desperately I wish for this to be so! For, until recently, I felt the same way about him. His sweet words are strung together in such a way that I could easily find them sincere.

But I have already believed his supposedly heartfelt words once before, and what did that bring me aside from pain? Every part of me that still cares for Sav wishes for his words of apology to be honest ones, but I also cannot ignore the wrongs already done to me.

Saverio Moretti is a con man, and as they say, the leopard cannot change its spots.

SAVERIO

June 07, 1899

O happy day, what joy is mine! My sweet young Thomas has finally agreed to see me! It would seem my words have gotten through to him. All I needed was a little bit of patience!

I have not prepared what I am going to say to him yet, but I suppose there is only so much that I can prepare. A great deal of what I say will be entirely dependent on what Thomas says to me. I must tread carefully, though. I am immensely grateful that he is going to see me, but in taking this meeting, I am risking my neck. One misstep and I could easily set off his temper, thus setting off his otherworldly abilities. I have known the beauty of his magic; I have no desire to know its wrath.

With my continued work at McEwan & Clarke's, I have managed to save a small bit of money. I know my coin should be going toward more practical things such as food and clothing and keeping a roof over my head — survival does not come cheap — but I am toying with the idea of purchasing a small gift to present to Thomas when we see each other again. Would he appreciate that or find it annoying? Perhaps he would think it insulting, an implication that I assume his love can be purchased.

It is quite possible that I am overthinking this, but I don't care. Everything must be perfect if I am to win back my love. I certainly will not be bringing him flowers. At this rate, his apartment likely looks like a defective greenhouse, overcome by decay (that is, if my tokens have not simply been discarded straightaway to the waste basket).

I have never been so nervous for a meeting. Before Thomas, I never much cared about the opinions of others. It is an entirely stressful affair! Life was so much simpler back when I did not trouble myself with matters of love. But now that I have felt it for myself, I mustn't give up on it. And I will not let Thomas give up on it, either.

June 08, 1899

Thomas and I had our meeting tonight; it was the first time I had seen him since the middle of last month, and even getting to be in the same room with him helped to relieve some of the pain that had been plaguing me these past few weeks.

I cannot say that the encounter went particularly smoothly, nor did it go nearly as poorly as I had been anticipating. I suppose the best way to clarify this would be to recount events:

Thomas came to me, here at my apartment. I had been wondering if he would not ask me to meet him somewhere more public so as to keep either one of us from making a scene—but I suppose that was ultimately the point of meeting in private. If things were to get unintentionally escalated, it would not be simply my neck that would be at risk. Not to mention the risk of eavesdroppers getting their cheap thrills from our conflicts.

I attempted to make the place somewhat presentable. My favorite silk scarf, dip-dyed to look like a watercolor painting, was draped over my table rather than around my neck. There were a few articles of clothing Isabella had managed to leave behind that were still lying out. I stashed them in the tiny closet by the front door.

I had my apartment looking tidy and had made a fresh pot of tea—that's right, a *pot*. I actually procured myself a proper teakettle. I had been up since nearly dawn readying myself for the encounter. Well, a slim part of my day was spent preparing. A good majority of the rest of it was spent fidgeting and pacing and not knowing what to do with myself. I can imagine that I looked about as nervous as Thomas does on any given day. I do not mean this as a criticism of him; it is quite honestly one of the things I have always found to be so charming about him.

When Thomas did finally arrive, it was a relief, for my nerves had been building to a point that would have caused me to burst if I had been left alone with my thoughts and anxieties for a moment longer.

He looked better than he had when I had seen him last. His hair had finally been washed and combed and had its usual spring. His clothes were pressed. His eyes were not so red as they had been before. More sleep? Less crying? Both?

"Come in," I said in greeting but immediately cursed myself. I sounded far too eager.

He slowly stepped into the apartment, warily, as if he were treading into unknown waters rather than a place he had already been countless times. He looked around, almost like he was inspecting the place, and his eyes gave off a similar sense of unfamiliarity, as if he were seeing it all for the first time. He flashed me a similarly measured look, and it was then that I understood: he was wondering what new secrets or treacheries were awaiting him this time.

It broke my heart.

"I made tea, if you would like some," I said.

He looked cautiously at the kettle on the stove. This look of caution was not the same he had been regarding me and the entire apartment with but the caution of someone who had tasted my watery concoctions in the past. Smart man. But oh how I wanted him to say yes. I was eager to surprise him with a beverage of much higher quality.

He eventually nodded, and it gave me a small thrill. 1) Because I was going to prove him wrong and 2) because it was a small gesture of positivity.

I poured him a cup and watched him take a sip. Satisfaction

surged through me when his eyes widened in surprise.

"So you read my letters, then?" I asked. I figured we might as well get on with it.

He nodded.

"All of them?"

Another nod.

"And…?"

He looked somewhat annoyed that I was pressuring him to speak, but was that not the point of this meeting? To finally speak to each other?

His lips parted, and what sounded like the start of a consonant escaped with a breath but was cut off. He looked to me feebly and finally asked, "If Neville had not connected you to Paolo, would you…would you have ever told me?"

"I wanted to. You have no idea how much I wanted to."

"Well, then why didn't you?"

I searched my mind. No answer I could give him would excuse what I'd done. "Because I was afraid of losing you. You had become so important to me—you *are* so important to me. I feared revealing what I had done would ruin everything. Turns out it was my lying that did exactly that."

We sat in silence for a moment or two. If Thomas found what I'd said acceptable, he made no effort to show it. So I added, "I do like to think that, if Neville hadn't found me out, I would have eventually told you myself."

He scoffed and shot me a look of disdain. This dismissal of my honesty caused my pulse to quicken, and I shot back, "I cannot know for certain—how am I to read the future? Or I suppose, in this case, the past. We don't all have magic."

Stupid. Stupid, *stupid*. He was finally giving me a chance, and my first impulse was to pick a fight with him. I looked at him, apology in my eyes, but my pride kept my lips locked, waiting for him to say something further.

"Does Paolo know my secret?"

"Of course not," I said. "And he never will."

Of course not. As if it were obvious. As if he were supposed to just take me at my word. I would not if I were in his position.

"You really haven't told anyone?"

I shook my head.

"Why not? I am sure there would be plenty in it for you."

"I thought you said you read my letters." That one was genuinely not meant to be so snide, but the sharp look Thomas shot me informed me of my misstep. I took a breath and continued. "I care for you. At first, you were convenient—a path to what I thought I wanted. And then, along the way, I realized you were what I wanted." *Note*: his lip trembled here. "I may not be so great at expressing what exactly it is that I am feeling, and that is because I have never felt anything close to it for another being on this earth."

"It does not erase the fact that you used me," Thomas breathed. I could almost feel his resolve thinning.

I shook my head. "It does not. Indeed, nothing I can do now will. My treachery and lies will always remain, stuck to the past like dried honey. But I can try to atone for my mistakes, something I intend to do for the rest of my life."

"This is all quite lovely," he said. Hope fluttered within me. "But you have said lovely things to me in the past." Hope vanished. "How can I possibly trust that things you say now are not merely further lies? Before, I was under the impression that you were a tailor's apprentice, only to find that you're a performer—and a good one at that. All you wanted was to be on the stage. How am I supposed to believe that you no longer desire that?"

"What purpose would lying to you now serve?" I folded my arms, genuinely curious about what he would say next.

"What?" he asked, as if he hadn't heard me.

"Why continue the charade? I know your secret. I obviously can't steal it, not for myself or Paolo, and I have not told a soul. Why would I choose to continue down this path we have started on just to con you? I would have nothing to gain. Is it so unfathomable that the feelings I developed for you are sincere?"

I was getting a bit perturbed. If he actually had read my letters, like he had claimed to, he would have known all this already. I thought I had done a somewhat decent job of explaining myself and making a case for my sincerity.

To my questions, Thomas looked baffled. He had no words, no way to combat the points I was making, and it seemed to irritate him. He looked defeated, as if we were in a heated debate over politics or some social issue, and he had just been backed into a corner. I merely wanted him to see that, maybe, this was a debate that was worth losing.

Finally he managed more words. "You're one of them!"

"What?" I asked.

"Neville, Paolo…you're just like them. They lie and manipulate and use information to get what they want. It's no wonder you're a part of their world."

This time I was the one who could react only with silence. Before ever meeting Thomas, a comparison to Paolo il Magnifico would have been met with joy. It would be high praise. Now it was exactly what Thomas had meant it as: an accusatory insult. And a comparison to Wighton? Well, that was just cruel. Deserved cruelty, of course.

Words were not going to be enough to get him to forgive me, so I stood and approached him, reaching out to touch his face. I had prepared myself for him to flinch or to turn away, but he remained still, allowing my hand to stroke his cheek.

"I love you," I whispered.

His eyebrows lowered, softening his gaze, and he looked

near tears. But he quickly stiffened and came back with, "I hate you."

I did not lose heart, for his voice faltered as he said it. Thomas is not as good of a liar as I am. I brought my other hand up and used both to cup his face, bringing it close to mine. He did not hate me. He would not be there in my home if he hated me.

"No you don't."

"I do," he persisted. "I hate you and I think that you should leave London."

"No you do not."

"Yes I do! Go back to Italy. Run off to another country and try your luck conning some other poor, unsuspecting victim. As long as you're away from here, what you do or where you go matters not."

"Thomas, I—"

It was here that he recoiled from my touch, trying to pull away from my grasp. I did not want to accidentally hurt that darling face of his. I removed my hands from his face and wrapped my arms, instead, around his waist. But he continued to push and yell until out of nowhere, I felt something…a force behind me. It was like a pair of large, invisible hands grasping at my shoulders, plucking me up off the floor, and flinging me against the wall.

The air rushed out of me as my body crumpled and collapsed onto the floor. Once I was down, I coughed uncontrollably while my lungs fought desperately to replace the oxygen they had just lost. It took me a few moments before I properly regained my vision. I craned my suddenly sore neck to see that Thomas had also collapsed on the floor in horror. He was on his knees and was bringing his hands to his lips, but before covering them, I saw him mouth, *Sav*.

I had to lie there for a moment, but as soon as I could, I

reached out my hands and pulled myself forward in a sort of crawl/dragging motion until I was right beside my love.

I laid my head on his lap, and he did not try to push me away. He put his hand in my hair, and I felt his body rise and fall as he sobbed while stroking my hair.

You know what? I take back what I said earlier in this very entry. Tonight went perfectly.

THOMAS

June 09, 1899

Last night I wept in front of Sav, and honestly, it felt even more intimate than making love to him.

 SAVERIO

June 14, 1899

Thomas is starting to relent in his resolve to keep me outside his walls. He tested me today, though. Something that was wholly unexpected, and I can only hope that my own resolve to win back his heart served me well enough to prove my intentions.

He called on me for another meeting, although this time it was not at my apartment nor was it at his own. He wanted to meet me at the Criterion Theatre. I thought it strange, since Neville and Thomas do not have any shows booked with the theatre currently, but after knowing the purpose of our meeting, I suppose the specific venue was of little importance—any theatre could have easily served Thomas's purpose.

He specified noon as the intended meeting time, but I was so eager for the chance to see him again that I arrived well before the first of the twelve bells. I waited in front of the large doors, and when Thomas did finally stroll up, I was thrilled to see a small smile playing across his lips. There was something else, though. Something about his demeanor that was harder to read.

"Are we getting a private show?" I nodded at the marquee, which was advertising the current production of *King Lear*.

Thomas didn't respond. He raised a bony knuckle to one of the doors and rapped against it. I was certain that if anyone were inside, there was no possibility they had heard a knock so light, but to my surprise, the door swung open to reveal a bespectacled woman with dark hair pulled into a tight bun atop her head.

She offered Thomas a familiar smile and myself a more curious one before standing aside and allowing us to enter the theatre. I followed Thomas past the grand lobby and into the empty auditorium.

It was dark, most of the house lights were dimmed, but with what little light was on, I could see set pieces and props lining the stage, likely from a prior or upcoming rehearsal.

Thomas continued, still without a word, toward the stage, and the silence was more than a bit unnerving. I watched as he hoisted himself up onto the stage, rather than simply using the stairs at stage right or stage left.

Once he was standing up on the platform looking out at me, my mind flashed back to that night so long ago at the West London Theatre when Thomas kept me in the audience after his performance with Neville and we got to know each other better. I could almost hear him reciting sonnets in the empty space once more. My heart warmed with the thought that maybe he had brought me there for precisely the purpose of recalling the memory of that night.

I now know his intentions were not quite so sentimental.

He waved to me and said, "Come up here."

I made my own way to the stage, though I elected to use the stairs, so it took me a little while to join him center stage. As soon as I was standing but a few feet away, Thomas closed his eyes, seemingly muttering something to himself.

The already dim stage lights went out, and my breath caught in the darkness. But it lasted only an instant before a pale white spotlight was on, illuminating Thomas and myself. At first, I had to shield my eyes with an arm so as not to be blinded.

"What is this?" I asked.

He kept his eyes closed but brought a finger to his lips, motioning for my silence. I did as commanded and remained silent. And that's when I heard it...

It started soft and low, like the muffled sound of rain outside a building, but it grew in intensity and clamor until an overwhelming sea of applause washed over the space. Uproarious cheers began to pierce the air. Though I knew Thomas and I were the only souls in the auditorium, the blinding spotlight made it impossible to make out the figures of the empty seats, and it was remarkably easy to let myself believe the applause was coming from real patrons and not merely the work of living, breathing magic.

How many times in my life have I stood in the wings during one of Paolo's performances, pretending that the cheering and standing ovations were all meant for me? But this...this was different. I was right in the center of it all as the sounds of awe and adoration enveloped me. I closed my eyes and welcomed it.

When I opened my eyes once again, I noted that Thomas had opened his as well, and he was watching me.

Fool, I cursed myself. I should have known better than to allow myself to get swept up in the facade.

I waited for the magical applause to quiet before asking once again, "What is this?"

"I'm giving you a taste of what you've always wanted," Thomas replied, as if it were the plainest thing in the world.

It was a time for thinking on my feet, something I am normally so skilled at. There was no denying that I had been backed against a wall. Thomas is not blind, and clearly, he'd seen the pleasure on my face.

I took another moment to gather my thoughts, then I took Thomas's hand in mine. I was near certain he would wrench it away but, to my surprise (and delight), he left it limp.

"I will not insult your intelligence by telling you that the desire for fame does not linger still. For so long, I have dreamed of being so beloved as to receive applause such as that." I could feel him retreating, but I gave his hand a small squeeze. "But why would I want to be beloved by hundreds of strangers for a single night of their lives when I could be beloved by one for a lifetime?"

I watched as he considered my point, still so much uncertainty hanging over him.

"But what if that one is not enough for you?"

So much vulnerability in one question. His defenses were lowering once more, and in that moment all I wanted to do was pull him close and kiss him as assurance. I wanted my lips on his to be the answer for any doubts in his mind. But I also did not wish to push his boundaries too far too soon, otherwise I would risk him distancing himself from me even further.

"I always thought what I was seeking was adoration," I responded, "but that was only ever a placeholder for what I truly wanted…what I truly needed: love. You just told me that you were giving me a taste of what I've always wanted, but you've already done that—and without the use of magic."

He smiled and, however faint, his grip tightened on my hand.

Forgiveness is a salve,
A balm that heals the wounded soul.
Forgiveness is a guiding light
In a never-ending hole.

Forgiveness is a mockingbird
That sings a song so sweet.
Forgiveness is a safety net,
To save thee from defeat.

It does not come easy nor cheap,
Weaker hearts, how they like to suffer!
But allowing the heart to hold its grudges,
O, that would be much rougher.

—An original poem by Thomas Pendleton

Thomas

June 28, 1899

Sav's and my meetings are becoming more frequent once again, and I am starting to be glad for it. The hurt has not healed entirely, and there is a part of me that is always wary when I am around him now—I do not know if this will ever go away—but I cannot deny that I am immensely happier with him as my friend, rather than my enemy.

Who am I trying to fool? Sav will never be just a mere friend to me. He has known me closer than anyone has known me, cared for me more deeply than anyone has cared for me. He has seen the hidden parts of me that others would find strange or even monstrous, and he has come to love every secret and fault I possess.

I should have known it would not be long before I forgave him. To put it frankly, I need him.

I cannot claim to have come to the decision to allow him back into my life fully on my own. There was something my mother had told me some months ago: "Forgiveness, she is a holy maiden." Now, it was clear at the time that she was saying this with the intention of warming me to her further, but her words have been ringing in my mind of late.

Sav has revealed to me that he does not believe in a higher power, but the idea that there is not some force beyond our control seems absurd to me. At first glance, it may seem that what brought Sav and me together was his lies and my foolishness. But what drew him to London, and ultimately into my world, was that first illusion. Like a moth to flame, he had to have the trick.

Instead he got me.

Tracing that back even further, one would ultimately surmise that it was my magic that brought love into my life. And who could have possibly gifted me with such otherworldly skills than the Lord himself?

These scribblings about my beliefs are not to prove my piousness. Who would I be trying to prove such things to in a personal journal? Myself? I note these thoughts only to underline why my mother's words had resonated with me.

Forgiveness, she is a holy maiden…

Holy. The stuff of angels. It seemed an apt description, since without Sav in my life, I felt as if I were in a waking hell. And just how long could I continue to keep myself trapped there, with nothing more than my own misery?

I must also thank Neville in helping me come to this change of heart. Yes, Neville. For in him, I have an example of what a loveless life can lead to. If I were to allow myself to cling to my anger, then I would end up no better than he. A bitter old man who allows greed and ambition to fuel each decision that he makes.

Neville also played a part in my forgiving Sav because without Sav, without love, there is no joy. There is no light in the dark. Circumstances have grown worse and worse with Neville. Abuse, torment, blackmail. The man has made actual threats on my life by threatening to expose my secret to the world. What sort of misery would I be subjecting myself to if the only person in my life was Neville Wighton? The time I get to spend with Sav is my relief, my escape. He is what keeps me going.

I choose forgiveness, for though it is hard, in doing so, I am also choosing love and joy.

SAVERIO

July 07, 1899

When Thomas first let me see his magic in an intimate setting, he created a small galaxy for me. Today he made me an enchanted garden.

After finishing an absolutely grueling day of standing around and looking pretty at the shop, I had a sudden urge to visit Thomas. He was not expecting me and I considered that I might be overstepping my bounds. Were we at the point yet where surprises were welcome? Or would it simply agitate an already fragile situation? Even so, I decided it was worth the risk. I hate how trapped Thomas has been by Wighton lately, and I figured a visit would serve to cheer him up.

When I arrived, he smiled, and not with hesitation or uncertainty. He was genuinely happy to see me!

I had no prearranged plans for the day, but that was sort of the point. Quite often, before the rift that temporarily divided us, I would take Thomas to explore London with me. I have always found that the most memorable of experiences come from having no plans whatsoever. Who does not love a little spontaneity? And in Thomas's case, I often feel that the boy *needs* it.

I asked him if he had any desire to wander the streets with me. He responded to my lack of a plan with an idea of his own.

"I know just the place we can go! It's somewhere I've wanted to show you for a while." The excited smile was unendingly charming, like that of a child with a secret he is eager to share.

A willing participant in whatever adventure was about to unfold, I followed him out into the day. He nearly sprinted, and I had to break into a light jog just to keep a few paces behind him.

It wasn't far, though, and when we reached our destination, I fully admit that I was a little less than impressed. It was a tiny bookshop nestled between a cobbler's workshop and a pub whose windows, upon first glance, still seemed to be frosted from winter's chill. Closer inspection revealed that it was actually a layer of dust coating the windows from the inside, leading me to suspect it had been closed for some time now.

Thomas reached out, almost like he was about to grab my hand and lead me inside. Then, remembering himself, he glanced down either side of the street and continued inside, keeping his hands to himself. The disappointment emanating from him was rivaled only by my own.

Inside, the shop was cozy but cluttered. The bookshelves lining the wall reached from the floor to the ceiling going all the way back (it was hard to tell if there even were walls behind them). Seeing as every inch was covered with books, there were no windows to let in the daylight. Even so, the oil lamps filled the entire space with a warm amber glow. It felt like a sudden shift into evening, though outside the shop it was still the afternoon.

It was charming, to be sure, but I could hardly tell why Thomas was so excited—I supposed his love of literature was reason enough. More specifically, though, I could not tell why he was so excited to show the place to me. No one else seemed to share his enthusiasm about the little shop, for we appeared to be the only living souls there.

"Mr. Wexler?" Thomas called out.

On cue, an old man with glasses and a jolly sort of look

about him popped up from behind a desk on the far end of the room.

"Well if it isn't my favorite customer!" The smile on his round face quickly turned to a frown. "I wasn't expecting you to stop by so soon. I am afraid those collections you ordered have yet to arrive."

"Oh, do not worry yourself! That is not why I've come." He gestured to me, so I took a few steps deeper into the cavern of books. "This is a friend of mine, Saverio. I figured I should show him my favorite bookshop in the city!"

His enthusiasm was delightful.

"Well isn't that just—" A low rumbling gurgle coming from the shopkeeper's stomach interrupted the man's response. Thomas and I looked to each other, both biting our lips to keep down the laughter. Mr. Wexler laughed off his own embarrassment.

"Pardon me, boys. The wife was supposed to drop by with lunch, but she is…" He pulled out a pocket watch. "Nearly an hour late!" His stomach groaned. He looked to Thomas with a sheepish smile. "Do you think I could trouble you to keep an eye on the shop while I fetch a sandwich from the café just down the block?"

Thomas nodded. "Of course!"

"Thank you, lad." On his way out, he nodded at me and shook my hand vigorously. "Any friend of young Mr. Pendleton here is a friend of mine."

Once Mr. Wexler was out the door, Thomas rushed over to twist the lock on the doorknob. My mind was racing at all the fun we could have in an empty store, but I played coy. "Now, how will any of the fine, paying customers be able to get in?"

Thomas smirked but ignored the question, joke or no. He swept back into the store until he was standing in the center of the room. He turned back to look at me, but only for a moment before closing his eyes and pulling in a deep breath. I was rapt. Whatever was about to come next, I knew it would involve his gift.

The already cluttered shop became even more so as books started falling to the floor. A slight panic came about instinctually, but watching Thomas, I knew I had little to fear and that this time I would not be flung against the nearest wall. This was intentional, purposeful. Not something to fear but to be in awe of.

All the books that were now lining the floor flipped open, and from them, the pages began rising on their own. They all began to fold and morph, taking the shape of various flowers. The printed type decorated the petals of roses and paper sunflowers that were nearly as tall as I am. Vines of paper and ink sprouted from the tomes and crawled across the floor as well. They also sprouted from books still on the shelves, winding their way down the mahogany. The yellowed pages of an old recipe book turned to a bushel of tiny tulips. In moments, the place had gone from a quaint little bookshop to a forest of paper flora.

I was overcome. It started with a laugh, then I brought my hand to cover my mouth in astonishment, then I felt the need to be near him. I made my way to his side but did not stop there. I grabbed him and planted a firm kiss against his lips, letting my physical affection show my astonishment.

I then returned to the picturesque scene unfolding before my eyes. I had an impulse to bring my nose close to one of the imitation roses and give it a sniff, but I resisted, for it would have been silly. This is not to say that books do not have an enchanting aroma of their own. Some books you come across carry more than just the standard smell of ink and pulp. Some smell of history, and memories, and secrets, if such things could ever be captured by scent.

"The magician's apprentice," I whispered to myself, then to him I said, "You never cease to amaze me, Pendleton."

In the face of such magnificence, it was hard not to also feel sorrow tugging at me. Sorrow for Thomas and the fact that Neville was keeping Thomas's magic all to himself and for what? His own selfishness. Fame, fortune, acclaim. Thomas could do amazing, beautiful things. But instead of adding his beauty to the world, his gift is wasted on the likes of the old magician.

I did not want to place the weight of my worry on Thomas, so I smiled. Then he smiled.

"Is there anything you can't do?" I asked, and it was a genuine question.

Thomas snorted and let loose a boyish laugh, as if it were the silliest question he'd ever heard. "Well of course—plenty of things."

"Like what?" I asked, "Have you tested the limits of what your magic can do?"

Thomas nodded. At first his expression was focused and stern as he thought on his reply, but then he smiled. "Well, I cannot fly, that much is for certain."

"Wait…you've actually tried that?" I could not help my laughter as I imagined sweet Thomas leaping up into the air, flapping his arms like wings. Thomas's smile widened as he nodded, so clearly he was in on the joke.

"What about other people?"

"What?"

"Can your magic…can it *control* other people?"

Thomas bit his lip. "That one is a little more…complicated."

"Oh?" I felt one of my eyebrows rise, almost as if the act were involuntary. I was intrigued by the vague answer, if not a little frightened, I must admit.

"I can control people physically. Like with the illusion, how I teleport Neville. Or when I get emotional I can sometimes lose control…as you experienced when I flung you across the room."

I rubbed the back of my head, suddenly remembering the soreness and the aching in my body as if the incident had just occurred.

"When I'm performing the illusion with Neville, I've also noticed that it takes a toll. Using my magic to control another person's physical form, or to make them disappear entirely – it takes all of my focus, my energy, my magic. It takes all I have and there is little else I can do in the moment, magically speaking, anyway.

"I can also alter perception—how others perceive *me*. Let us say, for instance, I am having a day where I am particularly cross with Neville and no longer wish for him to pester me. We could be sitting in the same room, but I could alter his perception so he doesn't even know I am there. To him I would be practically invisible."

"That's incredible. And I'm sure highly useful…but…I thought you said it was complicated. Nothing about that sounds complicated to me."

Thomas's expression grew somber, and he reached for a paper flower on the nearest shelf, fondling the print-covered petals. "I can't control human emotions. My magic can't make someone love me."

I looked down to the floor, suddenly sorry that I asked. I tried to keep my mind from wondering about who exactly he had tried that failed magical ability on.

Then we heard the doorknob twisting as someone worked it from the other side. Knocking. "Boys, it's me! I did not bring my key."

I shot Thomas a look of concern. How was he supposed to make our secret garden dissipate? But Thomas looked far less worried than I. He waved his arm, and in seconds, the paper flowers flattened out into their normal state, the pages finding their way back to their bindings.

I was still watching everything return to normalcy as Thomas rushed to the door, unlocking it for the owner. I was not looking at either of them, but I heard the confusion in the old man's voice. "There was no need for you to lock up."

"Apologies, Mr. Wexler, I must have misunderstood."

I still wasn't looking at them, but I was surely still wearing a look of disbelief and wonderment, for Mr. Wexler chose to address me next. "Everything all right, lad?"

"There is just…there are…so many books."

Was it brilliant? Not at all. But to my credit, I was lucky to even get any words out at all.

THOMAS

I woke up in Sav's arms today and a thought struck me: this is what I want my forever to look like. I want to start and end my days by his side. I want him to hold me when I am sad or afraid but also when I am glad or excited. All the secrets that I cannot shout to the world, I will whisper in his ears as we fall asleep, side by side.

This is everything I've dreamed about, everything I've read about, everything I've wanted!

And yet, even though I have Sav back in my world, I cannot truly have the life I want. Not completely. Not when I am forced to serve Neville in the interest of self-preservation. I am so close to the happiness I desire. But how can one be entirely happy when one is not free?

SAVERIO

I am the greatest fool the world has ever known. Everything was going so well with Thomas. I just had to open my mouth and ruin a good thing once more. It is as if I am cursed!

After the glorious gift of Thomas's forgiveness, I have been spending the past month ruminating, trying to come up with a plan. Now, I know how that sounds…Saverio up to his old ways, scheming once more! But the plans I have been making are not against Thomas but *for* him. For the both of us.

Standing around in a shop all day gives me a great deal of time to think, and it had occurred to me that Thomas and I will never be able to be truly happy while he is under the magician's thumb. Neville's crimes against Thomas's freedom and happiness have mounted and only continue to do so. And Paolo, though he is out of my life, the ghost of our relationship still haunts Thomas and my current state of bliss.

And so it struck me: What would serve to punish both Wighton and Paolo while still allowing myself and Thomas the life we so rightly deserve? (I am acutely aware of the fact that I am deserving of very little, all things considered, but that is beside the point.)

Rather than having poor Thomas bound to Wighton and using his beautiful gifts to win acclaim for a man even less deserving of happiness than I, Thomas could use his magic to bring about fame and notoriety for a new up-and-coming stage magician.

Myself.

Much like when I first concocted my plans to win Thomas's heart, the end goal would be to become a renowned performer, famous beyond even my wildest dreams. But this is no longer a selfish desire. The wealth that would accompany such fame would be enough to keep Thomas and me living comfortably for the rest of our days. We could travel the world, eat the finest foods, drink the most flavorful wines, live in a stunning home rather than making do in poorly maintained apartments. We could have true happiness, not the kind we must forage for ourselves in secret.

Before, when my plans were more devious, they involved using Thomas. But this—this would be a collaboration. Two partners, working together on the stage and in life. But when I posed the idea to my love last night, he failed to see it this way. I was at Thomas's apartment, and as he reclined, I told him of my plan, with wild hand gestures and the showmanship that I was becoming so known for once upon a time. I figured it would only serve to further prove my point that we could really pull this off, he and I.

I am now uncertain of what I was expecting upon finishing my proposal. What I was met with at the time was a stern silence and lack of eye contact. My heart tightened, and I felt as though I would become ill. Finally, he looked up, but not to me…to the door.

"I think you should spend the night in your own flat…and in your own bed."

Without seeing me to the door or waiting for me to leave on my own, he rose from his spot on the settee and made his way silently back to his own bedchamber. I had *angered* him. After all that time and effort spent finding my way back into his heart and into his life. I knew that going against his wishes would only worsen my situation, so I did as he suggested and made my way through the night and back to my apartment.

It is only now that I have had time to reflect on the incident that I realize how ignorant I was not to explain my position fully. Of course he was angry. Of course he assumed the worst of my intentions. With all the pain he has been put through…

Almost every person in his life has taken advantage of him or lied to him (I am accounting for myself in that lot; I know I am no better). Every person who has seen his inner darkness and secrets has tried to exploit that which he fears most and use it for their own gain.

I am not fooling myself or Thomas, nor am I trying to. I know that I have a great deal to gain, myself, from the arrangement I proposed. The money, the adoring public, and, of course, my wildest dream would come to fruition.

I will not lie and say that there have not been days when I have been in the back room at McEwan & Clarke's, desperately wishing that I were instead backstage at some grand theatre.

But the more I have thought upon it, the more I realize that that old dream of seeing my name in lights on a marquee means little to me now when I think about a future without Thomas. It is quite easy to imagine; all I have to do is think back to just recently, when Thomas was not speaking to me. The pain in trying to imagine an entire lifetime of that sort of emptiness is unlike anything I've ever experienced in nineteen years on this earth.

Thomas is my own true dream now. A life with Thomas by my side.

Now I just have to convince him of that and that my intentions are pure.

THOMAS

July 28, 1899

I should have known better than to let my guard down around Sav. Once a trickster, always a trickster.

He is now suggesting that I use my magic to propel him to a career of greatness on the stage, just as I have done with Neville Wighton. A near-identical arrangement. How dare he stoop so low? He knows what Neville has put me through. Sav tried to claim that he and I would be equal partners in the endeavor, but I am no fool. Well, I may have been once, but no longer!

And after all he did and said to prove his plans of using me were in the past. All his heartfelt letters…

It pains me to admit that maybe he does have a promising future as a performer. He is quite the thespian, with how he keeps convincing me that his feelings for me are genuine and that I am not just a means to an end, as I have been for so many others.

I simply want someone to love me for the person I am, not what my magic can gain them.

Obviously, that is far too much to ask.

SAVERIO

July 30, 1899

Paris.

The answer is Paris.

Or Prague, or Salzburg, or Budapest, or Porto, or anywhere that simply is not London.

My most recent idea caused Thomas to retreat and put his walls up with me once more. He likely fears that my intentions were purely selfish and that I was thinking only of my own future. I needed to make him see that it is *our* future I am concerned with. We are meant to spend it together.

Today I returned to his apartment, and he seemed guarded, at best. He swung the door open but stood in the doorway, blocking my entrance.

"What do you want?" he asked quietly. His arms were folded over his lean chest and his fingertips were drumming against his biceps impatiently.

"You," I said with a genuine smile, "and only you. Forever."

He was fighting back against a smile. I knew it because I could see the faintest hint of it forming at the corners of his pink lips.

"If this is some sort of trick—"

"No tricks," I interrupted him with a promise. "No more tricks, lies, illusions, masks…that's all in the past now. I realize that you, dear Thomas, are my future." I moved in closer and cupped my hands around his pale cheeks.

It was only at this point that he let me into the apartment, but that was likely due to the risk of being spotted by one of his neighbors.

All the same, I was in.

As soon as Thomas closed the door, I could not wait another moment to tell him my new and improved plan. "Come away with me!"

"Sav…" he started with a sigh. I knew what he was doing. He was making assumptions about my intentions once again. No doubt he believed I was making some grand yet impulsive gesture just to win back his good graces.

"I am speaking truthfully," I replied. "Let us leave this place. We can escape your parents, Wighton, the crowds, the expectations. It can be just the two of us against the world. Run away with me, Thomas Pendleton."

"Where would we even make off to?" Thomas's voice was skeptical, but even beneath that skepticism, I could sense his curiosity and interest.

"Paris? I have been many times, and it is lovely. The art, the cuisine, strolling along the river—creative and literary types like yourself are drawn to the city like moths to a flame. You would simply adore it."

There was a twinkle in his eyes, and I could tell that in his mind, he was agreeing with me; he knew he would love it. But after another moment or two, he frowned and said, "Neville has connections in Paris. He would certainly find us."

I merely shrugged. "Who says we have to stay in the city? We could make our way to a smaller, quieter town… Hell! We could live in a tiny village in the Alps and raise goats for all I care! As long as I am with you, anywhere will feel like home."

His eyes softened and his smile warmed. I knew I had convinced him that my heart was true. All the same, he asked, "And what of your dreams of becoming the world's greatest illusionist?" but the playful tone flavoring his words assured me his fear had subsided.

I smiled. "That's not what I want now. Love has brought me more joy than fame ever could."

I am happy to say that Thomas did not send me away last night.

THOMAS

July 31, 1899

All my life, all I've ever wanted was a love the likes of which is written about in poems by the greats. Now, not only have I found such kinship, but I will soon find a similar sense of adventure to that which I have read about in epic poems and sprawling novels.

Sav is whisking me away and we are venturing off to Paris.

He came to me with the idea just yesterday. At first it was easy to get lost in the allure and romanticism of the notion: young loves running off to France. And I cannot deny that my senses were humming at the very thought of finally getting to travel to the very city where so many of the writers I try to emulate hail from.

But it did not take long for me to remember what happened the last time I tried to leave England's borders.

I had to explain this all to Sav: my plan to steal away to Edinburgh and how, after discovering I had purchased a ticket, Neville had threatened to reveal to the world the secret of what I am.

Sav did not seem concerned in the slightest, even at mention of Neville's threat. Instead, he looked me in the eye and asked me if I truly believed that a man so wildly vain would really destroy everything I had built up for him in a move of self-sacrifice, just to keep me caged like a bird.

And to be honest, the answer I came to was no. I do not

believe that Neville's ego would allow him to shatter his reputation and throw aside his fame, not even to get his way.

He had been bluffing the whole time and I, being the naive fool I am, believed him.

Still, it was hard to shake the uneasy feeling that Neville's old threats had managed to sink into my bones. Sav must have seen this, for he continued to assure me that he would protect me from my old master.

Still, I argued that Neville would try to stop us, or, even if we did get away, he would follow us. Sav pointed to our shared history in the theatrical world and noted that this is where such skills would be coming to good use. He informed me that we would be traveling under different names, as entirely different people. He believes that by the time Neville catches word of our intentions to leave, we will already safely be far gone from London.

The more Sav worked to assure me, the harder it was to fight against the idea, especially considering it is already something I've wanted with all my heart (even without realizing it). I want to be with Sav, I want adventure out there in the world I have yet to fully know, and, of course, I want my freedom.

It is about time I stop wanting and start doing.

August 05, 1899

This pattern with Neville is exhaustive and yet all too predictable. Anytime I start to glance at any sort of glimmer of happiness, his shadow manages to drown out the light. The way fate has bound me to this man is cruel and torturous.

The one good thing that has come from our association was meeting Sav—a fact that is hard to appreciate when Neville seemingly tries to hurt us with each new step forward we take.

I have let Neville control me due to my own cowardice. With his abuse and his threats, I have allowed him to captain the ship of my life, but now he has crossed a line that I simply will not stand for. He has threatened that which is most dear to me in this world—far more precious than my parents' good names or my secret (even if exposure could cost me everything).

I was out for most of the day, running small errands here and there. One included a stop at a local clothier where Sav has been working. I must say, it was quite fun getting to see him in such a setting where he was under another's employ and being made to do mindless, trivial tasks.

After returning to my flat, the lightness I was feeling took a sharp turn into confusion and concern. My door was ajar, allowing a small crack of light to filter out into the hallway.

I was certain I had locked the door before leaving this morning. Even if I had forgotten, I would have at least had the good sense to close the door after me.

Hesitantly, I pushed the door open and, to my horror, there was indeed a figure standing at the opposite end of the room. The man's back was turned to me, but I recognized the wild wisps of graying hair.

Neville whirled around. "Ah, my apprentice has returned!"

Looking back, I should not have been so surprised. He was the one who had found the flat for me. Of course he had a set of keys made for himself. It was so very characteristic of him.

"You should not be here," I managed in a low, soft voice.

He shrugged, as if breaking into my flat was no worse than showing up unannounced at some social function. "What option did you leave me? I have been calling on you relentlessly to come to my studio so that we may discuss our next theatrical endeavor. Theatres from all across the globe have been vying for my attention."

Across the globe? I raised an eyebrow and shook my head. How many times had I told the man that I would not be doing any performances with him that fell outside of London? "I will not be doing any traveling with you, Neville."

He played at looking wounded by my words. "And yet, you will travel with Paolo il Magnifico's dirty little spy?"

He knew. He needed my help to perform his impossible illusions and yet, as if he really did possess his own magic, he somehow knew every move I was to make before I made it.

"How? But I... But...how..."

"You think Paolo is the only one wise enough to utilize spies?" Neville spat in triumph. "Mine are simply better at concealing themselves."

This new revelation left me feeling naked and vulnerable. Just how much did he know about my life through such methods? The man really is obsessive and controlling.

He met my stunned silence with a smile—well, Neville's twisted version of a smile, anyway. "Oh, Paris, such a lovely city indeed! Most lovely in the summertime, especially for…lovers."

I gulped down my own discomfort and straightened my shoulders. "You're not going to stop me this time."

He didn't say anything using his words, but his face flashed me an expression that asked, *Oh?*

"I do not believe that you would reveal yourself a fraud— destroy your entire career—no matter how desperate you are to keep me here. And even if you are not bluffing, I no longer care! You have threatened me so many times, and I cannot do this any longer, I cannot be enslaved by your greed and your ambition. My magic is mine alone, and it will no longer be used to benefit a man as callous as you! I do not care what you do to me or what you tell the world of me. I shall face the consequences and be glad of it, for I will be free of you!"

"Who said I wanted to stop you?" The flat quality in Neville's tone was unnerving.

"What?"

"By all means, go to Paris—in fact…" He reached into the lapel of his tailcoat and pulled out a long envelope. He extended it to me, nodding for me to take it.

I stood there, frozen. It was a trick…a trap…whatever it was, I wanted no part of it. He was not to be trusted, and whatever was in that envelope, it would likely only be used as another way to harm me. I know how this man operates.

After a few moments, he sighed when he realized I was not going to take it. He slid it back and pulled out the contents, waving them about in the air. They looked to be some sort of tickets.

"Are those…" I began, though I was already certain I knew.

"Train tickets," he said simply. "London to Paris. They are open tickets that can be used at the end of the month. Whether or not you choose to use them is of no concern to me."

He set them down on the table and started to make his way to the door to leave, but when he was no more than two feet away, he paused.

"Although, it certainly would be unfortunate if some manner of tragedy were to befall that pretty Italian boy of yours. You're dining at a café and all of a sudden—oh no!—the poor boy is choking on his meal. Or say, he decides to venture out on his own, take a relaxing stroll along the Seine. It can be slippery down by the water...what if the boy were to fall in and never come back up?"

There have been many instances in the relatively short time that I have known Neville Wighton that I have felt utter hatred toward the man—this journal alone contains plenty of evidence of that. But there has never been an instance quite like this. The idea of him daring to harm a hair on Sav's head sent rage coursing through my veins, which quickly transformed into the all-too-familiar supernatural current of energy. The furniture began to shake, the walls began to rumble, and for once, I did not concern myself with controlling it.

Neville looked about the room, but he did not run for the door. He did not even look frightened. On the contrary, he looked...amused.

The bastard.

He grinned that smug grin at me. "You always were so easy, Thomas. Timid individuals like you always are. And even as your confidence has grown, your love has made you weak... even weaker than before, I would venture to say."

He knew better than to risk his own safety further, so he left. Shortly after his departure, the rumbling within me and around me ceased and I slumped to the floor, nearly in tears.

I had finally been ready, finally been brave enough to meet Neville's threats head on. But what I would never be ready for was for those threats to be aimed in Sav's direction. If anything were to happen to him... Oh I cannot even think on it!

Neville may have found my weakness yet again, but this is not defeat. Sav and I will escape. I may not yet know how or when, but we will be together and we will be happy.

I will find a way.

THE  TIMES

LONDON SUNDAY   AUGUST 20, 1899

LOCAL BOY ACCUSED OF WITCHCRAFT; INVESTIGATION TO ENSUE

THE EDITOR'S SCRAP BOOK.

THE EDITOR'S CALENDAR

SAVERIO

August 14, 1899

Something horrible has happened. The most horrible thing that could have possibly happened! And I am helpless to do more than sit here scribbling when I should be by my love's side. My hope is that transcribing it here on paper will help to clear my anxious mind. With that clarity, maybe I can start thinking of ways to help Thomas.

What is worst of all is that it is my own fault.

Thomas had a rehearsal with Neville tonight at Covent Garden, and so I wanted to surprise him. I gave myself plenty of time and waited outside the theatre, not sure how long their practicing would take. I had brought a book with me to pass the time, but as evening set in, it did little good, so I stashed it away in my coat pocket and waited for my Thomas.

I looked at the different buildings up and down Bow Street, wondering if I had time to do a little exploring of my own, but I caught movement out of the corner of my eye. Expectantly, I flashed a smile toward the doors of the theatre, but it was Wighton who emerged.

Wighton has always had an odd look in his eye, something manic and tense, but even so, he was giving me an odd look as he considered me, then he walked off into the night. Shortly after, the man I had been waiting for emerged.

He asked what I was doing there, and I asked if he wanted to take a walk. He looked around. If he was worried Neville or someone else had already spotted me, he was a little late for that. Eventually, though, he smiled and nodded.

We made our way down Southampton to the Strand, then we crossed over to the Thames. A cool breeze danced off the river as we were crossing Waterloo Bridge. I saw Thomas shiver (well, more than usual), and I wanted to alleviate the chill—plus I was thinking selfishly and wanted to have him close to me. I wrapped an arm around his shoulders, certain that the cover of night would keep us safe.

I had not even heard the footsteps.

"What have we got here, Mickey?"

Thomas and I whirled. Two men, not much older than us by the looks of it, were standing at the end of the bridge but then slowly started making their way over to us. From their dress, I could tell they were working class. Suspenders held up loose pants that they likely could not afford to have tailored. One was gaunt, with dark-red hair that was tied back behind the nape of his neck, and had grease stains on his shirt. The other hid what little hair he did have beneath a threadbare wool cap and was shorter but broader, with thick muscles.

"Looks like a pair of sods to me," the thin one jeered.

Closer and closer they got. I had already removed my arm, but I could already sense the discomfort coming from Thomas for the impending confrontation.

"You boys headed to the pub, I presume? By all means, don't let us stop you." I stepped to the side and fanned my arm out, presenting the clear path I had just made for them. But they were not interested in my mock chivalry.

"We don't like your types 'round here," the big one grunted.

The thinner one stuck his hand out in front of him. "What my friend here is trying to say is that we are just a couple o' good Samaritans. As I am sure you must know, buggery is considered a crime. And we can't have you out committing crimes on our streets. Think of the families that might be out and about…the children. Can't have 'em witnessing your foul display."

I could sense Thomas's anxiety rising, and apparently so could they.

The big one with the cap moved in toward Thomas and nodded to him. "This one don't look much older than a child himself."

The redhead stroked his chin, pretending to consider his friend's statement. "That would make your actions especially lewd."

I ignored him and focused on the gorilla. "You leave him alone, you blundering oaf!"

He grinned, revealing some gaps where teeth should have been. "And what's a couple of Nancies like yous gonna do about it?"

At the time, I did the most unintelligent thing I could have done in that scenario—and now looking back on what it has brought about, it is an action I regret more than I can say. I stepped forward and, even though his mass far outweighed my own, I took a swing at Mr. Wool Cap.

"Sav, no! Don't!" But Thomas's pleas were too late. In a surprisingly fluid motion, the oaf grabbed the arm I had tried to strike him with and bent it in a way it was not meant to bend, pinning it behind my back. He quickly grabbed my other arm and brought it back to join it.

A thin, triumphant smirk spread across the face of the redheaded man, and he moved in. In a fair fight, I might have stood a pretty fair chance, but I was properly restrained, and the way the big guy had my arms twisted, it felt like one of them could snap under the pressure at any moment. He landed a punch, fist connecting with my cheek. In this instance, his thinness worked as an advantage, his bony knuckles a weapon.

The man almost laughed in satisfaction and immediately continued to punch at me. Some aimed at my face, others right to my gut. Thomas was crying out behind them the whole time, begging them to stop and to let me be, but his cries fell on deaf ears. The trickle of something warm and sticky descended from my brow.

I had closed my eyes and was bracing myself for the next punch, but it did not come. I opened my eyes and the man had stopped, but he was far from still.

His hands, no longer balled into fists, were now clutching at his own throat, grasping at it, and gurgling noises came out. His cheeks were turning purple and his eyes were wide with fear. He was choking. His lips, which had been clenched together tight, sputtered open and water came dribbling out over his chin—an unbelievable amount of water. But no matter how he emptied his mouth, more continued to pour from his lips.

He was not simply choking...he was drowning.

I looked to Thomas and, sure enough, his eyes were giving off a subtle glow. Nothing so bright as to call attention to himself, more like the moonlight shaded under a passing cloud.

The ogre finally released me to try and help his friend, not realizing how utterly futile it would be. My muscles ached, my face was even wetter with blood, and I was certain some of my bones had been shattered, but I gathered what little strength I did have and rushed to Thomas's side. I shook his arm, hoping that a distraction might break the magical bonds. "Thomas, you have to stop," I whispered.

"I can't." Desperation clung to his words. "I've never done something like this before...I don't know how."

I had only to watch as the redheaded man fell, first to his knees, then face first against the pavement. Wool Cap looked to his dead companion, breathless, then looked back to Thomas and me before lurching away in horror. As he ran, he cried out,

"Witchcraft! There's witchery afoot! Someone help!"

Just as I had feared, a group of passersby out for the evening gathered at the end of the bridge. They watched as the oaf stumbled forward and, after hearing his accusations, turned their attention toward us and the damning evidence in the form of a corpse. I had no time for horror or to process that a dead man was now lying at our feet. I needed to act.

"Thomas, go!" I urged. "You need to get out of here. Run!"

But he didn't flinch. He was not even shaking. It was probably the most still I had ever seen him, as if he were encased in ice. I could not even be entirely certain if he was hearing me anymore. That was, until he looked up at me.

"No, you have to go. Go now."

"What?"

Thomas's eyes were wide with terror. "You have to get out of here, please! This was my fault, but they'll blame you, too. And you're a foreigner; who knows what they will do…"

I shook my head. "I am not leaving you. Not a chance!"

The tears were already spilling down Thomas's cheeks. "Sav! Please! Just go!"

"Not without you."

My next impulse was to grab him from the underarms and just drag him away from the scene, but that is when two police constables arrived to do the dragging.

"He is the one who did it!" a woman with dark hair shouted. "He killed him!"

"He did it using nothing but his mind!" shouted another.

There was no way to be certain whether these men believed what the crowd was claiming, but they restrained Thomas all the same, pulling his arms behind his back and guiding him away. Thomas attempted to make their task more difficult, kicking and thrashing.

I reached out for him and tried to insert myself between

him and one of the constables. But neither of the men bothered to try and restrain me, let alone arrest me. It was as if they were looking right through me.

As if they couldn't see me at all.

I looked down, and I couldn't see my own form. It was Thomas. He was using his magic to make me invisible. He knew I would never willingly hide. He knew I would not abandon him. And so he made the choice and hid me from view. I watched as they dragged him away, looking more frightened than I had ever seen him before. It was not until he was completely out of view that I became visible once more. Luckily by that point, the crowd had already dissipated.

Now Thomas sits in a cell across town, and I have never felt so powerless. I do not even know who I can turn to for help. Neville? His parents? There are so few people in Thomas's life who he trusts, and I have only just recently been counted among the trusted once again.

All I can say for certain is this: this world will not use its prejudices and fears to take my magic boy away from me. I will not allow it.

August 15, 1899

They will not let me see him. I went to the police station today, demanding that they let me see Thomas Pendleton. The man I spoke to informed me that due to the "unusual circumstances" surrounding the murder investigation, visits were strictly limited to immediate family.

For once in my life, I cursed my Italian blood. My genes have gifted me with good looks but unfortunately looks that would never let me get away with claiming to be Thomas's brother.

So once again, I am helpless, pacing about my apartment while Thomas needs me most! I had considered going to his parents to discuss what options we have for helping Thomas, but when I went to the house, a man outside of a house a few doors over told me that the Pendletons no longer resided there and had not for months (a fact Thomas had neglected to mention).

There must be something I can do.

August 16, 1899

I found my courage, swallowed my pride, and went to see the magician.

I stood outside Neville Wighton's studio, thinking of how months ago it had been my desire to break into this very place and steal the secret to the greatest trick I had ever witnessed. Nostalgia and shame washed over me in waves until I finally gathered the nerve to go to the door. But before I could knock, the door burst open and Neville came waltzing through.

"Mr. Wighton, I was hoping I could speak with you!"

He looked me up and down but continued walking. "Forgive me, Mr. Moretti, I am a busy man and I simply do not have the time."

I trotted after him, keeping pace easily. "You know my name?"

"You have been my apprentice's companion for the better part of a year, Mr. Moretti, are you really that surprised? I make it a point to know who Thomas spends a significant amount of time with, and you are quite literally the only person on my list." He stopped to smile at me, but it was unnerving how out of place it seemed on his face. "Besides, my old colleague Paolo has told me much about his protégé." He turned and continued walking.

I held back the urge to take a swing at him, and instead trotted after him like one of the horses towing carriages around the city streets.

"Thomas is in a great deal of trouble."

He let out something between a scoff and a laugh. "Trouble? Is that the word people are using to refer to murder these days?"

"It was an accident," I breathed through clenched teeth.

"He was provoked!"

Neville stopped. "I know all about last night's little incident. My studio was the first place the police came to this morning. I have heard the accusations Thomas faces." He looked me over. "And guessing from that shiner you are wearing, I'd reckon Thomas was not the only one being provoked."

I ignored his comment on my battered appearance. "Well, if you know what the people are saying, then you know we have to do something! We must free him from prison."

"*We* mustn't do anything, Mr. Moretti."

"But think of it, you have more at stake here than anyone! More to lose. If Thomas is proven to have magic, or is a 'witch,' as the zealots like to call it, then you will be proven to be nothing more than a fraud."

"All stage magicians are frauds. You should know that better than anyone. We con the people out of the price of admission to the theatre night after night. And deep down, each audience member knows this, but they willingly accept the lie and allow themselves to believe for an hour or so that maybe, just maybe, what they are seeing is beyond explanation. They all know what they are signing up for in the end. I appreciate the concern, but my reputation will be just fine."

"And what of your conscience?" I asked.

"What of it?"

I stopped dead in my tracks, stunned. What sort of answer can one even supply to something like that? Thomas had oft complained of Wighton's cruel heart, but only then did I get to witness it firsthand.

Neville didn't even blink, didn't miss a step. Not that I knew what to say, had he given me the chance, so instead I just let him walk away.

I am on my own now, and uncertain what move to make next. But my Thomas needs me.

August 17, 1899

The police made their way to my doorstep today for questions. Honestly, I figured I still had a little more time before the trail led to me. I was about to leave, with no real destination in mind, just determined to do *something* to help. When I opened my door, my landlord was standing there, preparing to knock. Accompanying him were two men: one was dressed in a standard police uniform, the other in more casual dress, but his presence was more commanding and authoritative. His dark goatee was peppered with graying hairs.

My landlord left the men in my company, and I had little choice but to invite them in.

The goateed man examined me for a moment. "I hope we did not come at an inconvenient time." I highly doubt he cared.

"Actually, I was just heading off to work, so if we could keep this brief, that would be ideal."

"Where do you work?" the man I was assuming was a detective asked.

"McEwan & Clarke's."

The man in the uniform pulled out a small notepad and jotted something down. I was not actually scheduled at the shop today (even if I were, I would have no intention of standing around as a human mannequin while Thomas is locked in a cell), but I figured it would be best to give them the name of my employer. That way if they follow up, I'll have someone to vouch for my credibility.

"Where are our manners?" the goateed man asked, stroking

his chin hairs. "My name is Detective Branson." He reached out a hand to shake mine then nodded to his colleague. "This is Constable Higgens." The constable did not move to greet me but stood still as stone.

There was no point in playing the fool and asking what business they had with me. It was likely they had heard all about my tirade at the police station, demanding they let me see Thomas. Even if they somehow had not heard about the incident, surely the bruises and cuts on my face were evidence enough that I had things to answer for.

"Shall we get on with it, then? Ask me whatever it is you came to ask me so that I can be on my merry way."

Branson frowned. He was likely used to being a much more intimidating presence when confronting persons of interest in his cases. Something told me he did not enjoy having a young man step on his toes and take the lead.

Good. The questioning had not even begun and I already had the upper hand.

"Will you please state your name for us?"

Higgens was ready with his notepad and tiny pencil.

"Saverio Moretti."

"Not from around here, I am guessing. Forgive me for being presumptuous, but that accent tells me you hail from Italy."

"Your powers of perception are incredible." I looked to Higgens, nodding toward Branson, "Quite bright, this one. Just like that Holmes fellow." The stoic constable remained unaffected. Not even so much as the quirk of a smile. What fun he must be at parties!

Branson was even less amused. "How long have you been in London, Mr. Moretti?"

"Less than a year."

"And what was it that brought you here in the first place?"

"Work. There's little of it in the town I came from, and I

needed a change of scenery." I gestured sweepingly about the apartment. "So here I am."

"Here you are," Branson muttered, more to himself than to me. "And what is your connection to Thomas Pendleton?"

"We are friends."

"And in what *manner* are the two of you friends?" Branson's eyebrows raised, and I could tell he was sure he had me in a corner.

"He is one of the first and only friends I have made since arriving in London."

"And just how does an Italian migrant working in a clothing shop meet a wealthy magician's apprentice?"

"I was lucky enough to attend one of Wighton's performances last year. One of the very first, actually, when he premiered his big act at the West London Theatre. The ticket was a gift from a well-to-do relative in Rome. Have you gotten a chance to see the show yourself?"

"I've had the pleasure, yes," Branson said, indulging me.

"Well, then you must know how spellbound I was. A fascination with illusions and with the theatre led me to want to get to know the Pendleton boy better. We have been spending time together over these past few months—we became companions in no time at all."

"And in all this time that you have been spending with young Mr. Pendleton, did you ever notice anything…strange?"

Higgens was still scribbling away.

"Not a thing." I smiled, perchance a bit too smugly.

Branson frowned. "Let us not play games, Mr. Moretti; we know you were there the night Mr. Edwards was killed."

"Mr. Edwards?" This could have passed for genuine confusion. I mean, it was not as if I had known the red-haired man's name at the time.

"You might not know him by name, but perhaps you'd

recognize him as the one who did that"—at the word "that" he gestured toward my eye—"to your face."

"Ah yes, lovely fellow."

"Do you think this is funny, Mr. Moretti? A man is dead!"

At this, I took on a more serious tone myself. "No, I do not find this funny. The only thing 'funny' about it is that you have my friend locked up because some heretics on the street cried, 'Witchcraft!' Do you even realize how absurd that sounds? The man stopped breathing right there on the bridge, likely from some internal ailment. Maybe he had a heart condition, who knows? But rather than looking into the deceased's medical records for further investigation, you are taking the lazy man's route and blaming it on magic—what's next? Are you going to blame all those prostitute murders on faeries? Perhaps Jack the Ripper is actually a sorcerer!"

"That is quite enough, Mr. Moretti," Branson said.

"Is it? Is it enough?" I choked back what felt oddly close to tears. "Because my friend is an innocent man on trial for ludicrous charges because assuming the impossible is somehow more manageable than doing your damn job!"

"That will be enough questions for today, Mr. Moretti. We appreciate your time, but we should really let you be getting off to work." Branson nodded to Higgens, and they both made their way to the door. Just before leaving, Branson turned to peer at me over his shoulder.

And with that, they were gone. I wanted to find something more productive to do with my time, something that might benefit Thomas, but I was worried they might have an officer try to keep an eye on me, so I went to the shop, for continuity's sake. Harold was confused but seemed happy for the help, all the same.

A wasted day. I must do everything I can to prove his innocence (even if it is an innocence that does not exist). I can only imagine what he must be going through in the prison but cannot help but to wonder why he has not attempted an escape with his gifts. He managed to make Neville disappear and teleport him night after night! Why does he not simply do the same for himself? It confounds me!

August 21, 1899

I still cannot locate Mr. and Mrs. Pendleton. I am certain that the police have already spoken with them and that they are well aware of the danger Thomas faces, but I have no means of communicating with them to try to form some sort of strategy.

The best I have been able to come up with is research. I have spent the last three days at the library—more than I have spent in months—scouring over everything I can find related to old witch trials. Mostly, I have been finding accounts from America, but it seems there have been similar such trials all around the world. Each more ridiculous than the last.

Doubtless, the murder trial will be taking place in only a matter of time. My theory is that if I can prove just how foolish these accusations sound, then maybe Thomas might stand a chance. It will not be easy, though. People are stubborn when it comes to their superstitions.

Then again, it does not quite make sense for me to be criticizing others for believing in the unbelievable. If Thomas has taught me anything, it should be that nothing is quite as it appears. Who knows? Maybe some of the testimony from these witch trials in a little town called Salem was truly caused by paranormal phenomena. Now that I know I live in a world where magic is alive and well, anything is possible.

This being said, for the sake of keeping Thomas alive, I must prove such thoughts to be laughable garbage, just as I would have thought this time last year.

August 30, 1899

I am at a loss. Stunned. ~~My hope~~~~My Thomas~~
Having read about witch trials until I was certain my eyes might bleed, I figured it was time to visit my friends down at the police station. Armed with the knowledge that the last known execution for witchcraft in this country took place more than two hundred years ago, I was certain that I could convince someone there just how absurd this whole thing was.

When I arrived, I once again demanded that they allow me to see Thomas Pendleton. The uniformed officer stationed at the clerk's counter left wordlessly, and I assumed I was being blatantly ignored.

"If you think I will simply leave, you are a fool! I have all the time in the world! I shall sleep here if I must!"

But the man returned, not alone. With him he brought along a distinguished-looking gentleman with dark eyes and a groomed goatee.

Branson.

"Ah, Mr. Moretti. I was wondering just when you would show up."

"Detective, you must release my friend."

"Oh, must I?"

"You cannot just hold a young man in prison with no trial; it is unjust. If you have plans to formally charge Thomas with murder, then the very least you can do is inform me when his trial is set to take place so I can procure an attorney."

Branson seemed amused at this, but his tone remained serious. "There will be no need for any lawyers."

"Then you are releasing him?"

"We have sufficient evidence to move forward without a trial," Branson continued.

"Move forward?" I asked.

"The accusations against Thomas Pendleton have been confirmed. He will be executed publicly for the murder and for practicing witchcraft, both serious crimes deserving of an equally severe sentence."

The oxygen escaped from me as the world tilted in a violent spasm. I had to slam my palms down against the wooden desk to stabilize myself. I lowered my head, fighting against the pounding sensation. "*Executed?*"

"I apologize; I know this cannot be easy to hear about someone you—"

"You cannot do this! You cannot simply execute someone without a fair trial! This is madness!"

"Under normal circumstances, yes, but these are not normal circumstances. People are in danger."

"Yes, Thomas Pendleton is in danger! You are about to end a young man's life over evidence that is speculative at best!"

"Mr. Moretti, the man's lungs had filled with water. Explain to me how a man drowns on dry land."

"We were right by the Thames. The river—"

"There was a handful of witnesses who never saw him enter the river."

Rage roared in me like a flame. "And this is somehow enough to put him to death?"

"We have something else." Branson gave me a measured look, as if deciding whether he should reveal it to me. "We have testimony from someone close to Thomas, someone who has been able to validate the claims of his magical abilities."

"Who? Who told you this? Whoever it is, they are lying! Did you offer them a reward for the information? They likely would have said anything for the money."

But I did not need Branson to tell me to know exactly who had revealed Thomas's secret.

What of your conscience?

What of it?

The words from our previous conversation rang in my head—screamed, more so, like an alarm bell. But why? *Why?* Thomas is only good to him if he is alive!

"There was no reward money. And I certainly cannot give you any names. This is a matter of public safety. Thomas has used his magic to murder an innocent man, and he shall pay for his crimes at the gallows. We have express written consent from Parliament allowing—nay, *urging* a hanging as soon as possible."

Hanging... Thomas is going to be...

What little sturdiness was keeping me upright gave way, and I collapsed right there on the station floor. A pair of officers rushed over to assist me, and I screamed at them to keep their filthy, bloodstained hands off me. After a few moments, I was able to sit up on my own. I turned my attention back on Branson.

"If you will not give me the name of the person feeding you these lies, at least tell me where I can find Avery and Katherine Pendleton so that I may speak to them regarding their son."

"Mr. and Mrs. Pendleton are currently under investigation."

"On what grounds?"

"Their son is a witch," he said. "These powers did not simply come out of thin air. And even if they did, Mr. and Mrs. Pendleton conspired in hiding a living witch in their household for seventeen years. A secret that has now cost a man his life."

Yes. Thomas's.

The hanging will be in five days. *Five days.* If I could only see Thomas. Speak to him. There is no secret to cover up now; they have all already made up their minds about him. He has to use his magic to gain his freedom. It is the only way! There is still time—there is still hope.

THE  TIMES

LONDON SATURDAY   SEPTEMBER 02, 1899

APPRENTICE OF NEVILLE WIGHTON THE GREAT FOUND GUILTY OF WITCHCRAFT; PUBLIC EXECUTION IN 3 DAYS, THE FIRST IN LONDON IN MORE THAN 30 YEARS

SAVERIO

I have never known agony such as this. Every time I breathe, it feels like ice is filling my lungs. Every time I try to walk, it feels as if I am stepping on broken glass. It feels like a hole has been ripped open in my chest, and now I cannot find the missing piece, no matter how I search.

I am nineteen years old. I should not know this kind of grief. I should not know the pain of losing my one and only love — not yet. I should not know what it is to hold the lifeless body of the one you love most in this world.

And yet here I sit, barely able to collect my thoughts in a way that seems legible.

I did everything I could. He was right there! But I...I was too late...

The day of the execution was mad. I made my way to where the police had erected the new gallows for the occasion: Manchester Square. What a cruel irony, that the very first place I laid eyes on my love is where I would also watch him die!

One would think Wighton was about to put on one of his grand performances with how many people had crowded into the square. As I trudged into the crowd, I scanned the masses helplessly for a familiar face; even with how long I have been in London permanently, I still have very few of these here. That said, I did spot the girl who had stormed into the Pendletons' Christmas party. That wintery night she had been all wrath and rage. Today she was still beautiful but full of sorrow and anguish. She did not have any right to these feelings — not the way I did!

Others in the crowd did their best to appear equally morose. Then there were the few who could not contain their thrill at the entertainment that was about to befall them. Animals! Heartless heathens! Throughout the crowd, whispers and murmurs broke out in waves. In hushed tones people gossiped about the murder, lying about things they thought they had seen at Neville's shows or how they always thought the Pendletons were peculiar folk. I heard one woman ostracizing Thomas, referring to him as a monster. But *they* are the monsters. Every last one of them!

Then the murmurs and the whispers ceased. Utter silence. My body tensed. I knew it meant that Thomas had arrived. A black carriage pulled up just behind the crudely built platform where the noose hung waiting for Thomas. Two constables stepped to either side of the carriage door, ready to haul out their prisoner. It was the first time I had seen him since the night of the incident. All I had wanted was to see him, but not like this, not under these circumstances. And nothing could have prepared me for what I saw.

Thomas had always been slight and frail, but the boy they pulled forth was near skeletal, bone and skin, a creature barely living! His eyes looked hollow, only highlighted by the redness lining the whites of them. His fair hair, which normally sat in lively curls atop his head, now lay flat and dry against his scalp. He had to be dragged forward, and I could see raw, red marks underneath the shackles on his wrists. It took everything in me not to cry out.

And then it struck me: why was I holding back at all? It was certainly not the time for that!

"*Thomas!*" I screamed. Many in the crowd turned to face me. I paid them no mind. I was not there for them, and I cared little for their judgments.

Recognition sparked within his sunken eyes, and he stood alert, as if my voice had broken him free from some accursed trance. "Sav?" But that is only a guess as to what he said from watching his lips for whatever he did say, it came out as little more than a whisper, his voice dry and thin.

"Thomas!" I screamed once more, then took off in a sprint toward the platform, though it was difficult weaving through the bodies all gathered so tightly together. My heart was pounding like a drum and every beat was a message, urging me forward: *Go! Go! Go! Go!* "Thomas! Use your magic, do it *now*!" Murmurs and gasps erupted all around.

One of the constables had been preparing to place a hood over Thomas's head. Thomas turned his eyes on him. Seeing him then, how weak he looked, I was suddenly doubtful that he could muster any power at all.

The man attempting to place the hood on Thomas flew across the platform, landing on his back with a sickening crack against the wooden planks. Screams from the crowd filled the air and, with that, I was no longer the only person in the crowd running. Thomas turned his attention to the constable who had been dragging him forward. This one went flying out into the crowd, just like Neville's illusion. Though instead of disappearing, the uniformed man fell to the cobblestone street below, nearly missing a mother and her small child. If the first landing's sound was sickening, this was utterly revolting and somehow loud enough to be heard over the chaos that had consumed the gathering.

A third constable, somehow unfazed by the state of his two colleagues, reached for the noose with one hand and for the collar of Thomas's shirt with the other. Thomas turned his attention to the rope. It came to life, like a dangling brown snake. The noose head looped around the man's wrist and tightened. The man yelped in pain, trying to pull his arm away.

Thomas saw his opportunity and took it, moving out toward me. His weak knees would not allow him to run, but he was making his way toward me all the same. "Sav!" he tried calling out once more.

"*Thomas!*" This time it was not in desperation or fear but pure joy. He did it! He had used his powers and was now going to make it into my arms, alive.

A shot rang out through the chaos, silencing the screams and stopping people dead in their tracks, including myself. Thomas's gray eyes widened and his mouth opened in a trembling oval shape. We both looked down where the crimson stain had started to form on his shirt.

No, no, no.

So much blood.

He fell to his bony knees.

"No!" I screamed. The rest of the crowd somehow managed to remain silent, though many of the faces looked nearly as horrified as I felt. They had all come to watch an execution as if it were a street performance and yet were shocked the moment they witnessed actual bloodshed. As if a hanging were so much more dignified than watching a young man be gunned down in the street.

I did not look to see who had pulled the trigger. All I could see was Thomas. I rushed to him, then knelt beside him and cradled him in my arms. There was no use stopping the tears, for they were already staining my cheeks with their salty, cruel warmth.

"Sav," he croaked again.

"Shh, I am here, Thomas. I'm here! Please just hold on."

He used what little strength he had left to clasp one of my hands within his. "I love you," he whispered, voice rasping as the words escaped his throat. It sounded so final. Like a farewell.

But this could not be farewell!

"No, no," I pleaded, begging him to stay on this earth with me. "Thomas, please, you are going to be fine. You can use your magic. You can *fix* this!"

He lifted his head, his mouth right beside my ear as he croaked, "You will find me. I know it." He then smiled sweetly, looking almost serene as his chest fell for the last time. I shook his body, as if I could somehow rattle more breath into him, more time! When it did nothing, the tears started coming faster and each of my own breaths came in short, sharp bursts.

I pulled his cold, limp body closer to me—one arm wrapped around his slender frame, the other covering my own mouth as I coughed out horrified sobs.

Seconds felt like minutes. Minutes felt like hours. And hours felt like years. When the crowd finally did disperse, a group of policemen approached and had to pry Thomas's body away from me. I was brought in chains to the police station, where I sat most of the night in a cell. Detective Branson was the one who eventually showed up to release me.

As he led me out of the police station, he looked from side to side, as if making sure no one was watching us. Once he was satisfied, he turned back to me and discreetly pulled a leather-bound journal from the interior pocket of his wool coat.

I knew who it belonged to without him telling me, but he felt the need to say, "It belonged to Mr. Pendleton—Thomas." The correction was unnecessary. Obviously the small tome had not belonged to Thomas's father. "We should really be returning it to the boy's parents, but all things considered, I thought it might provide you with comfort during these trying times."

It was strange; he was acting as though he were giving me a gift, yet the words "Thank you" were the furthest ones from my mind.

He then muttered some nonsense, giving his condolences

and whatnot, took credit for getting me released, and proceeded to tell me I was lucky that I was not being charged for inciting a riot.

Lucky? *Lucky?* How dare he or anyone else try to tell me that I am anything near fortunate? The love of my life is dead. I could not protect him nor could I save him, hard as I tried.

Thomas did not simply possess magic; he *was* magic. He was pure starlight. Neville was a monster for trying to harness it, and I was a fool for ever thinking I could re-create it.

September 18, 1899

¶ feel utterly numb.

October 01, 1899

I have barely slept, eaten…hell, I have barely moved since Thomas's death.

What is the point?

If this is the kind of agony love brings, I may have been better off never seeking it out at all.

October 15, 1899

Today I considered taking my own life. Not out of sheer misery, you see. But out of a twisted kind of hope.

What if I was wrong all along? What if there truly is an afterlife and I am wasting precious moments that could be spent reunited with Thomas? And in a far better place than this forsaken city, no less.

I wanted to do it…oh how I fantasized about it.

If there is an afterlife, Thomas is likely ashamed of what a coward I am.

THE  TIMES

LONDON SUNDAY   OCTOBER 15, 1899

THEATERGOER PULLS GUN ON STAGE
MAGICIAN DURING PERFORMANCE

On Saturday night, Neville Wighton the Great was performing at the West London Theatre. The performance marked his first since the revelation that his previous apprentice was a practicing witch and was publicly executed. The performance also marked the one-year anniversary of Wighton's performance where he performed a vanishing illusion that has since brought him a great deal of fame and renown.

The show on Saturday was sold out, and Wighton vowed that a portion of the money from ticket sales would be going to Mr. Avery and Mrs. Katherine Pendleton, the parents of the deceased who have been exonerated of any wrongdoing.

In the middle of the performance, after completing a trick involving making a volunteer from the audience appear to levitate, a young man stood and hollered at the magician, "Fancy trick, murderer!"

When audience members turned to the young man, they were shocked to see a pistol in his right hand, aimed directly for the stage. Attendees of the performance describe the young man as having olive-toned skin, unkempt black hair, and a thick Italian accent.

Police were called on to the scene and were let into the theatre by the staff, but the magician waved at them to pause and addressed the man. "Do it."

The crowd gasped, but later, many attendees claimed to have wondered if it was not a part of the act.

"Excuse me?" the young man reportedly asked.

"Shoot me," Wighton said.

It is said that there were a few moments of tense silence before the young Italian man eventually lowered the weapon. The police disarmed him, and the patrons were all safely evacuated from the theatre.

No one was harmed in the incident. Mr. Wighton has refused to comment.

SAVERIO

October 19, 1899

Neville called on me for a private meeting today at the West London Theatre at around noon. There was a matinee scheduled today. The request struck me as odd, considering I'd just recently made a threat against his life. Most of that week had been spent inside a prison cell for me. Eventually, I was released, and to my utter disbelief I found that it had been Detective Branson who had paid the bail money. I think the man feels pity for me, which is odd, considering that he was the one so eager to fit a noose around Thomas's neck.

I met Neville all the same. My hate brewing inside me was both the thing telling me to stay away from him as it was the fuel urging me to go to him. To spit in his face and demand he answer for what he has done, to Thomas and subsequently to me.

I was let into the theatre and told by an usher to proceed to the auditorium. It seemed empty. I made my way to the stage expecting him to be waiting in the wings.

"Mr. Moretti, so good of you to come."

He was sitting in a chair in the second row, directly in front of stage right.

"Seems a bit foolish to ask for a meeting with a man who held a gun at you in this very space."

"I do not fear you, Moretti," Wighton said. "I pity you."

I did not want his pity. Any pain I was feeling was *his* fault.

"Ahh, pity? How very…human of you. Be careful, someone might start to think you have some empathy in you…or a soul."

Neville found this amusing. What he did not realize was that I was not joking. I meant every word I spoke.

"First time I have ever had a gun pulled on me during a performance," Neville admitted. "It was rather thrilling."

"You pretend to pity me yet mock my grief?"

"Mocking? No. I am simply commending the fire you possess, boy, but it is wasted on trying to make an enemy out of me."

"You are already my enemy," I told him.

"And why is that?"

"Are you really so thoughtless, Wighton?" I asked. "You dangled Thomas's magic in front of thousands who came over the course of this past year to watch you perform. Dangled him like a rabbit before a pack of hungry wolves. Every moment he spent on that stage with you was another moment in jeopardy. And then when he was in trouble, did you protect him after all he had done for you? The fame and fortune his gift earned you? No, you sold him out! And do not try to weasel your way out of this; I am well aware that it was you who told Detective Branson of Thomas's secret, and you gave him Thomas's journal as proof."

"I will not deny that I confirmed what the police already suspected, yes. What Thomas had, as you know, it was a beautiful thing, but it was also a dangerous thing—a weapon if not used correctly. Rumors were going around after that night on the bridge. People were starting to wonder, and bad things happen when people wonder. What if someone nefarious had attempted to use Thomas's skills for a dark gain?"

The hypocrisy in his words was enough to make me laugh.

Neville frowned but continued with the nonsense he was spewing. "You are too close to the situation. The nature of your relationship with Thomas blinds you to the reality and the scope of the measure I took. If you cannot understand why I did what I had to do, I can live with that. I can also live with Thomas's ghost, which will likely haunt me as it will you.

"I may have been the one masquerading his magic as illusion work night after night in various theatres across the city. But I will ask you to think on this: Was it at one of my performances that he was discovered? Or did something else lead to that?"

I was going to be ill.

"Anyway, a discussion of blame and who is at fault is not why I called you here. I have something that belongs to you. I do not owe you an apology for what transpired, but I do owe you this." He held out an envelope.

I looked at it with suspicion in my heart. What could he possibly have of mine? Or what could he possibly offer me that I would even want at this point?

"What is it?" I asked.

"They were not so cruel as not to grant Thomas a final request," Neville explained. "Apparently all he asked for was a pen and paper so that he may write a letter. When he was finished, he told the police that they were to give it to the one person who actually cared about what happened to him. They mistakenly assumed it was me, but as soon as the constable explained this to me, I knew who it was truly intended for."

As soon as I knew it was from Thomas, I grabbed it out of his hands. Before I could say anything about it, he gave a stiff nod in farewell before exiting the auditorium.

The letter is now sitting on my kitchen table, and it feels strangely fearful, the idea of reading Thomas's final thoughts before his execution.

My Dearest Sav,

They tell me that my days are numbered now. That the charge of witchcraft against me has been validated and I am to answer for it. Answer for what I am.

Doubtless, the thought has crossed your mind and you have wondered, out there in the free world, while I sit here in my cell, why I have not made some daring attempt at escape. The only answer I have is this: it is all true, and I am guilty of everything of which I am accused. Though I do not much care for the term "witch," I do possess magic, and with that magic I, however unintentionally, ended a man's life. There shall be no more deaths on my accord. There are no roads that will lead us back to each other.

But do not fret for me, Saverio Moretti. Yes, I am scared. Of course I am. And of course I would want to continue living a life with you by my side. But know this: I was happy.

You gave that to me. Before you entered into my life, I was a sad man forced into a future he did not want and with no person to talk to or understand me. Not only did you understand me, but you saw who I was and you loved me for it. And you helped me to love myself. I have felt more joy than I have ever felt in my entire existence. Even the period spent fighting with you and thinking that I hated you, I was still happier than I had been for ever knowing you existed.

My one saving grace has been thoughts of you. Such thoughts are the only bits of light that filter into my dark, dank cell. Just the other night I dreamed for the first time in what feels like eons, and do you want to know what I dreamed of? The Christmas party at my parents' house. Only my parents were not there, and neither were any of the other insufferable guests. Just the musicians and you and me, and we danced—oh how we danced! In the dream, it seemed the moment would likely last forever.

But there is no true forever; everything must end.

And before I am forced to leave this world, I must make one final request of you: Live your life. Be happy—as happy as you managed to make me! You deserve that much. And you have such a unique, vibrant spirit—if you did not continue to let it sparkle, the world would be darker for it.

You showed me what love is, a fine accomplishment if I do say so myself. If I am indeed gone, please know that I died a happy man with a full heart.

Thank you so much for all you have given me.

Yours forever,
Thomas

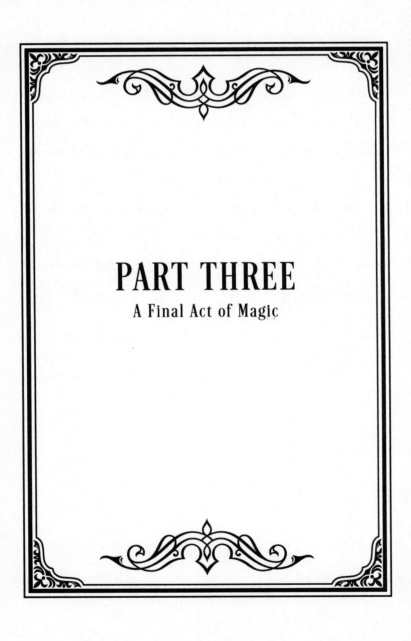

PART THREE

A Final Act of Magic

A week had passed since Neville had called Sav to the theatre and delivered Thomas's final letter to him. His pattern of sleeplessness and neglecting to eat persisted, only now it was also paired with an obsession over a piece of paper.

Thomas's final thoughts, his last piece of writing—poetry in its own right, for it was his heart, his sweetness, emptied out onto the page. Most poets, at least the ones Sav knew of, were notorious for putting their torment into their writing, and poor Thomas had the lingering cloud of his own death hanging above his head when he penned the note.

Ever since opening the letter, Sav had been compulsively reading line after line, like an actor reciting lines for a play. Each time his eyes traced the words, he imagined Thomas speaking them to him, and it provided some comfort.

Now it was a source of maddening confusion and quite possibly…

…hope.

Sav had read the letter more times than he could count, and one of the first things that had caught his eye was that the letter had been dated. It struck him as odd that Thomas would find dating the letter necessary. Whose benefit was it for? But it did not take long for Sav to dismiss it. After all, it was the contents within the letter that mattered.

He did not pay notice to the date atop the letter again until, out of the corner of his eye, something seemed different about the lines and curves of Thomas's penmanship.

Sav inspected the date to find that it was from nearly a year ago: *October 04, 1898.* It was not simply a case of mistakenly written numbers, for the month itself was not even correct!

Sav blinked in disbelief. He was so certain that *September 01, 1899* had been written there previously.

But that could only mean that it had been altered somehow, and that was…impossible.

Impossible.

The word made his heart feel heavy as hot tears irritated his eyes. For so long he had considered many things to be impossible — and then he met Thomas. If anyone should have learned by now not to discount anything as impossible or unbelievable, it would be him.

In Sav's mind, there were two possibilities: Thomas's mind had started to fade while in prison and he simply had no sense of time or reality, *or* there was something more to this story. Something Sav was meant to find.

He sat at the wooden table in his apartment, cradling the paper in his hands. He was always worried that if he clutched it too fiercely that it might disintegrate into tiny bits. He searched the confines of his mind, trying to recall anything of significance that might have happened on that particular day. It was precisely around the time he had arrived in London with Paolo and Isabella, he remembered that much. But for the life of him, it had been so long ago…

His eyes wandered over to the bookshelf, to the journal that remained untouched. Ever since the detective had given it to him, he had kept it stored away on the shelf, like some cursed tome to be avoided. In less than a week, he had clung to Thomas's letter like a lifeline, but those words had been intended for his eyes. To peer inside Thomas's private journal had felt too much like an invasion to Sav — trespassing into secrets that Thomas had not elected to share with him.

Now the leather-bound journal looked far more inviting. It was a key—a tool in this instance. If Thomas truly had left some sort of message for him, then certainly he would want him to use the journal.

He leafed through the pages until he found the entry from October fourth of the previous year, and he noted that it was quite the milestone occasion, indeed: Thomas and Neville's first rehearsal for the performance that served to change the course of their lives forever.

He scanned the details of the rehearsal's happenings. Though it did not surprise him in the least, reading of Neville's cruel behavior and insults toward Thomas enraged Sav, and he had to admit that he received a sick sort of satisfaction when he got to the part about the magician landing on the row of chairs, his limbs splayed out like those of a marionette doll's. What Sav would have given to have seen that!

As he read, Sav attempted to keep his eyes and mind open to anything of significance—anything that might stand out as a sign or a hint. It was not until the final line that something caught him as bizarre. At the beginning of October in 1898, Thomas had ended this particular entry by stating that if his secret did not kill him, then Neville Wighton likely would. What had surely been a joke about his mentor at the time had turned into a dark prophecy.

And clearly someone else had noticed.

In the margin, beside the prophetic words, a note had been hastily penned then crossed out with runny black ink, but by squinting, Sav was able to make out the words: *I was right. On both counts.*

Sav gaped at the message. *I was right.* It was as if Thomas was confirming that a combination of his magic and his mentor's treachery had led to his demise. But when would he have had a chance to make such a note? And why?

Sav sincerely doubted that Branson would do Thomas the kindness of allowing him access to his journal whilst imprisoned, given the fact that it was their only true evidence backing Neville's claims.

Did Thomas know his fate prior to the incident at the bridge? If so, would he not have been more careful? Questions bloomed like wildflowers in Sav's mind. He brought his fingers to the journal page, brushing them over the peculiar message. It certainly looked to be Thomas's penmanship.

"What are you trying to tell me?" Sav said aloud in the empty room, wishing more than anything that he would hear Thomas's voice in response.

His sore eyes turned back down to the journal. Perhaps this was not the only instance of strangeness—perhaps more messages were buried within. Sav was uncertain of where to begin but decided that surely the beginning would be best.

That evening, he pored over each page by the light of the fading amber glow of a candle nearly at its wick's end. When the last of the wax had melted down and the tiny flame extinguished, Sav determined that he would not be getting any sleep that night all the same, and so after a failed attempt at trying to read in the dark, he brought Thomas's journal out for a "stroll."

Down just two blocks on the street, Sav situated himself beside one of the gas streetlamps and continued to read fervently.

༄ॐ ॐ༄

Night transformed to morning, and by the light of day, Sav continued his search. Over the span of a day, he had read the journal from front to back multiple times.

His melancholy heart had lingered on the passages

depicting some of his own favorite memories, such as sampling salted meats at the market in Whitechapel or their first meeting at Simpson's among the sea of black-and-white suits and chess sets. It was as though he were reliving each moment now that he was getting to witness them all through Thomas's eyes. His heart warmed at reading just how captivated and excited Thomas had been when they had first encountered each other. Sav had been equally excited, of course, but at the time it had been for reasons Sav no longer wished to think on.

Decidedly, one of his favorite passages to read detailed that frigid night in November they had migrated with Arthur and Roger—Sav spared a moment to wonder what happened to those charming old men—from Simpson's to the White Lion Pub. Sav remembered thinking that night how Thomas had finally seemed to be letting his guard down and allowing himself pure enjoyment. Thomas's words in the passage served as evidence that his assumption had been correct.

Sav closed his eyes and thought back to the life that had sparked behind Thomas's. The sweet smile on his face as they skipped around the room, arm in arm. His chest ached at the memories, but he did not stop—did not force himself to think of something else. He would rather live in an escapist dream of the past than wake to the reality that his Thomas was no longer with him.

This was his third time reading this particular entry, and though he already knew it held no clues or vital bits of information to feed his rising suspicions, he took his time reading it, letting the words dance on the paper as joyously as they had danced with each other. But when he arrived at the section where Sav had initiated the revelry by pulling Thomas out of his seat, he *did* find something peculiar...

It was just as they got up to dance, Thomas was no longer using the words "he" and "him" when referring to Sav in the journal, or even calling him by name.

Instead he used the word "you."

It was written more like a letter directly to Sav in those couple of paragraphs, as if he had intended for the words to be read by Sav's eyes—as if he had foreseen it.

The confusion felt like a physical burden on his mind in that moment, a weight suddenly pulling him down, demanding he rest. Sav had already gone over this and every other entry in the journal more than once, and yet the two prior readings had not brought about this revelation. If asked, Sav would have sworn on his life—well, perhaps not his, maybe his father's… that way he would be good to him for something—that before, Thomas had written the words "he" and "his" and "Sav."

Not only that, earlier in the very same entry were words like "he" and "his" when speaking in reference to Sav. It was only that small, strange section toward the end that seemed to be addressing Sav directly, as though they were engaged in a conversation with each other.

Sav could not remove his eyes from one line: *The pub was nothing more than a blur of lights and sound and all I could see was* you.

⚬⚭⚬ ⚭⚬⚮

Days passed and there seemed to be no further activity. Sav surely would have noticed if there had been, for his eyes were transfixed on Thomas's pages as though he were an anxious university student certain he would fail his final exams if he ceased reading his coursework for but a moment.

When the nothingness persisted, it filled him with frustration and fear—fear of his hope being misplaced and fear that he would have to return to the version of his life where Thomas's death was an immutable fact.

Until he found a new peculiarity. There was still a fear in him, only this was a fear that he was slowly going mad and that these "clues" might only be his mind playing cruel tricks on him.

It was another crossed-out message. Sav had been spurred on by the memory of the tiny galaxy Thomas had created in his bedroom when he first asked him to perform magic. Though he had read it already, multiple times, he felt the need to know just what Thomas had been feeling after such a lovely, intimate night.

On March twenty-third, his sweet boy had written out on the page just how elated he felt. That he had showed Sav his darkest corners of himself, the side people would likely fear, and the fact that Sav had been so amazed and awestruck…it had meant so much to Thomas! And knowing that now meant so much to Sav.

It was a short entry but filled to the brim with glee—the kind of glee Sav had not known for a time, and so he reread the passage, hoping to get even just a small taste of that happiness back.

It was either eight or nine times through (Sav had lost count) when something struck him as peculiar. With such a short passage, there was a great deal of blank paper before reaching the end of the page, but there at the very bottom of the paper was a tiny note that had been crossed out multiple times.

Though it took some strain, Sav was able to make it out: *Your eyes always saw me for what I truly was. I need you to find me again.*

Sav rubbed at his eyes, angry with himself for allowing himself to go this long without sleep—of course he was starting to become delirious! He had been reading the same passage over and over in the same sitting, and only moments ago the tiny message had not been there.

Even so…even if it had been and Sav had simply missed it due to its size or how thoroughly it had been crossed out, it was just too perfect. It read far too much like exactly what Sav wanted to see: a sign that Thomas was waiting for Sav to come find him, even though he had held his cold, limp body with his own hands.

Sav lay awake that night, not on his bed but on the floor, wondering why he was subjecting himself to such grief and torture.

∽◉◐ ◑◉◐

It took several more days before Sav was able to find another irregularity. It was particularly difficult for him to find during his first handful of passes through the journal, for it was within the section where Thomas was not speaking with Sav—a section Sav preferred to merely skim at first.

In May, Thomas had been planning to depart from London, a fact Sav had been wholly unaware of until they had started making plans to flee to Paris together. Whilst discussing potential cities that he might flee to, Thomas had written: *There is no paved road that will lead Sav back to me now.*

On its own, the line would simply seem to be Thomas putting his anger toward Sav into poetry, but the moment Sav read the words, they struck a chord of familiarity. Sav turned his attention back to the final letter from Thomas, which he'd left at its usual place on the table, and though he had it practically memorized, he read through it again, just to be certain.

Just as he knew he would, he came across the line: *There are no paved roads that will lead us back to each other.*

Sav's eyes darted between both pieces of paper. The lines were nearly identical, and every bit of sense and reason Sav possessed was screaming at him, telling him that this was no coincidence.

⋆⊙⟋⟍⊙⋆

When Sav had made his way to the train station that morning, his whole plan was to find Thomas still alive at the end of the journey. To hold him in his arms and stare lovingly into those big gray eyes. What he had not been expecting was to spot Thomas's eyes among the crowd at St. Pancras Station.

They were not really Thomas's eyes, of course. This pair of eyes belonged to Katherine Pendleton. His mother. The striking resemblance caused the air to exit Sav's lungs all at once and for his own eyes to water and sting.

It had been so long since he'd actually seen Thomas's parents in the flesh. All that time while Thomas had been incarcerated, he had searched for them, and when he needed them they were nowhere to be found. Now here they were, Avery and Katherine Pendleton, making their way down the platform to board a train, as if it were just a normal day. As if their son had not been plucked from their lives and from the world.

Their sense of normalcy filled him with insurmountable anger. For all he knew, they were going off on some indulgent holiday.

He was not about to miss the chance to say everything he had told them at one point or another in his mind these past few months.

"Stop!" he hollered through the noise of the bustling crowd. Many heads turned but not the ones he had intended. Perhaps he needed to be more specific.

"Avery and Katherine Pendleton!" Their heads turned.

There were murmurs and whispers all throughout the crowd as they watched on, waiting for events to unfold that would fuel the next day's gossip.

If they recognized him, it did not show in their expressions, Avery's stern and focused and Katherine's calm and poised. Sav was certain that even if they did recognize his face, they would feign ignorance and pretend not to know anything about the Italian boy shouting at them in a train station.

As he neared them, he grew even more infuriated. Avery was dressed in maroon and beige and Katherine in a floral dress.

"Interesting ensembles," Sav said, making a point of looking them up and down.

"I beg your pardon?" Katherine said, bringing a dainty hand to her chest.

"Well, it is no news that you both have experienced the worst thing any parents ever could: the loss of a child. One would assume that black would be a more appropriate color."

Avery's brow furrowed. "It was months ago now that we lost our Thomas. You will forgive us for trying to move forward with our lives."

"So you no longer mourn him, then?"

Katherine's eyes grew wide and she bit her lip. The sad, pathetic look was enough to almost cause Sav guilt. *Almost.* All he had to do was remind himself of everything they'd put him through. Avery, meanwhile, was growing red in the face.

"Boy, I do not know how close you were with my son or how you even met, but do not pretend to know anything about our grief."

Sav's fists clenched. "I knew your son well enough to know what you did."

He waited, to see if they would comprehend his meaning without getting into the specifics. Sure enough, they both put on neutral facial expressions, like armor, but in their eyes he saw the pain…the guilt. He easily recognized it, for he, too, had felt his share of guilt when it came to Thomas.

It was Katherine who spoke up this time. "Everything we did, we did for our son."

"You may be able to fool yourselves with lines like that, but you will not fool me." The anger heated his words like a fire. "You were being selfish. Doing what you could to protect the style of living in which you are accustomed and your precious reputations. If you hadn't been so afraid of a little honest work or more modest living, Thomas would have never even met Neville. He'd probably still be alive today! Thomas was lonely and scared and didn't know what was happening to him. He needed your guidance, your understanding, and, most of all, your protection. And what did you do? You led him to the hungriest lion in the pack."

The guilt still surfacing and tracing the lines of Avery Pendleton's face told him that these were all things they had already considered…possibly even dwelled upon. But Avery just stiffened. "It would be easy to sit here and throw around wild accusations about who is truly at fault. But let me ask you this, if you were so close with Thomas, what exactly was it that you did to protect him?"

"I loved him," Sav said in a low voice, though those listening in carefully still let out a few surprised gasps. It likely was not the answer they were expecting, nor was it the one they wanted. But it was the only one he had.

Avery's already dark expression somehow managed to grow even darker. "A lot of good that did our son."

It was one of the coldest things that had ever been said to Sav. He realized in that moment that Thomas's father and Neville Wighton were two men cut from the same cloth.

Avery turned to his wife, but not before shooting Sav one

last look of disdain. "Come now, Katherine, we will miss our connection."

He moved forward down the platform, but Katherine lingered a short while longer and leaned in to whisper, "He really did love Thomas, in his own way, as did I." She then pulled up her skirts and trotted after her husband in heeled boots that clattered and clunked along the wooden platform.

The fact that she needed to tell him that confirmed what he already knew: their love for Thomas was not unconditional.

He could have told them where he was going. He could have told them of what (or rather, who) he intended to find when he got there. He could tell them of all his theories and the strange occurrences with Thomas's journal and letters.

But he did not feel they deserved this sort of hope. And besides, if Thomas was alive, then he was making a point to hide himself away. In addition to Wighton, Avery and Katherine were likely also on the list of people Thomas would be hiding from.

And besides, if he was wrong, and Thomas was not waiting on the other end, then it would just be another heartbreak anyway, one he would have to endure alone.

❧ ❧

The train lurched to a halt upon its arrival at Gare de Bruges, the screeching of the wheels on the tracks pulling Sav out of something resembling rest. He still hadn't had a night of sleep since Thomas's…since the *incident*, as Sav was referring to it in his mind. Not his death—death was final, after all.

Somehow, though, he had been able to drift off while traveling. Something about being in constant motion soothed him.

After disembarking from the train, he gave the locomotive a final glance over his shoulder. This was it, the end of the line. The last of his money was spent and there would be no way for him to buy another ticket, whether it be back to London, to Italy, or anywhere. The thought did not concern him much. The thought of returning anywhere at this point seemed pointless.

Back when he had been traveling the world with Paolo, nowhere felt like home. There was no specific place where he belonged and no one he belonged to.

Until he met Thomas. Thomas had become his home, and without him, he would never know another.

But he had to believe that he was right this time. He had to believe that all the paths, all the clues, had led him to Belgium for a reason. Then again, that was exactly what he had thought when he had showed up in Salzburg and in Stockholm. He had even returned to his homeland of Italia, searching for the magic boy. Trains, buses, taxis across town — he was like an explorer searching the world for his long-lost treasure. His map? A letter folded with care, tucked away in his left breast pocket with Thomas's dainty signature at the bottom of the page and a journal tucked beside it, pages marked and bent from exhaustive study.

Sav pushed his dark locks away from his weary eyes and dragged the same hand along his face. His lack of sleep surely showed in his appearance. He had not actually had the bravery to look into a mirror for weeks.

He examined the crowd filtering out and around the train station, his heart suddenly sinking in the futility of it all. A whole sea of people was in front of him, as was a winding city with plenty of nooks, crannies, and crevasses for Thomas to be hiding in. He could be right under his nose and Sav could so easily walk right past him without even realizing. What if he already had in one of the other cities?

The thought was enough to make him want to drop to his knees and curl up there on the street, but a small bit of movement above the rows of heads kept him standing upright. It was the fluttering of wings. A moth floated through the air and landed on the city map situated just outside the station.

He felt drawn to the small creature. Normally his eyes would have passed over something so insignificant and mundane, but there was something peculiar about this moth. As he neared it, he noticed that its wings were not a standard gray or white, like one would expect to see. The wings were covered in black markings, as if someone had written upon them like parchment.

As if the small thing were made of paper.

The moment the thought crossed his mind, the moth took flight off the map and out into the city. Sav's heart fluttered as fast as the moth's small paperlike wings—faster, even—and he took off in a sprint after it.

As he ran, he briefly acknowledged how bizarre it probably appeared to the people lining the cobbled streets, a young man chasing after a moth. But Sav was gripped with the inexplicable feeling that he could not let the insect get away from him. For what if it truly was made of paper? What if it was a sign?

Thoughts of paper flowers blooming before his eyes set his feet to run even faster, keeping his eyes locked on the moth as it floated away. He nearly ran into a vendor selling fresh pears and apples, a couple out for a stroll arm in arm, and, more than a few times, he nearly tripped over small children who were well below the line of his vision as he looked to the sky. Angry shouts and remarks in Dutch filled the air and trailed after him, but he did not look back. He kept going. Faster. Faster.

Eventually, Sav's chest began to tighten and breath became harder to summon from his lungs. But the moth continued to get farther and higher, and it was growing more difficult to make out the lines of its wings, so he pushed forward in spite of his weariness.

Down winding streets and even through alleyways, he obediently followed. He turned around corners and bends until one turn led him to water. The moth was now floating over one of the city's canals, and rather than flying straight across or diverging back over solid ground, it went along with the bend and flow of the canal, flying directly above it as it continued.

Sav finally allowed himself a chance to catch his breath, and with what little of it he had, he whispered, "This better be you, Thomas."

He looked to either side and spotted a small wooden boat that looked a little rickety for his liking, tied up nearby. He then looked over each of his shoulders. Though there were plenty of people around to witness the theft, none seemed to be paying him any mind now that he was no longer sprinting through the streets, so he did his best to look casual as he untied the boat and hopped inside.

He had to squint and strain his eyes to finally track down the moth. He'd lost a decent amount of time, and now it was a good distance ahead of him with no signs of slowing. He plunged the oar into the murky water and propelled himself forward furiously. The boat kept veering in terms of direction, so Sav had to turn his eyes back down to the water to steady himself. After the third instance, he was unable to find any sign of the moth when he looked back up.

"No, no, no! Come on. Come on."

His eyes darted in every direction, looking to the sky, the buildings lining the canal, even the water, but he could not find the wings that looked to be patterned with delicate script. Sav blew out a sigh and put his oar back into the water with a sense of resolution. He had come this far. Surely, if he continued down the canal, he would be able to locate whatever it was the small creature had been leading him to.

But soon there was nowhere for him to go.

The canal led into a stone wall with only a half circle lined with iron bars to allow the water to filter out into some outlying area that Sav could not reach. He flung the oar into the water, too distraught to worry himself with the fact that it was not his property or that he would need it to travel back down the canal. He could feel the heartbreak setting in. The disappointment of another failed attempt. The darkness that had started to descend over the city as the hour grew late felt grimly appropriate to Sav in that moment, but with the lack of natural light, he noticed the warm glow that was now flooding out of a nearby building and reflecting against the mirrorlike canal.

Sav looked up to his left. There, what looked to be a small shop with a doorway leading out to the water, whose doors were flung open. Sav strained his bleary vision and saw that rows of bookshelves lined the walls inside.

A bookshop.

If he were looking for a sign, there would be no clearer one than this. Trepidation crept in, and Sav knew he should keep his hope at bay, that continuing his search would likely only further his disappointment, but in spite of his own logic, he dipped his hands into the water and began paddling himself toward the canal storefront.

There was a bar along the open doorway, allowing those entering by boat to access the entryway, and so Sav hoisted himself up. It was small and overcrowded with books, many having to sit in stacks on the floor beside the shelves. The room smelled as warm as it felt, with welcoming hints of wood, wax, and, of course, old paper.

Sav stopped in his tracks, and the corners of his lips fell as he remembered the day in the bookshop in West London. He felt a pang of guilt for not remembering the name. He knew it was named after the man who owned it, and he knew it had been one of Thomas's favorite places in the world. It could now easily be counted as one of Sav's favorite places as well, for it held the memory of the secret garden of print and page Thomas had created for him. He remembered the awe he had felt witnessing such a display of raw, beautiful magic and he remembered how happy Thomas had seemed, allowing himself to be free with his gift, even if it had been behind a locked door.

His knees buckled at the memory, and he drew in a sharp breath. This was not the time for that. He could not allow himself to mourn Thomas's memory while searching for him at the same time.

"Hello?" he finally willed himself to call out. Even though the space was so tiny, there were few places one might hide. "Is anyone here?"

"Mmm." A cross between a moan and a grumble came from across the room. Encircled by book stacks of varying lengths, an old man with long white hair tied into a braid and eyes a similar shade of milky white was sitting at a stool, his shoulders hunched.

Sav stepped closer, and the man's back stiffened. He said something in French, but Sav knew only enough to catch specific words such as "welcome" and "browse."

What is a blind man doing running a bookshop? Sav thought to himself. He could not help but think on how if he had been someone else with different intentions, it would be unsatisfyingly easy to steal from the old man.

"Is there anyone else here?" he asked. "Anyone who works with you in the shop?" When he did not receive an answer, Sav made an attempt at translating his words, but if the man's continued silence was any indication, he was not doing a satisfactory job of it.

Sav turned back around to reexamine the room. It was so small and so cluttered. There were no hallways leading to other rooms, and though from outside Sav had seen that there was another story to the building, there were no stairs leading to the level above.

Sav's heart felt hollow, like nothing more than a cavity in his chest. The pieces to the puzzle had led him to the canal, which had then led him to a bookshop. Of all the coincidences, this was a cruel one. He decided he would not waste another moment there and made his way back toward the door, hoping that the tiny boat had not drifted away.

Just as he was reaching for the bar to lower himself, both the doors that had been sitting open flew shut. Sav's heart stopped and then began beating again but at what felt like twice the normal speed. Not because of fear but because he was entirely positive that there had not been a breeze that night.

He did not turn around, not yet, but he heard the sound of air whirring behind his back and books slamming against the wooden floor. He then heard pages turning and paper folding and he finally allowed himself a glance.

It was happening again. All around him, books were open and from them the pages were being morphed into meticulously crafted paper flowers while, from the higher shelves, paper was coiling and rolling together to form vines that then wrapped their way down the bookcases. The old man in the corner was unable to see the impossible garden forming around him.

It was as if the memory that he had been thinking on only moments before was coming to life before his very eyes. He had not noticed the precise moment when the tears began to slide down his cheeks, but there was no stopping them once they started. He covered his mouth as he choked out sobs. His Thomas. His sweet little magic boy.

He reached out with a hand to touch one of the nearby

flowers. He was afraid of what might happen if he plucked it, as if it were an illusion and removing a flower would shatter it all and send him back to his lonely reality, so he merely caressed the delicate paper.

The sound of a floorboard creaking gripped Sav's attention, and he turned to face the corner of the room opposite of where the old man was sitting. A staircase had appeared where there had only been a wall before, and descending the steps was...

Thomas Pendleton.

Sav had to lean all of his body weight against the nearest bookshelf to keep from collapsing entirely. The boy was as pale as moonlight, and any other person in Sav's shoes might have thought they had happened upon a ghost. But Sav knew it was him. Flesh and blood Thomas, looking more beautiful to him than he ever had before.

"Thomas?" he whispered. His voice was so hoarse from the sobs, it no longer sounded like his own. This was everything he had been wanting, everything he had hoped would happen, and yet, now that he was faced with this new reality, he found it impossible to compose himself.

Thomas did not look as overwhelmingly joyous as Sav felt. In fact, he looked absolutely gutted.

"Hello, Sav," he said.

Hearing Thomas's voice after all this time sent another wave of shock through Sav, and he had to flatten his hands against the wooden shelves to stay up on his feet.

"I can only imagine what I have put you through these past months or what you must be thinking now. You must hate me, and I would not blame you if you did; you have every right to."

Hate him? Oh poor, sweet Thomas. Hate was the furthest thing from Sav's heart in that moment. He wanted to tell him as much. He wanted to take him into his arms and never let go. He wanted to climb atop the roof above and sing, sing for the people of Bruges and all the world to hear. He opened his mouth to say something—anything—that might properly express his joy, but as his lips parted, no words came to him, leaving only silence to fill the room.

Thomas looked further pained. "I should have told you what I had been planning."

Planning? There was still nothing that Thomas could say that would make Sav hate him, but this remark did throw him. "Are you saying you orchestrated the whole thing? You planned everything to happen the way that it did?" It seemed unlikely… impossible, really.

"No, no, not all of it." He spoke quickly, in a way that made it clear he also acknowledged how impossible that sounded. "My only plan was to make sure that everyone thought I was gone for good—most importantly Neville. He knew that threatening me to keep me in line would no longer have the same effect it once did. So he threatened something—someone much more important to me…"

Thomas did not need to say any more. Sav only wished that he had known that the vile magician had been making threats against his life so that he could have eased Thomas's troubled mind. They could have faced the threats together, side by side. After all he had been through, Wighton was far from frightening in Sav's eyes.

"I had to disappear. It was the only way…with so many eyes on me. I was in danger because of what I was…what I am. But I was also putting you in danger because you love me."

Thomas looked at Sav, and the last part was said as something more of a question than a statement he knew to be true. Sav almost felt reason to be insulted. Had he not just spent the last of his money while out searching the world for Thomas? *Of course* he loved him! But rather than voicing any of this, he remained silent, still frozen in place standing in the middle of the bookshop. In part, his silence was due to the fact that he was still stunned by his love's presence after all this time, but mostly he was silent out of respect. It was time to hear him out. Not enough people had taken the time to truly listen to Thomas while he was "alive."

Thomas drew in a wavering breath. "But your love for me was not the only thing putting you at risk. Yes, I planned to make it so that everyone believed I was dead, but — "

"How?" Sav interrupted. "How did you do it? How did you convince everyone you were actually dead? For that matter, how are you *not* dead? A bullet pierced through you. You were bleeding all over the square."

Thomas was silent for a moment, then reached down into the pocket of his trousers. He removed his hand and held out his palm, presenting a small metal bullet.

"It never actually hit me," Thomas said quietly.

Sav tried to form the start of a question, but there were no words for what Thomas was revealing to him.

"As soon as the pistol was fired, my magic lashed out. Usually it's much slower...gradual. But this...this was instantaneous, like some sort of impulse. I transported the bullet, just like I had transported Neville all those nights. I was never actually bleeding. Do you remember the first time I made a paper garden for you?"

Sav nodded. "How could I forget?"

"You asked me about the limits of my powers, and I told you that I had the ability to alter perception. And so that's what I did."

Sav blinked, uncertain of what to say. After everything he had been through, the explanation seemed overly simple yet impossible at the same time.

"To anyone who looked at me, I made it appear that I was bleeding, that my skin was draining of color. To anyone who touched me, I made it seem that my skin was colder…that there was no pulse. It was my magic the whole time."

Sav fought back tears as the gruesome images from that day flooded back into his brain. And Thomas had been pulling the strings the whole time.

"The plan to fake my own death only materialized after what happened at the bridge. The way I lost control—that was entirely real. I'd hurt people with my magic before: I sent Neville flying through the air once; I slammed you up against a wall. But this was different. This time I lost control and it cost a man his life. Murder, Sav. I murdered someone!"

Thomas choked back a sob, and it took a great deal of restraint for Sav to stay silent while Thomas struggled with so much pain.

"I wanted to escape London, to keep myself safe, to keep you safe…but in a way, I think I also needed to keep others safe. Who knew when I would lose control like that again?" Thomas sighed. "I *still* do not know." He gestured around the shop. "Even here where I hide away, I worry about hurting someone once again. The guilt is something I will have to live with every day, as is the fear. You should fear me, too."

"Fear? Thomas, your magic has always just been another part of you that I have loved. One of the many things that make you who you are."

"But I can't always control it."

Sav finally found his strength and his words, and he rushed to his love's side, then clutched his soft, pale cheeks in his hands. "Shh, shh," he soothed, stroking his cheek with a thumb. He had been waiting so long to see Thomas again, something that, for a time, he did not even think a possibility. The last thing he wanted was to see him anxious and plagued with guilt.

"You have controlled it enough to fill a bedroom with glowing stars. You have controlled it enough to create a literary garden. The rest? That is the unknown and yes, it presents a great risk. But so does love itself. Now that we are together again, I shall stand by your side, no matter what happens. My darling Thomas. I could *never* fear you. Do you not understand the relief I feel now? To find you alive…I…I am the happiest I have ever been in my existence!"

He could feel the tension melting from Thomas's muscles, and now Thomas was the one weeping, a sad smile painting his face. Had these been normal circumstances, Sav would have taken care to wipe each and every tear away, but there was only one thing Sav now had on his mind. With his hands still on Thomas' cheeks, he pulled his face in toward his own, pressing his lips firmly against Thomas's. Thomas reached around his back as his hands moved up his spine to the back of his neck, one hand continuing farther into his hair, tugging lightly as they moved in unison.

In Thomas's lips and fingertips he could feel his want, and desire, but, most of all, his love.

When they finally pulled away, Sav began choking out more sobs, and this time it was Thomas who moved to comfort him, stroking his hand through Sav's hair.

Sav looked back up at Thomas. "I am so, so sorry."

Thomas looked perplexed, but he flashed a sweet smile. "I faked my own death and forced you to mourn me, and it is *you* saying that you are sorry?"

"Not only has our relationship been a danger for you, forcing you to stage something so gruesome…it was also founded upon lies and schemes. I like to think of myself as better than Wighton or your parents but really, I am no better. I tried to use you for my own gain, and I still cannot believe you chose to forgive me. I am not deserving of your forgiveness."

Thomas squared himself so that he and Sav were looking each other directly in the eyes. "You think you are part of what

I was trying to escape? Saverio Moretti, your love has set me free. The old Thomas Pendleton, the one you met so long ago, he is a stranger to me now. A miserable stranger who did not know what it was like to experience true happiness. All the scheming of my own recently...it was for us—for you! It was so that I could be with you! That is all I want—all I've ever wanted."

Thomas brought a hand down to stroke Sav's cheek and dry the rolling tears.

Sav could not help a playful little laugh as he sniffled. "You know, you would have saved me a whole lot of time and money if you had just sent a message telling me exactly where you were."

Thomas looked him square in the eye, and in a particularly terrible Italian accent, he asked, "Did you not like *my* mystery?"

He had remembered every detail from that conversation, and it warmed him to know that Thomas had, too.

Thomas gave a nod. "In all seriousness, I could not be certain of who would be rummaging through my private journal—you, Neville, the authorities...I had to be careful."

At this, Sav pulled out Thomas's journal and handed it back to its rightful owner.

It was not until a low cough from across the room interrupted them that Sav remembered that the blind old man had been sitting there the whole time.

Thomas let out a sheepish laugh and took Sav's hand, guiding him over to the man. "Where are my manners? Sav, this is Maurice; he owns the shop and has for the past fifty-five years." Thomas then offered an introduction for Maurice in French, using Sav's full name.

Though Sav was quite certain the man could not understand English, he still whispered when he said, "Thomas, my darling, the man owns a bookshop and he is blind."

Thomas nodded. "He was not always this way. When he started to lose his vision, he could not bear the thought of losing the shop or the stories it possessed. To this day, he still misses getting to read the books with his own eyes. After finding this place and offering my help for room and board, I took to reading to him each night before closing the shop. It seems to comfort him."

Sav beamed. Thomas always did have the biggest heart of anyone he had ever known. Sav leaned in and placed a tiny, appreciative kiss on Thomas's forehead.

Thomas's smile grew even wider and his eyes shone. Sav was positive he would endure another bout of sobs, so to keep himself from breaking down once again, he pulled him into a tight embrace. Thomas buried his face in Sav's chest, and Sav kissed the top of Thomas's head, the familiar scent of his golden curls intoxicating him more than any perfume could.

Sav counted all the ways in which he was fortunate as he stood there, holding what he loved most and what he thought had been lost to him forever. There he was, breathing, his heart beating, so near to Sav's. He was his own little miracle.

His magician.

꧁ ꧂

The bell tower chimed four bells, and Sav perked up from his position behind the counter. Under normal circumstances, Gericho's Unisex Clothier was open until five bells, but Sav had received special permission to lock up early, for this particular day marked exactly a year since Sav had first arrived in Bruges and made the greatest discovery of his young life. He and Thomas of course had to commemorate the occasion.

Closing up was always a fairly simple process, as soon as he was able to get Sophia out the door. She was always lingering around the shop during his shifts. Sometimes she was looking for pieces for herself and other times she was picking out a little something for her "husband." Sav was seriously starting to doubt if Roger truly existed and if he did, Sav wondered if he would love the idea of her spending so much time at a clothing store for no other purpose than to ogle the clerk. For his own part, Sav made sure to always drop mention of his beloved waiting for him to get done with the workday. She was harmless, though, and actually had a delightful sense of humor about her, so Sav did not mind her company.

There was an extra bit of skip in Sav's steps as he hopped along the cobbled streets he had now come to know so well. The late afternoon sun warmed his cheeks, and he nodded his hellos to familiar faces and strangers alike.

He entered the bookshop through the street entrance and was greeted, as he was every day, by the sound of Thomas reading aloud to Maurice. He listened closely before walking over to them. The day's selection was Mary Shelley. A bit dark, but even so, being read in Thomas's voice, it sounded sweet and innocent as a lullaby.

He strolled across the room and kissed one of Thomas's hands. "*Mon amour.*"

"*Il mio amore,*" Thomas replied in Sav's native tongue, putting on his best attempt at an Italian accent. It had become a routine, and one that Sav cherished.

Sav turned his attention to the old man. "My dear Maurice, may I borrow young Thomas from you?" he asked in near-flawless French, if he did say so himself.

Maurice chuckled. "My boy, *I* am the one who is borrowing him. You know he is yours to keep."

Thomas grinned. "I am." He then winked at Sav. Ever since his return from the grave, he had this inexplicable air of confidence about him. Sav had decided long ago that Thomas wore it well.

They made their way up two flights of stairs to the top level, a quaint little apartment that Maurice had already been letting Thomas stay in. It was even smaller than Sav's apartment in London, but the space was the only thing about it that was lacking. The cream-colored walls and chestnut wood lining the floors made each room feel warm and inviting, the view looking out over the canal from their rooftop like something from an old oil painting, but most important was the person he got to share such close quarters with. Thomas was the first thing he saw when he arose in the morning and the last sight he gazed upon before drifting off to sleep. He had never known such perfection in his life.

He set about boiling water over the gas stove while Thomas began chopping vegetables…using his magic. Once the food was prepared, they brought their dishes with them to the roof terrace, their favorite place to take meals. They filled their bellies and told each other stories as the evening descended over Bruges. Sav went inside only once to retrieve a bottle of wine he had purchased specially for the occasion.

Once the night sky was glittering with the lights from stars above, Thomas used his gift to make it appear as though the stars themselves were forming into various shapes and words. Sav watched in awe, just as he had that night when Thomas had brought the stars directly to him.

That time in their lives seemed like an eternity ago. And now, after all their searching and all the pain that the world had inflicted upon them, they were finally free. Finally home.

ACKNOWLEDGMENTS

Where to even start? I've been writing stories ever since I was a kid and now, to have a story I wrote become an actual book is a pretty surreal feeling. It's nothing short of a dream come true, and there are so many people who helped to make this dream a reality.

First to my family. I wouldn't be here without you, and you all helped shape me into the woman and writer that I am today. To my dad, Stephan; my momma, Liz; my sister, Abby (aka Abberz); my grandma Patricia (aka Gukkerz) and Louie. I love you all so much! (I wish I had enough pages and time to list out my entire extended family, just know I love you all, too, and am so grateful for all of your support.)

To my love, Eddie. You've been there for me through this entire journey, and I can't wait for all the future journeys. You're so incredibly sweet and supportive of all my dreams. Through the highs and the lows, you've had my back and have been my number one fan. Your love and support means the world to me and I'm so lucky to have you!

To my writing group, Roz, Stef, Zoe, Daniel, and Lee. You guys are the best writing family and support system anyone could ever ask for. You have all helped me grow so much as a writer and honestly, without you guys, this book would have never even come into existence. Your feedback and support has taught me so much and gotten me through this whole experience. You're all so amazing, and our writing retreat is by far one of my favorite weekends out of the year. I'm so glad we all took that class at StoryStudio.

To my best friends in the world, Kate, Destini, and Katlin. You ladies give me so much strength, and I don't know where I'd be without you. You're amazing, and I feel so lucky that I get to call such talented, brilliant, creative women my friends. Thank you for all the support! I love you guys!

To my super agent, Whitley Abell. I knew from that very first phone call that we were on the same page, and I feel lucky to have you in my corner and championing my words. Thank you for being my advocate, one of my biggest fans and supporters, and a voice of reason. You've helped me so much through this process, and I can't wait for all the books we will get to work on together moving forward. You're the best!

To the amazing team at StoryStudio who helped make me a better writer, with a huge shout-out to both Jill Pollack and Rebecca Makkai for all your support as I entered into the publishing world. The sense of community I have found at StoryStudio has meant the world to me.

I've been so lucky to work with not one but three amazing editors on this book. Stephen, thank you so much for loving this book with all your heart and making my dreams come true. The way you fought for this book touched my heart, and I can never thank you enough. Kate, thank you for sharing your incredible insight and helping to make this book the best it could be. And Lydia, thank you so much for all your guidance, for adopting me and my book baby, and for all your hard work. And to the entire team at Entangled Teen. Thank you so much for everything!

And to anyone and everyone reading this book now. You're the reason I do this, and you picking up this book and giving it a chance has helped to make one of my biggest dreams a reality. Thank you.

GRAB THE ENTANGLED TEEN RELEASES READERS ARE TALKING ABOUT!

STAR-CROSSED
BY PINTIP DUNN

Princess Vela's people are starving. She makes the ultimate sacrifice and accepts a genetic modification that takes sixty years off her life, allowing her to feed her colony via nutrition pills. But now the king is dying, too. When the boy she's had a crush on since childhood volunteers to give his life for her father's, secrets and sabotage begin to threaten the future of the colony itself. Unless Vela is brave enough to save them all…

KEEPER OF THE BEES
BY MEG KASSEL

A Black Bird of the Gallows novel

When the cursed Dresden arrives in a Midwest town marked for death, he encounters Essie, a girl who suffers from debilitating delusions and hallucinations. But Essie doesn't see a monster when she looks at Dresden.

Risking his own life, Dresden holds back his curse and spares her. What starts out as a simple act of mercy ends up unraveling Dresden's solitary life and Essie's tormented one. Their impossible romance might even be powerful enough to unravel a centuries-old curse.

FREQUENCY
BY CHRISTOPHER KROVATIN

Fiona's not a kid anymore. She can handle the darkness she sees in the Pit Viper, a DJ whose wicked tattoos and hypnotic music seem to speak to every teen in town…except her. She can handle watching as each of her friends seems to be nearly possessed by the music. She can even handle her suspicion that the DJ is hell-bent on revenge. But she's not sure she can handle falling in love with him.

TOXIC
BY LYDIA KANG

Hana isn't supposed to exist. She's grown up hidden in a secret room of the bioship *Cyclo* until the day the entire crew is simply gone. Fenn is supposed to die. He and a crew of hired mercenaries are there to monitor *Cyclo* as she expires, and his payment will mean Fenn's sister is able to live. But when he meets Hana, he's not sure how to save them both.

entangled teen

an imprint of Entangled Publishing LLC